broken
homes
&
gardens

a novel

rebecca kelley

Blank Slate Press | Saint Louis, MO

For information, visit us at www.blankslatepress.com
Cover design & original art by Elena Makansi
http://www.elenamakansi.com
Cover photo from Shutterstock
Cover font: Lemonade, designed by Rachel Lauren Adams

Library of Congress Number: 2015935314

ISBN: 9780991305889

For Andy & Audrey

broken
homes
&
gardens

1

those nooks and crannies

Joanna blinked away the sleep and waited. Her clothes hung limp off her body. One ring, two, then three before her sister picked up. She almost laughed with relief.

It was past midnight and she had been traveling for over twenty hours. First to Prague, on to Frankfurt, San Francisco, now here. She had withdrawn money during her layover in San Francisco, and then bought a stale muffin and cup of coffee—her first meal on American soil since last summer. The muffin was too sweet, tasted like nothing but sugar. She had tried to reach her sister from the San Francisco airport—no answer. Joanna had been forced to leave a message. She had considered calling her mom but thought better of it. She would call later, once things had settled down.

"Joanna?" her sister said.

"It's me."

"Where are you?"

"At the Portland airport. Didn't you get my message?"

"I got it. But why are you *here*? This doesn't make any *sense*."

"Laura." Joanna closed her eyes and rested her head against the wall, holding the black receiver of the payphone against her ear. She could picture her sister exactly, so distressed by one little hair out of place. "Can you just come get me?"

Her sister sighed—then relented. An entire lecture in a single sigh.

♩

Laura lived in a one-bedroom apartment in Northwest Portland, in an old house divided into six living units. Laura's was on the third floor, facing a narrow alley, looking out at the building behind it.

"The good news is, I never bought a washer and dryer for this room," Laura said, flicking on the light in a large, empty closet off the kitchen. Laura had already set up an air mattress on the closet floor, complete with sheets and a quilt. Joanna had to smile at this. Her sister did not want her here, but she still cared about proper hospitality. After getting over the initial confusion of Joanna's unexpected arrival, she'd snapped into shape, switched into gear. "The bad news is we have to do our laundry over at the Laundromat."

Joanna sunk down onto the mattress. She wanted nothing more than to change her clothes, brush her teeth, wash her face, and sleep for years.

♩

Joanna spent her first three days in Portland doing

nothing. Jet lag, she told her sister. She would wake up sometime long after the sun came up, shower, then pull on her uniform of leggings and oversized T-shirt. She spent her days skimming books off of Laura's bookshelves and looking up jobs on Laura's computer. But without her own address or phone number, it hardly seemed worth it to apply. At night she'd go right back to bed without changing her clothes.

On the third night, her sister knocked on Joanna's door and peeked in. Joanna was sitting on the blow-up mattress, leaning against the wall, reading under a dim light. "I talked to Mom," Laura said. "I told her you're here."

Joanna sat up straight. "*I* was going to tell her! I was waiting until I had a plan."

"What *is* your plan?"

"I don't know. That's the whole point—I wanted to figure something out. Mom will tell me to go back to Reno. But I can't go back."

"Because of Dustin?"

"Dustin?" Joanna widened her eyes in surprise, as if she had trouble placing the name. She laughed. "Please. I should have let Dustin go last August, before I left. A clean break, no hard feelings."

"You broke up? I thought you were trying to make the long-distance thing work."

"We were," Joanna said. "Until we weren't." A little more than a month ago, Dustin had sent her a handmade valentine: a cartoon bumblebee holding a heart-shaped sign in its little insect legs. *Bee mine.* Inside he included the lyrics to the song he was writing about her. "Oh Joanna / I keep your bandana / wrapped around the neck of my steel guitar." Never mind that she never gave him a bandana. Or that Dustin did not play the steel guitar. Or that Joanna /

bandana was a facile, ridiculous rhyme.

A week after that, he dumped her via email postscript: "P.S. I'm seeing someone."

"I wish him the best," Joanna said to her sister. That was not true, of course. She'd ripped the valentine into four pieces and stuffed it in the trash the day after she arrived in Portland. She took his photograph out of its frame and threw it away, too. She didn't experience any ritualistic pleasure from these acts. Simple housekeeping—no more to it than that. There was no anger left. It was easy to move on in Portland, another world. She was starting over. She was proud of herself. This is how you do it. This is how you move on. She could write a book about it. If only she could harvest the time squandered over limp-haired guys in earsplitting garage bands. She could have learned Czech better. Maybe another language, too. Read more books, earned an online PhD.

"Go back to the Czech Republic and finish the school year, then," Laura was saying. "Those poor kids—"

"I can't go back there!" Joanna said, too loudly. "Even if I had the money for another ticket, I couldn't go back. Don't you get it? I *tried*. It didn't—it didn't work out."

"You're young, beautiful, and speak two languages!"

Laura had spent a semester in Spain her junior year and had a wonderful time. Joanna had seen photographs of her sister, the fastidious one, with the perfect pale skin, smooth blonde hair, and blissful, half-closed eyes, holding mugs of beer to the camera. She ate octopus and drank sangria and smoked unfiltered cigarettes. She had an affair with a Dane. She learned to speak Spanish with a Castilian lisp and saw the Guernica in real life. This is what "going abroad" did for people—for other people. Loosened them up, exposed them to new things, made them more interesting.

It was a horrible thought—that she, Joanna, was incapable of enjoying the very best moments of her own life. It was like so many other experiences she'd been told to savor because they would only happen once: her entire childhood, her first kiss, first love, college. Not only had she not enjoyed those milestones, she'd been relieved when they'd ended.

"Well, maybe it would be good for you to be on your own for a while," her sister was saying. "I mean, you've been living with Mom your whole life. You're twenty-*four*—"

"I wasn't 'living with Mom.' Tess and I rented that apartment *together*—"

"You even had the same *job* for a while—"

"What do you think that whole work abroad thing was about? I was *trying* to be on my own."

"Don't go back then! You still have to call Mom sometime."

"But I don't have a job or a place or anything."

"You can stay here," Laura said. "I mean, until you find a place of your own. I'm sure you don't want to live in a windowless room forever, right?"

Joanna tried to keep her expression neutral. She had, in fact, been thinking she could get by pretty well in this little closet. Staying seemed so simple. It would take no effort. "Are you sure?"

"I wouldn't have offered if I wasn't sure. You do need to look for a job, though. You'll need to move out eventually."

Joanna let her face open into a grin. "Yes, yes. I know. Thank you."

"So you'll call her?"

"She'll be hysterical. I can't deal with that right now."

"Why would she be hysterical? You're acting like she's some kind of nut."

Joanna gave her sister a look. "When's the last time *you* lived with her?" No answer. "I think I know her a little better than you," Joanna said.

Laura handed her the telephone. "I promised I'd make you call her." She shut the door behind her.

Joanna took a breath and dialed her mom's number.

"Joanna!" her mother screeched into the phone. The barrage of questions began: What happened? Why did you leave? What did the Czechs do to you? Why Portland? What are you going to do now? *What were you thinking?*

Joanna couldn't explain any of it. "I don't know, Mom, okay? You know they say how going abroad changes your whole perspective? How you'll have the time of your life and never be the same? Well … I didn't. I wasn't out there living it up. I was sitting inside my apartment watching American television dubbed over in Czech. Nothing really *happened*. I just decided to visit Laura for a while." This was not the picture she'd painted earlier. She'd written home about how amazing everything was—the church made of bones, the crispy potato pancakes she bought from street carts, the delightful children eager to learn how to conjugate English verbs.

The reality of Joanna's work experience abroad was something else entirely. The *gymnázium* where she worked was somewhere in the middle of Moravia, hours away from Prague. She taught conversational English in the mornings and had most afternoons to herself. At the end of every day, she crossed off the square on the wall calendar, like a prisoner. The highlight of each week was going to the village's tiny grocery store and choosing one of the five waxy, yellow peppers available. She taught herself Czech expressions she would never have the opportunity to use: *Jak se jmenutete? Dáte si něco k pití? Miluju tě!* What's your name?

Would you like a drink? I love you!

"Why didn't you just come home?"

"No flights from Prague to Reno, Mom."

"You can come home now, though. We could talk to Anita about getting your shifts back. And you should see my new place—I've got it all fixed up. And your room! I have it just how it was in our old place, with all your things. The bed with the black and white quilt Grandma made you, your *Little House on the Prairie* box set. Everything's the same, but better! It has a view—"

"Laura said I could stay with her for a while." Joanna braced herself for hysterics. Instead she heard nothing but silence on the other end of the line. "Mom?" Any second her mother would start crying or moaning. Or maybe she had fainted. "Look at everything you did while I was gone, Mom. You're doing so well at that job, you bought a townhouse—that's amazing! And I was only gone seven months. I need to be on my own some more—we both do." Joanna stopped and listened for her mother to react. She didn't hear anything, not even breathing at the other end of the line. "Mom?"

"You're right," her mother said at last. Her voice sounded low and calm, not hysterical at all. "We should be on our own."

Sometimes the sisters stayed in. Joanna had started making regular trips to the library, returning with stacks of books about mail-order bungalows and vintage kitchen design and Pacific Northwest cottage gardens. Joanna pored over these books while Laura graded her fifth graders' homework under lamplight. Other evenings Laura invited someone over, and then Joanna would tiptoe out of the apartment. She didn't know what to do with herself at first, but she didn't want to hang around Laura's friends or hide out in her little laundry room while Laura entertained some guy she was trying to impress. At first Joanna would hole up in coffee shops, nursing a milky coffee beverage and reading outdated magazines. Later she took off on walks around the neighborhoods, trying to learn the city.

"Don't go because of me," Laura said one evening. She had set the kitchen table for two.

"Wow," Joanna said, eyeing the cloth napkins, the vase full of flowers, the two tall candlesticks with freshly-snipped wicks.

"Too much?" Her sister placed her hands on her hips, assessing the tabletop. Then, with an air of decisiveness, she relocated the vase to the coffee table in the living room and retired the candles to a drawer in the kitchen.

"Better," Joanna said. She slipped into her sister's raincoat and stepped into her boots.

Portland in spring was misty and fragrant with cherry blossoms. The air cool but thick with fog, the sidewalks wet and shiny with rain. She moved quickly, gazing up through the tree branches outlined against the sky. She walked until it grew dark, taking in the wood smoke from chimneys, the fresh scent of laundry from dryer vents, the smell of rain and new grass. She inhaled greedily, almost gulping the air down. As she walked, she looked in the windows of houses, lights glowing gold inside all of those rooms. She could walk all night, squinting through wavy glass.

Her favorite houses had what she thought of as nooks and crannies: tiny four-paned windows on an upstairs dormer, winding staircases leading to a turret or widow's walk, upstairs balconies covered with plants and wicker furniture, sunrooms lined with books, attics with sloped ceilings and skylights. For the first time Joanna saw that houses were more than walls and rooftops, yards more than grass and trees. She was astonished to find they were more complicated than that, that all this time she had missed these details and that the details had names, a whole vocabulary she hadn't known existed: soffits and rafter tails, clematis and delphinium.

She returned to the apartment building with a flush in her cheeks. The carpet on the stairs leading up to the third floor was soft and green, like a bed of moss. Her arms brushed against the jacket of a guy coming down the stairs. They both looked up at each other and nodded. He seemed to be smiling over some secret joke, his eyes bright. Something in his amused expression made her sure he was Laura's visitor. He looked different from the boys her sister had dated in the past—guys Joanna had secretly called "business school douchebags," with sculpted haircuts and fake grins. She watched this prospect, with his slight build and wispy light-brown hair, as he whistled down the stairway then pushed the doors open and slipped out.

Laura was in a good mood when Joanna entered the apartment, humming as she tidied the kitchen.

"How was your date?" Joanna asked.

Laura sat down at the table and smiled. "How was your walk?"

"Good."

"What do you do out there? Where do you go?"

"Nowhere in particular." Her sister was looking up at her as if she really wanted to know the answer to her questions, so Joanna elaborated. "I like it. Walking through the rain, peeking into all those windows, looking into the houses."

"So you're a voyeur."

Joanna shrugged.

But that wasn't it at all—it had nothing to do with other people's lives. It had to do with hers. She needed to be out there, devouring the air and running her fingers along the mossy walls. She peered into houses and imagined herself tucked away in those nooks and crannies. All those windows were glimpses into all the ways her life could take shape.

2

this was the kind of flattery that worked at three o'clock in the morning

Out tending her tomato plant, Joanna was struck with what seemed, at that moment, to be a brilliant idea: she could move out onto the balcony. The warmer, dryer weather made it possible to spend more time outside— she practically lived out there anyway. As her bare hands loosened the soil along the edges of the pot, she took in an invigorating breath, inhaling the sharp scent of the plant, the compost's complex odor of damp leaves and earth.

Already in June the plant was rewarding her diligence. Its delicate yellow flowers shriveled up, revealing hard, green marbles: her first tomatoes. By July or maybe August the tomatoes would sustain her, starting with a Bloody Mary for breakfast. For lunch, a salad of sliced tomatoes, mozzarella, and basil. (She needed to get a basil plant!) For dinner, gazpacho. (And a cucumber plant—it could curl around the railings of the balcony.) A blender, electric skillet, and a hot pot would allow her to cook everything right out in the open air. And with a cot and a sleeping bag, she could sleep under the stars. When the rains started she'd have to construct a kind of large eave or overhang—

"Joanna?" Her sister was standing in the doorway. Joanna had been sitting on the balcony floor—her legs around this giant terra cotta pot, her hands in the soil—for the last five minutes. She cleared her throat and patted down the dirt. Laura was staring at her. "Well?"

Joanna blinked up at her sister, trying to retrieve the thread of conversation she'd dropped while daydreaming about relocating to the balcony. It wasn't even a romantic balcony overlooking vineyards or an elaborate yard. It looked out over the top of the building next door. The lids of dumpsters clanged shut in the alleyway three stories below. A few phone lines crisscrossed in front of what would be her view.

"You're still coming, right?"

Joanna sighed. "You know me and parties." She yawned. "And I'm really tired. I didn't sleep too well last night."

"Please," said Laura. "Just this once. You owe me."

"He's not cheap with the liquor," Joanna said with admiration. She had expected a cooler full of beer. Maybe a keg in the bathtub. This was top-shelf stuff, plus mint picked from the front yard and arranged in a glass of water. The limes were cut into half-moons and assembled in a small bowl. "Nice touch," she added.

"Are you sure you should be drinking that?"

Joanna raised her glass up for her sister's approval. "It's mostly ice and tonic water. Relax. I can handle this." Laura issued a half-confident nod, and drifted into the crowd in search of Ted Michalski. This party marked their fourth date, and it would be a test of sorts, for both of them. Laura would see how he lived, meet his friends. And Ted would finally make the acquaintance of Laura's little sister.

Joanna made her escape to the bathroom and locked the door. It was in the bathroom that she knew Laura would end up marrying this man. The hexagonal tiles on the floor gleamed. He'd folded his towels in thirds and draped them over what looked like very expensive towel bars. Peeking in the medicine cabinet, she found bottles of multi-vitamins and containers of dental floss arranged with precision. Laura was always tidying up the contents of the cupboards or sorting her socks by color and heft. She and Ted could spend hours together, organizing things.

When she ventured back into the party, her sister was nowhere to be found, and Joanna parked herself by the built-in bookshelves near the fireplace—familiar territory. Many a college house party had found her sipping Cokes and studying the book or CD collections—as if by picking up a copy of Plato's *Republic* and narrowing her eyes intelligently, some dashing philosophy student would approach her and engage her in a passionate discussion about justice. She'd pass the time trying to come up with insightful witticisms that referenced the allegory of the cave.

Ted's titles revealed an eclectic reading repertoire: old college text books, some of the classics (high school required reading?), a large collection of graphic novels. He subscribed to the *New Yorker*. She and her sister read it cover to cover every week. He also had a large stack of old *Sports Illustrated* magazines. Maybe he got it for the swimsuit issue.

An oversized paperback caught her eye. She turned it over in her hands.

"Put that book down," commanded a stern, deep voice.

She jumped up, nearly spilling her drink all over herself.

The grim reaper stared her down. That was her first thought: a skeleton peering out from a black, hooded cape. His bony fingers reached for the book, slowly, as if she were a suicide risk and he was attempting to take a loaded gun from her twitchy fingers. He snatched the offending object and issued an audible sigh of relief. Crisis averted.

Her initial shock passed, and she put her imagination in check. This was not the grim reaper. This was a guy with the black hood of his sweatshirt pulled up over his head. Big dark eyes—not so threatening now—stared out from under a fringe of straight brown hair that swept across his forehead. He was pale and thin but not really skeletal. "What's your *problem*?" she asked him.

"Sorry." He extended his hand for her to shake. "Malcolm."

She took his hand in hers. It was dry and cool—papery. "Joanna Robinson," she said, withdrawing her hand. Instead of withdrawing his, too, depositing it back by his side or in his pocket where it belonged, he extended it further, closer to her. He reached for her stomach, rested his whole hand on it, gently.

She jumped back, this time careful not to spill her drink. "What is *wrong* with you?"

"You're not pregnant," he said.

"*What?*"

"Expecting?" He gestured towards the book he still had in his hand. It was *What to Expect When You're Expecting*. Why on earth did Ted have a copy of *What to Expect When You're Expecting*, snuggled right next to *To Kill a Mockingbird* and *Sin City* on his bookshelf? This question had inspired her to pick it up in the first place. She had been examining the hugely pregnant woman smiling beatifically on the faded, pastel cover when Malcolm had interrupted her.

She shook her head. She opened her mouth, but she couldn't think of anything to say.

Malcolm was smiling, looking less like the Grim Reaper and more like just a twenty-something guy at a house party. "Never read this," he said, placing it back on the shelf and patting it like a little dog. "It's alarmist. It will give you a guilt trip about eating so much as a bagel."

"Well, I'm not pregnant."

"Future reference, then."

"So … you have kids?" Why else would this guy, who could not possibly be out of his twenties, have read *What to Expect When You're Expecting*? To impress women at parties by dazzling them with his knowledge of the reproductive system? It seemed unlikely.

"Believe me, Joanna," Malcolm said. "I have never sired—nor do I have the desire to sire—a child."

She was spared having to come up with a reply when a drunken blonde girl threw her arm around Malcolm and lured him back into a group of revelers, leaving Joanna standing at the bookshelves, temporarily rooted to her place on the hardwood floor.

Fifteen minutes later, a new drink in her hand, she exited through the back door and stepped out onto the deck. She saw Laura then, leaning against the railing next to a sandy-haired guy, laughing. She recognized her sister's companion at once—he was the guy she'd passed in the hallway a few weeks earlier. So this was Ted. Laura stopped laughing, placed her hand on his arm. She leaned close to him and said something. Ted watched her face, transfixed.

Laura caught Joanna's eye and gestured for her to join them.

"You have a beautiful house," Joanna told Ted.

Laura raised her eyebrows, undoubtedly surprised by her younger sister's sudden ability to make polite small talk. Joanna smiled.

"Thanks," Ted said. "I can't take all the credit. Malcolm did a lot of the renovations. He built this deck." He gave the railing an affectionate pat.

"Malcolm is Ted's roommate," Laura explained. She scanned the crowd—a few people leaned against the deck railing, drinking and laughing. No Malcolm. "Malcolm Martin … kind of thin, big eyes?"

"Oh yes. I met him." His name sounded like the beginning of a tongue twister.

Ted's face took on a wistful expression. "I don't know what I'll do without him. For two years!"

Joanna tried not to smile. It was cute, the way Ted wore his heart on his sleeve. Her sister needed someone like this. Earnest, sincere.

She excused herself by expressing an interest in the yard. She walked down the steps and onto the grass. She was starting to piece it all together. Her sister had mentioned the purpose of this party—it was a going-away party for Ted's housemate. Ted's housemate was joining the Peace Corps. Malcolm certainly didn't seem like the Peace Corps type. Peace Corps volunteers should be strong, full of enthusiasm for bettering the world. They should be brimming with optimism, a sort of do-gooder charm. Was Malcolm a do-gooder? He was, apparently, a carpenter. Maybe he planned to build shelters. Or decks.

In Portland it wasn't uncommon for tenants to let weeds take over their yards. But Ted—and Malcolm's—backyard was as neat as the medicine cabinet. A flagstone pathway cut through the lawn. Lavender, rosemary, and mint grew along the edge of the fence. And a vegetable patch! She restrained herself from running her fingers along the stems of their tomato plants. They were spindlier than hers, flowering but not yet bearing fruit. This pleased her. She may not have a steady job as a temp, she may not have her own place to live, but she had a very sturdy tomato plant.

Next to the garden beds stood a wooden structure she had at first taken for a shed. Upon closer inspection she saw it was a covered bench—a little hut with a corrugated tin roof, tucked into a grove of bamboo that separated Ted's house from the neighbor's. She sat down and scooted back, pulling her legs in so she disappeared into the hut. The sky grew dark and the air turned chilly. It was still June, not quite summer. By next month the warmth of the sun would toast the lawns, dry out the evening air.

The house seemed far away from her spot on the bench. Inside, people's heads bopped along to music she couldn't hear, their faces indistinguishable. Forget her sister's balcony. She could live in a hut. Just a simple hut in the back of someone's house. That's all she'd really need. Her eyelids felt heavy. She let them sink down.

"There you are." Malcolm stepped into the bench hut and sat down next to her. Her eyes flew open. She didn't acknowledge him; he didn't seem to be expecting her to.

They sat gazing out at the yard for several minutes without saying anything. A breeze blew through the bamboo; the leaves at the top rustled. Then he looked over at her. "Your sister told me all about you."

She stared back at him, her mouth open.

"She said I should talk to you about teaching English."

Her heart rate slowed down. "Teaching English?" For a moment she imagined her sister had betrayed her; told everyone about her recent failures. "Did my sister tell you that I left early?" Joanna asked him.

He shrugged. "She just said I should talk to you."

"I did a terrible, terrible thing."

"You killed someone."

Joanna didn't crack a smile. She inhaled sharply before speaking. "I got this job teaching English in this tiny little town. Two-hundred and fifty kids! I took off. Abandoned my post."

He was frowning. "That's it?"

She did smile at that. "It's okay if you never want to talk to me again." Her bare arm brushed against the sleeve of Malcolm's sweatshirt.

Malcolm stretched out and slung his arm over her shoulder, drawing her in. "Come here," he said. "I'm cold."

She tensed up for a moment, then relaxed in his bony arms. "You're the one wearing a jacket." She felt so comfortable all of a sudden. Not too cold at all—the perfect temperature. She let her eyes close again. He shivered and pulled her closer.

An hour—or was it two hours?—later, she woke to find herself curled up on the bench. Her head rested on her hands, her legs bent to fit on the seat. Her body unfolded. No one was in the backyard or out on the deck. Only one light was on in the house—the kitchen. The air felt cooler now, laced with a sweet, metallic scent. She pushed her arms through the sleeves of her jacket and stretched her aching limbs. The sleeves were a bit too long and worn out at the cuffs. This was not her jacket—it was a black hooded sweatshirt, smelling of wood shavings and soap. She zipped it up to her chin and headed towards the house.

Malcolm was sitting at the kitchen table playing solitaire. The rest of the house was dark and quiet. "What time is it?" she asked, her eyes adjusting to the light in the kitchen. He was slapping down cards three at a time. "Is my sister here?" For a panicked moment, she wondered if Laura had left her here on her own.

"Damn it!" Malcolm threw down his cards. "I can't win." He looked up at her. "She went to sleep."

"She went home?"

He tilted his head in the direction of the bedrooms upstairs. "With Ted."

"Oh." This seemed so out of character for her sister.

"I told her I'd take care of you," he said. "Come here." He patted the seat next to him at the table. He began shuffling the deck of cards.

She sat down.

Malcolm dealt the cards. "Rummy," he said.

She took her hand without comment and began sorting by suit. They played in silence.

"You and your sister look nothing alike," Malcolm said when the final cards went down. She nodded. She heard this a lot. Laura was petite with straight, blonde hair—the kind of hair that is almost white during childhood and turns golden as the years go by. She had a thin nose and a red mouth, just like their beautiful, pale mother. Joanna was a good four inches taller than Laura, and because of this, people often mistook her for the older sister. With hazel eyes and dark brown hair—almost black—people sometimes asked her if she was Italian or Latin American. "I'm just a mutt," she would usually answer.

When the girls were young, people used to come up to their mother and ask if Joanna was adopted. "Just switched at birth," her mother would reply. It was meant as a jab—a "mind your own beeswax" type of response. But Joanna didn't really mind. She enjoyed thinking about it, actually. *Switched at birth.* Nothing so exciting had happened to her since.

Malcolm looked over at her, then reached up and ran a finger down the side of her face, slowly. "Your sister is more beautiful than you."

She looked into his dark eyes. Part of her wanted to storm out of the house. Another part of her realized that his comment didn't bother her. It was true, wasn't it?

"But your face is much more interesting." He took her hand in his. "Come on. It's time to sleep."

This was the kind of flattery that worked at three o'clock in the morning, or whatever time it was.

"You know we just met." She was sitting on the edge of his bed, an island in a sea of boxes and suitcases.

Malcolm sat down next to her. "That's my sweatshirt." He unzipped it for her, nudged it off her shoulders. It fell off and landed on the floor.

"I can't wear this to bed." Her heart knocked against her ribcage, though she wasn't scared so much as nervous and—she had to admit—curious to find out what would happen next.

Malcolm went over to one of his suitcases and rooted around. He took out a gray T-shirt, neatly folded, and brought it back to the bed.

"Hands up," he said, lifting her blouse off her as if he were undressing a child. He pulled the gray T-shirt over her head and she poked her arms through the arm holes. "There."

Very business-like. She still had her bra on; she wondered if she should unclasp it, take it out through the sleeves. They sat at the edge of the bed, looking at each other.

"Malcolm," she said. She would thank him for the shirt, then find a nice couch to curl up on downstairs.

He leaned in and kissed her gently. She was too surprised to kiss back, at first. But when he kissed her again, she responded—even reached up to touch his face. She had no idea what she was doing. She wasn't at all drunk, so that didn't explain it. They wrapped their arms around each other, collapsed onto the bed. He felt heavier on top of her than she had anticipated, more substantial.

"I'm leaving tomorrow," he said into her ear, his voice so low she could barely make out the syllables. He kissed her hard on the mouth before she could reply.

"I know," she said forty minutes later.

"Listen …" He ran his hands down her bare back. (Somehow he'd solved her problem with the bra. The gray T-shirt, too, was lost in a tangle of covers. But she had stopped him when he'd reached down to undo the buttons of her jeans.) "I think we should sleep together."

She laughed. "We've known each other—what? Eight hours?" She began calculating but lost her train of thought when he tipped her head back to kiss her throat.

"Eight hours, is that all?" he said. "It feels like years."

"What a line," Joanna said, but she knew what he meant.

"You'll forget me otherwise," he said into her neck.

She pressed her body against his. Maybe this is what she needed—to succumb to her desires, to sleep with a total stranger the night before he left for another country. And it didn't feel like kissing a stranger at all. Maybe that's what every lonely person told herself in times like these, but she didn't think so.

But then she shook her head. "Too bad we didn't meet months ago." She sat up and began patting around the top of the covers.

Malcolm was looking up at her, smiling. "You're so cute," he said. "What are you looking for?"

"That gray T-shirt."

He pulled her back down to him and she nestled

against him. "You don't need it." He kissed her on the tip of the nose, then got out of bed to close the curtains over the open window. The curtains billowed up with cool, rain-tinged air, then deflated. He shivered and slipped back in bed. She pulled the sheets over them, settled into his arms, and closed her eyes.

"If we'd met months ago, I'd make you my girlfriend," he said, his voice drowsy. "If you were my girlfriend, you'd sleep with me."

She smiled. The hours weighed in on her. She was tired. "Yes. Every night. Maybe sometimes during the day, too."

"I'd have to work."

"We'd lose our jobs," she said. "We'd be unemployed. We'd have all day to devote to each other."

"Sounds nice."

"Write me while you're gone." The room was getting lighter, even with the curtains shut. In a few hours, she'd leave. She'd go back to the balcony, check on the infinitesimal growth of her tomato plant—another tiny sucker shooting between the stems, another yellow flower withering away.

"I will," he said, and they drifted asleep with their limbs tangled together.

3

this time with just the most essential posessions

In the entryway of her downtown apartment building, Joanna retrieved her mail from the metal box for the last time. Catalogs selling garish bras and underwear, flyers for nearby pizza delivery, credit card applications—all these went directly into the blue recycling bin. Underneath the layers of paper, there it was, the prize: a thin airmail envelope addressed to her in a now-familiar slanted scrawl. She placed the letter underneath a bank statement and tucked them both under her arm.

"Ready?" Nate was holding the elevator door open for her. It was one of those old-fashioned ones with a wrought iron gate that needed to click into place before jostling up to the fourth floor. Joanna tried to swat away her annoyance. It was the last time she would pick up her mail down in the lobby, and she had wanted to savor the moment.

Joanna chastised herself. She was being ridiculous. It was just mail. It was not a "moment."

"You sure you don't want me to stay and help?" he asked

her, standing on the threshold of her apartment.

Joanna smiled at Nate and reached up to run a finger through the wave of hair across his forehead. "Nah. I work better alone."

He kissed her lightly on the lips. "All right. We'll celebrate tomorrow."

When she was eight years old, her parents sold their little blue Audi Fox. She had crawled in the back seat and cried for an hour until the new owner came and drove it away. She felt the same way about leaving this apartment: sentimental beyond reason. She'd made a life for herself here. Or perhaps that wasn't the right phase—it implied settling down, growing roots. She'd lived here for a year and a half; can you make a life in a year and a half?

The place was not all that great. A downtown studio on the top floor, with a view of the building right next to it, ten feet away. It smelled like stale bread. Old toast. Joanna walked to the back and pushed open the awning windows, letting in a cool gust of air. The windows were old, metal with chicken wire inside the glass. When it rained, cold water dripped on her face as she lay in bed. But now it was a rare sunny day in early spring, and the whole room filled with light, fading the fabric on the bedspread. Pigeons roosted outside on the ledge, flapping close to the glass, staring at her with their red eyes.

This was where she lived when she started taking classes, after her sister insisted she "do something with her life." She signed up for a few graduate-level courses at the downtown campus and moved out of her sister's laundry room. By winter term she was enrolled as a graduate student in rhetoric and composition. After grad school she could give teaching another shot, redeem the whole Czech fiasco. She would carve out a niche for herself in adult education.

It was a solid plan. But the truth was, she didn't want it as much as she probably should.

As a child, Joanna had wanted to be a singer despite having no talent for singing and no real desire to perform. Ditto with acting, marine biology (the career of choice for every girl in the fourth grade), fashion designer, and archeologist (inspired by film enactments of beautiful women in khaki clothes and pith helmets). She was not the type of kid to settle on a future profession. Even as an adult, she could not help but think she could apply herself equally to any number of pursuits.

Right here on this horrible twin mattress, under the faded quilt, was where she and Nate had consummated their relationship. Their first time had been awkward, a fumble of belt buckles and buttons in the dark. They weren't overcome by passion, kissing frantically, then falling on the bed, ripping each other's clothes off. Instead, they'd more or less agreed that they'd like to "take the next step" in their relationship. And that was that.

They had spent the next three hours in each other's arms, talking about the failed relationships of their pasts. Nate was still suffering the emotional ramifications of his broken engagement to his high school sweetheart. They'd stayed together through their senior year and for all four years of college. In the months before his fiancée, Melissa, was supposed to enter dental school, they decided to "take the summer off" and date other people. How would they know they were meant for each other if they had such limited romantic experience? Following their agreement, they didn't see or speak to one another for three months. Two weeks before the deadline, she called him in tears, begging him to escort her to an abortion clinic.

Nate told Joanna all this in a rush, in one breath, as if he were making a confession. Then he had fallen asleep while Joanna lay awake, spying through the windows of the next building, making up stories about other people's lives.

Joanna stood in the middle of the apartment, her hands on her hips. The place looked deceptively empty—her bed under the window was the only piece of furniture. The folding card table she'd used as a desk, the overstuffed chair she'd found with a "free" sign on the curb outside her building, and the frayed rugs and pressboard bookshelves had already been carted off to the thrift store. A few boxes—packed and taped shut—lay stacked in the small entryway.

Under the surface, though, the place was a disaster. The kitchen cupboards contained a mountain of recycling she'd stuffed inside for the entire time she'd lived here: crushed cans, glass bottles, cardboard and paper. She should start with that; it would probably take eight trips down to the basement to get rid of it all. First, though, Joanna walked over to the bed and straightened the covers, then smoothed the wrinkles out of the pillowcase with her hands. She placed the pale blue envelope with the striped red edge in the center of the pillow and made a bargain with herself: After taking down the recycling, then mopping, scouring, and dusting the place until it would pass the building manager's inspection—then and only then, could she open the letter, as her reward.

She'd always thought she'd be the one sending letters from foreign countries. Now receiving mail postmarked from Kazakhstan had become the highlight of her days. She invested a little too much energy into the correspondence, scribbling out pages between letters. She had the sense not to send it all.

Her history with pen pals had left her cautious. In

fifth grade her best friend moved away, and they made a solemn oath to write. Joanna and Veronica had made forts in the sagebrush, read all the same books, played with dolls together long after everyone else their age had outgrown them. They'd concocted elaborate mysteries and solved them by using calculators, studying the clouds, and recording their observations in notebooks. After Veronica left, Joanna spent most of her allowance on stationery and stamps. For months they exchanged stickers, jokes, secrets, but eventually the correspondence tapered off. For every letter or postcard Veronica sent, Joanna wrote three. Sometimes she enclosed a self-addressed stamped envelope, too.

When the lapse between letters became unbearable, Joanna had no choice but to accept the possibility that Veronica had died. Joanna would lie down on her bed, stare up at the ceiling and let the sadness press down on her. She'd try to summon tears. After mourning her friend for what seemed like hours, she'd jump up with a renewed sense of purpose, sit down at her desk, and scribble out another letter.

In high school, she had a male pen pal: Geoffrey, from Chicago. He signed his letters "Geo," had a fake ID, went to bars to see bands they mutually adored. Their letters quickly evolved from confessing their love of British musicians to love for each other. They made plans to move to London after graduation and live together. Page after page detailed the apartment they'd rent, the graves they'd visit, the pubs they'd frequent.

He had written poetry about her, about yearning to gaze into her sloe eyes and touch her supple skin. So when Geoffrey said he had borrowed money from his older brother and bought himself an airplane ticket, she told her mother she wanted to go on a school ski trip over winter break. Geoffrey would find a romantic getaway in the mountains and take care of everything. On the day of his arrival, she packed a small suitcase, borrowed her mom's car, and drove to the airport to pick him up, clasping the snapshot of him in her hand. She'd studied that picture so much she had memorized his face, squinted to make out details in the background: the posters on his wall, an unmade bed.

He never arrived. She waited for him for five hours, until the next flight from Chicago came in, then drove home in a daze, called his house, and talked to his mom, who said he had certainly flown to Reno that day. She locked herself in her room, confused, crying. She told her mom she wasn't feeling up to the ski trip after all.

She heard from him a week later. Geo may have been the one person who enjoyed writing letters more than Joanna. He had three pen pals in the Reno-Tahoe area alone and had gone snowboarding with the first girl he recognized waiting outside the gate. Sorry he had missed her. He guessed he hadn't recognized her from the photo she had sent.

Of course most of her long distance friendships didn't end so badly. But they all ended eventually. First their letters would taper off, then they stopped coming altogether, then they were gone.

Joanna's phone was ringing when she came in from the basement. Her hands sticky with old jam and who knows what else, she let it go to voice mail. Trudging up and down the stairs had made her hungry. She retrieved a jar of peanut butter from the fridge. The refrigerator! How could a 350-square-foot apartment contain so many hidey-holes for empty cans and bottles, half-eaten jars of pickles and mustard? Oh well. She'd empty the contents of the fridge into a box or a laundry basket and take it all over to Nate's tomorrow. She'd deal with it then.

She couldn't find a spoon, so she ate the peanut butter with her fingers. In the distance, a siren wailed. Shopping carts filled with bottles clanged over the sidewalks. People shouted. These noises had created the soundtrack for her letter reading and writing for a year and a half. The next time she read a letter, she'd hear—what? Lawn mowers droning, children screaming?

She never thought Malcolm would actually write her from Kazakhstan—especially considering what a fool she'd made out of herself before he took off—but he did. His letters were filled with strange details; she could never quite tell when he was pulling her leg and when he was giving an accurate depiction of his life over there. The first winter he was gone, he told her it was so cold that the rivers froze over. He ice-skated under the bridges. "It's forty degrees below zero," he wrote. "That's the same temperature in Fahrenheit and Celsius." He later informed her that he'd taken to wearing a huge fur hat, a floor-length fur coat, and fur boots to deal with the elements. She had assumed he added a few creative flourishes to this story, but the next letter came with a snapshot of him wearing this very ensemble. "I have nothing on underneath this," he scribbled on the back.

On winter nights she'd walk on sidewalks wet with rain and think of Malcolm on the other side of the world. Through the crosshatch of tree branches she'd look up at the telephone wires, looming firs and cedars. The sky, always gray, so near the ground, the rain on her skin. She belonged here in a way she had never belonged at home, growing up. In the high mountain desert, the sky stretched out huge and blue, the dust-colored hills and the mountains vivid in the distance. Everything was wide open; she didn't know it then, but she longed to feel closed in. She had missed, without realizing it, the coziness of rain, early nightfall, cups of tea, ferns and moss growing on trees.

At times she wondered if her imagination had made Malcolm into this great friend, wonderful listener, sensitive soul who took in everything she said and understood it better than she did herself. She had a hard time piecing together how she viewed him. She knew parts of him, but those parts didn't necessarily fit together to form a picture she understood. The Malcolm from the party, the one with the hood up over his head, girls pulling at his sleeves, pulling him away from her. The Malcolm after everyone had left or gone to sleep, who lifted her shirt over her head and folded it neatly into a square and set it on top of his packed suitcase before he turned back and looked at her unclothed body—not lustfully but with a serious, almost studious expression before he kissed her.

And then the Malcolm in the letters, the vegetarian traipsing around in a fur coat and hat. Who also worried that he was in over his head, that he had nothing to teach his students who knew the rules of English grammar better than he did. Who had quit eating meat when he was twelve because of some childhood trauma involving a seagull but took the gift of the fur coat from his host brother because it would seem rude to turn it away. And because he was so cold that he curled up with two hot water bottles at night. One at his feet, the other cradled against his chest like a baby.

Through their letters they discovered that they'd been the same type of angsty teen, right down to the thick black eyeliner and dog-eared copies of *The Fountainhead*. They used the same brand of toothpaste. They both, by the most remarkable coincidence of all, owned the same New

American Heritage dictionary published in 1963.

One time Joanna mailed him a letter that contained only a list:

Words that Didn't Exist in 1963

air head
area code
astronaut
carjacking
disco
gentrify
glitch
junk food
pizza
sexism
supermarket

"Would we have been friends if we'd met in high school?" Joanna asked him once. Malcolm said they would have. They would recognize each other by their matching eyeliner, by their twin books. They would seek each other out. Joanna could imagine it perfectly, the two of them, skinny teenagers dressed in black clothes, hunched over their brownbag lunches on the bleachers, having those intensely sincere conversations about Camus or the *Communist Manifesto* that seem so exciting and relevant when you're young.

Every once in a while they would mention the night they had spent together. "I'm freezing here in Kazakhstan," Malcolm wrote her. "I could use a bed warmer. Someone like you, whose skin is soft and warm, like a pancake. But then I'd wake up wanting an American breakfast, and I can't get that here."

Malcolm mentioned other girls every so often, but their names were always changing. Once he mailed Joanna a photo of the Peace Corps volunteers in his group and he had his arm slung around a redhead's shoulder. He didn't say who she was, and Joanna didn't ask. She had told him about Nate, of course. A friend from grad school introduced her to him. He had seen Joanna around campus, pursued her. February was an odd time to start a romance, with the slick black tree branches crisscrossing over their heads as they walked down the park blocks together. Their first kiss took place under an umbrella in the rain. He took her by surprise, pressed too hard against her face, immobilizing her lips. But it was too romantic a gesture to dismiss, and after that, they were together. Of course she didn't tell Malcolm all that. She mentioned Nate casually at first—slipped his name in a sentence somewhere in the middle of a page.

Then later, she told Malcolm things about Nate that she never told anyone else. That she was going into this relationship with her eyes open. She was not going to make a fool of herself like she did with Dustin. These confessions didn't feel wrong because Malcolm was so far away. Things she couldn't imagine telling the strange guy she met at the party, with his big, morose eyes and sarcastic snicker, she wrote down on paper and flung into the universe. Kazakhstan! Thousands of miles away, over an ocean, high up in the air—it didn't even seem like a real place.

Moving out of her sister's apartment, attending graduate school, dating Nate—all these things made her feel slightly less ridiculous for the way she'd acted when Malcolm had left. Wearing her wrinkled clothes, she had tagged along when Ted drove him to the airport. And then—oh how she wished she had just gone home, bid him farewell after slinking out of bed!—she'd cried her eyes out as she waved goodbye to him. He was kind, though. He'd wiped her tears away with the sleeves of his hoodie, bent down and kissed her nose. "It's just two years, sweetheart," he said. Sweetheart! Later she wondered if she had imagined that part.

Ted had given her a lift back to Laura's apartment. Joanna went straight to the balcony. Through the panes of the French doors, she saw Ted and Laura sitting next to each other at the kitchen table, their heads bent together. They appeared to be whispering—probably about her. When her sister looked up, Joanna shut her eyes, still red and stinging from tears and exhaustion.

It had turned dark outside her downtown studio—and it was as clean as it was going to get. She owed it that much, she supposed. She took a long shower and changed into her pajamas before curling up under the covers. With the bedside lamp on, her place felt cozy rather than empty and stark. She could live like this. Maybe moving in with Nate wasn't such a great idea after all. They had been together just over one year; cohabitating could be a huge mistake. She could back out now, start over (again!), this time with just the most essential possessions: a bed, a lamp, a teacup, a pen, some paper, a letter. She would be like that character in a novel she read once about the woman who rid herself of everything she owned, item by item. She kept paring down, paring down until all she had left could fit in her handbag. Then she walked out the door and left the house behind, too.

Settled under the covers, Joanna was about to open the letter when she remembered something she forgot, had almost left hidden in the recesses of this apartment. She threw off the quilt and ran over to the tiny cupboard door off the entryway. When she'd first moved in, this mysterious cabinet on the floor had been painted shut, but she'd pried it open with a butter knife. Nothing was inside. She wrote Malcolm about it and he'd asked her if the cabinet was accessible through a door from the hallway, too. She had never noticed it before, but every apartment had one—a tiny door next to the big one, nailed shut.

It's a milk door, Malcolm had explained in his slanted handwriting. Milkmen would access the door in the hallway, depositing cold bottles of milk for people to retrieve in the comfort of their own apartments. She'd been keeping all of Malcolm's letters in there ever since, in a heap. She opened the door and reached in to gather them up. To think she'd almost left them for the next tenant to find! It was a romantic notion, in a way. Letter writing took effort; it was tangible evidence of their connection—ink on paper. They never called or emailed. And sometimes she sent him more than words: a book or a tiny packet of tea or a clipping from a newspaper or a feathery Japanese maple leaf pressed flat between the pages of the dictionary.

Maybe she *should* leave the letters here, to be discovered. Someone would find them in the milk cupboard, read them all, and see how she and Malcolm had something special, a deep friendship that went beyond ordinary romance. Like Jean Paul Sartre and Simone de Beauvoir! No, not them. Too messed up.

She went in search for a string, something to bind the letters together. A red satin ribbon would do the correspondence justice, but mint-flavored dental floss would have to do. She tied the letters in a neat bundle, as thick as a brick, then buried them under some clothes in her suitcase.

Back in bed, she could hear the muffled sounds of her

neighbor's television. She studied the envelope of her unopened letter. These letters would stop coming, one day— in half a year, to be exact. Then what? Well, she didn't need to think about it now. It was late, and she deserved a reward for the hard work she'd done. The cavities of the apartment had been scraped out, the baseboards sparkled—even the walls had a special sheen. She situated herself against her pillow and opened the envelope with a box knife.

4

after two years, an ocean, and all those time zones

"I never thought I'd live to see the day when one of my girls married," Tess Robinson said, overseeing her two daughters at the salon the morning of Laura's wedding. The sisters sat side by side while Tess paced behind them.

"So you thought we were un-marryable, or you thought you'd die an early death?" This was Joanna's attempt at joking around with her mother, but Tess was not listening.

"And who knows?" Tess said. In the mirror, Joanna observed her mother clutching her chest and smiling up to the ceiling. "I may be next!"

Joanna tried to catch her sister's eye in the mirror so they could exchange panicked expressions, but Laura was smiling. "We can't wait to meet him, Mom," she said.

"*What?*" Joanna wanted to whip around in her chair, but she had to settle for yelling at her mother's reflection. "What are you talking about? *Who* are we talking about?"

"Oh, I forgot to tell you," Laura said. "Mom is bringing a 'special guest' to the wedding." Again with the smiling.

"Just wait," Tess said. "You'll like him. He's been wanting to meet you."

"How long have you known this guy? Like a month? And already you're talking about *marrying* him?"

"Six weeks," said Tess. "And we're not getting married. Not yet, anyway."

"Six weeks? Laura, you let Mom bring some stranger to your wedding? Are you sure about this?"

"Calm down, Joanna. It's my wedding, okay?" Laura did not appear to be concerned at all. She was checking her phone. "Well," Laura announced a moment later, "it looks like Malcolm is in Chicago."

Joanna dug her fingers into the armrests. "Chicago?"

"Don't worry—he'll be here before we say our vows." The stylist's fingers twisted through Laura's gleaming halo of hair, pinning up strands with sparkly little bobby pins. Laura sat up straight in her chair, admiring her own transformation, as if the late arrival of the best man was of no particular concern to her. "Or at least by the reception," she added as an afterthought.

"Are you sure he'll make it in time? The best man has to do more than show up during the *reception*. He has to hand the rings over, make a speech ... "

"Don't worry about it, Joanna. He'll be here."

"Easy for you to say," Joanna muttered. She was the one who would have to pick up the slack if he didn't show, and speechmaking was not her thing. Last night she'd shot up in a panic, grabbing on to Nate's arm. What is it? he'd asked her. How could she be the maid of honor *and* the best man? She didn't have the rings. She didn't have a speech. She wouldn't have to make a speech, would she? Nate assured her that she wouldn't. If worse came to worst, *he* would make a speech. He'd even make it rhyme, he said, patting her hair as she closed her eyes and started to breathe again. Rhyming speeches always go over well.

"You're just nervous about seeing him again, aren't you?" Laura said. "Two years is a long time." She grinned up at their mother in the mirror.

Tess's face lit up. "You know Ted's best man?"

"I met him."

"They're like—pen pals," Laura said.

"Very romantic!" Tess trilled.

"I have a boyfriend, in case you two forgot."

"Ooh, Joanna, look at you!" Tess pointed at Joanna's reflection in the mirror. Joanna had barely registered the questions coming from the stylist. Tess had taken over, commanding instructions. So Joanna couldn't complain when she finally focused on her mirror image and found a wide-eyed version of herself, hair done up in braids and ribbons, dark tendrils curling out in several directions. Then everything disappeared under a cloud of hairspray.

An hour before the wedding, Joanna stood in a leafy courtyard lined with a hundred white chairs, studying the list Laura had given her. She had assured her sister she'd take care of it. But why did getting married involve so many flowers, so many ribbons, so many place cards printed on 200-pound cotton paper? She walked down the aisle, affixing a beribboned cluster of flowers to the end of each row of chairs. It was perfect wedding weather, a late summer day in Portland, the sky free from rainclouds. Overhead, a canopy of leaves rustled in the breeze.

"Any idea where this thing goes?"

At the sound of his voice, she turned around. Malcolm

stood no more than a foot away from her, holding a gigantic bunch of zinnias and ferns. After two years, an ocean, and all those time zones, there he was. He set the flowers on the ground and opened his arms. She went in to hug him. He felt bony and breakable.

"Mm," he said, pulling her closer to him. "You must have missed me."

"I'm just *so* glad I don't have to perform all your duties at the wedding."

"I thought all we had to do was stand up there and sign the marriage certificate."

"Well, there's a lot more to it than that. Flowers, rings … and if I didn't have enough to worry about, my mom showed up with some random guy she just met."

"That does sound stressful," Malcolm said. He was grinning down at her.

"Shut up," she said. "I'm not cut out to be a wedding planner. And my mom—well, you'd have to know her."

"Just met her, as a matter of fact. Jeremy, too."

"Jeremy? Is that his name?" Joanna asked, sounding bitter.

"What's wrong with Jeremy?"

She stood back and eyed him critically. If it was possible, he was even skinnier than he was before he left. He'd survived on nothing but boiled starch for two years—or so he had said in his letters. Boiled noodles, boiled potatoes, boiled potatoes *with* noodles. He was wearing aviator sunglasses and a tuxedo. He looked like he hadn't shaved in a week. "You look awful," she said.

"What did you do to your hair?" He crunched a tendril between his thumb and forefinger. He smiled or smirked—she couldn't tell which. "So where do I put these flowers?"

She consulted her list, the panicky feeling washing over

her again. "What are those? Zinnias? I don't see anything about zinnias here. There's supposed to be something on that birdbath thing under the archway, but this doesn't say anything about—"

"Hey, calm down. It's going to be fine." He stepped back and assessed her.

"Stop staring at me." She tugged her dress up. For months Laura had insisted that she didn't care at all what Joanna wore as her maid of honor, but then she "fell in love with" a green strapless gown she thought would go so perfectly with Joanna's coloring. Joanna had spent half the day yanking it back into place.

"You really don't have the chest to pull that dress off."

She frowned at him. He was still wearing his ridiculous aviator sunglasses. She told him to take them off. He did. He had rings under his bloodshot eyes. "You look awful," she said again.

He shrugged. "I know." They stood on the gravel path, grinning at each other for a moment too long. "Ted said you had the rings," Malcolm said.

The rings dangled from her wrist by a thin satin ribbon. After Ted had given them to her for safekeeping, she had struggled to find a place to put them, finally resorting to plucking a ribbon from her hair, threading it through the rings, and then looping it around her arm three times. Paranoid that the knot would come loose, she'd been clutching the rings in her fist. "Here they are." She lifted up her wrist.

He took her hand in his and raised it up to get a better look. The ribbon wouldn't slip over her knuckles, so he began to untie the knot. He picked at it with his fingers until it came loose, his face so close to her wrist she could feel his breath on her skin. "There," he said, unwinding the ribbon from her arm. He pulled the rings off the ribbon and slipped them into the inside pocket of his tuxedo jacket.

Then he took her hand back in his and turned it over to examine her palm. Her grip on the rings had marred her skin with indentations. "Look at that," he said, smoothing out her palm with his thumbs.

When they heard someone clearing his throat behind them, she dropped her arm to her side and took a small step away from Malcolm.

"Sorry to interrupt," Nate said, coming up to Joanna and putting his arm around her shoulders. "Your sister needs you." He nodded at Malcolm. Malcolm put his sunglasses back on and gave Nate a little eyebrow raise in return.

The reception took place on the top floor of a brew pub, with brick walls, exposed ductwork, high ceilings flanked with fir beams, and windows looking out at the twinkling buildings and bridges. It was such a departure from the weddings they'd attended as girls, in casino ballrooms decorated with balloons.

Sometime before midnight, Joanna found Malcolm sitting on the floor in the corner of the room, his back against the wall. He looked half asleep, his hair shooting out in all directions, his bow tie undone and hanging around his neck. Joanna balanced two cups of coffee on their little white saucers and lowered herself next to him. She set the cups on the ground between them and opened up her hand, which she'd filled with sugar and creamer packets. "I don't know how you take your coffee," she said.

He took one crumpled sugar packet and poured the contents in his cup.

Joanna stuffed the rest of the packets in Malcolm's jacket pocket. "I take mine with cream," she said. "No sugar. You know, if you were interested."

Malcolm looked into his coffee. "Where's the boyfriend?"

"He left. He had to take my drunken cousin home before she passed out."

"And you're okay with that?"

"Well, yeah. He's doing me a favor. I don't want to spend my sister's wedding babysitting my twenty-year-old cousin."

"Katie, right? Long straight hair, that short prom dress number?"

"That's her."

"You sure you trust Nate with your little cousin?" He accompanied his question with a lecherous look. Joanna punched Malcolm on the arm, and he winced, pretending to sway from the impact. "Ouch," he said.

"You deserved that. You're disgusting."

"I've been up for over twenty hours. My jokes are suffering."

"Yeah, no kidding. That was not even slightly amusing."

"Blame it on lack of sleep."

Joanna folded her arms in front of her and stared out at the party. Most of the attendants over seventy had trickled out after the cake-cutting, but a surprising number of guests were still on the dance floor.

"Hey, Joanna, seriously, I didn't mean—"

"Oh no," Joanna interrupted. She put a hand on Malcolm's arm to silence him. Jeremy had spotted her and Malcolm sitting against the wall and was making his way over to them. He was good-looking, in a Nevada cowboy kind of way, with rusty curls and an aw-shucks expression permanently plastered on his face. "He's going to ask me to dance," she said to Malcolm under her breath.

"Joanna?" Jeremy extended his hand to her. "Will you do me the honor—"

Joanna tried to muster an apologetic smile. "Sorry, Jeremy!" She scrambled up to her feet, pulling Malcolm up with her. "Malcolm *just* asked me. Next time!" She dragged Malcolm to the dance floor.

"Okay," she said, throwing her hands around his neck. "Pretend like we're dancing."

Malcolm placed his hands on her hips. "That was rude."

"I know. I—I just make it a policy not to get involved with my mom's love life." She didn't need to tell Malcolm that just hours before she had begun half seriously hatching a Shakespearean plot—involving handwriting forgery—to drive her mother and Jeremy apart. If only she could make Jeremy disappear without sending her mother through all the usual breakup-related histrionics.

"He's not so bad. Your mom seems happy with him."

"It's just … inappropriate. He's like, my age."

"Your age plus ten or fifteen years, maybe."

"I don't know why he'd be with Tess. And don't say she's hot."

"I wasn't going to. Your dad is remarried, right? I'm sure your mom—"

"It's more complicated than you think. And I don't want to talk about it."

"Okay," Malcolm said. They were silent for a few measures. "I like that dress on you," he said after a while.

"I thought you said I couldn't pull it off?"

He smiled. "You can't." Joanna looked down. The entire bodice of the dress, stiff with boning, was jutting out inches from her body. Malcolm was staring down at her strapless bra. "That's why I like it so much."

They stopped dancing while Joanna adjusted the dress. She pulled a few bobby pins from her hair and pinned the fabric to her bra.

He pulled her closer. She didn't push him back. A new song started up, and Joanna stopped. "What's wrong?" he said, nudging her. They resumed their awkward swaying.

"Nothing. I'd just hate to keep you from hooking up with some willing bridesmaid."

"You were the only bridesmaid."

"You know what I mean. Laura appears to have several available friends for you to prey on."

"So that's what you take me for."

"I know how it goes with you. You find some lonely girl at a party, then convince her to make out with you …"

"Then I write her letters for two years just to prove I'm not a total asshole."

"I'm glad to know I'm a special case."

"Yeah, that's exactly what you are." Their bodies—or rather, the edges of their clothes—were touching, polyester to polyester. A bundle of nervous energy fluttered out of her, but she managed not to fill the silence with breathy laughter. "Hey, your boyfriend's gone now," he said in her ear. "We could have a proper reunion."

"Ha, ha."

"So you and Nate are next then," he said.

"For what?"

"For this!" Malcolm waved a hand in the air. "You caught the bouquet, right?"

"Laura threw it straight at me."

"You've been together—what, a year?"

"Longer than that."

"Oh wait, I forgot. You two have an arrangement."

"It's not an arrangement. It's a real relationship. We just

agreed we won't be together forever. We'll end it when it dies a natural death. No toughing it out, making each other miserable. No messy, expensive divorce. We're in it because we want to be, not because of some promise we made in the beginning when it was all rosy and new." Malcolm was regarding her with an amused half-smile. "I don't believe in marriage," she continued. "Neither does Nate. I mean—"

"Joanna." Malcolm leaned down and lowered his voice. "Marriage exists whether you believe in it or not."

"But it doesn't last! Half the time, anyway. And what about the other half, the ones who stay married? What percentage of them are even happy?"

"So, Laura and Ted are doomed." The music stopped, as if on cue. They broke away from each other. When a maudlin romantic pop song began trickling out the speakers, Joanna tipped her head in the direction of the tables, and Malcolm followed her. They sat down at a table.

"Well, I hope it works out. I like Ted," Joanna said.

"Yeah, Laura's good for him. Big step up from his college girlfriend."

Joanna had heard about her. Ted had spent the better part of his sophomore and junior years engaged in screaming matches with a beautiful—but temperamental—ceramicist. Joanna could hardly imagine Ted in a relationship like that, pottery flying above his head. He was so even-keeled, always wearing that quiet, little smile on his face.

"There are exceptions to the rule, of course," Joanna said. "There's that one percent or whatever that make it work."

"One percent, huh?"

"Your parents are still married. So you tell me: Are they happy? Are you glad they're still married?"

"Sure. They're happy. They seem happy."

Joanna paused for a moment. "My parents were crazy

about each other when we were young. Now they're at their daughter's wedding, and I doubt they've even exchanged two words all evening."

Malcolm frowned. "This is depressing."

"What's *depressing* is staying in a horrible marriage for your whole life."

Malcolm chuckled. "Have you told Laura all this?"

Joanna squinted out onto the dance floor and found her sister with her arms around Ted's neck. She was laughing at something he said. Her golden hair was loose, and she had a flower from her bouquet tucked behind one ear.

"Nah," Joanna said. "I'll let her have her fun."

The music slowed again, and the lights dimmed. Ted pulled Laura closer to him. Only a few other couples remained—their dad and his wife Linda, some of Ted and Laura's friends. Joanna didn't see Tess and Jeremy; they were probably making out in a bathroom stall like a pair of teenagers.

"We could probably leave. No one would notice," Joanna said to Malcolm. His eyes almost fluttered closed for a second. "Hey, do you need a place to stay? I should have invited you to crash at our place, but—"

"No thanks," he said. "I have other friends, you know."

Joanna felt herself turn red. He probably had a whole slew of ex-girlfriends and future-girlfriends waiting to take him in. "How many pen pals did you have, anyway?"

Malcolm stared down at her, more awake than he'd looked since the ceremony. "Jealous?"

She wanted to say she had missed him, or that she was so happy to have him back, but it seemed ridiculous, considering. "No," she said. "Curious. Just want to know what I'm dealing with here."

"Not too many," he said.

All those letters, back and forth for two years, but in person, she had a hard time reading him. "I just realized we've spent less than twenty-four hours of our whole lives together. And that's including today, standing up for Ted and Laura, arranging zinnias and things."

"True," Malcolm said. "But I'm here now."

5

outside it was snowing

Joanna spent the month of December reading five-page student essays that "demonstrated an ability to quote, summarize, and paraphrase." Stagger deadlines and assign more exciting essays next time. Lesson learned.

She and Nate had agreed to spend Christmas apart, purely for logistical reasons. He hadn't been back home in two years, and one of his best friends was getting married on Christmas Eve. She insisted he drive up to Seattle without her. The end of the semester would require all of her time and energy, anyway. Then she would have to plan for spring term. She had syllabi to create, textbooks to adopt, assignments to write.

Malcolm called her on Christmas Eve. "What's the plan for tomorrow?"

Joanna was sitting on the couch under a quilt, drinking hot chocolate. The day had disappeared under a haze of televised Christmas movies and trashy magazines she would be embarrassed to read in front of Nate. The night before, she'd finished her stacks of essays and submitted her final grades, and she intended to celebrate by doing nothing that required any mental exertion at all. "I haven't planned a thing."

"But we're still on for tomorrow, right?"

"Of course." She took a spoon and began eating the chocolaty sludge at the bottom of her mug. She hadn't seen Malcolm since Thanksgiving. It seemed like months ago. "Is Christine coming?" Christine—tall and thin, wearing a ruffled vintage blouse—had accompanied Malcolm to Thanksgiving dinner at Ted and Laura's. Joanna pictured the three of them—Malcolm, Christine, and Joanna— eating Christmas dinner together in a fancy restaurant, then exchanging gifts by a roaring fire.

"Christine? No."

"Did she go home for Christmas?"

"I have no idea."

"Oh." She smiled to herself. He said he'd come over in the morning so they could open presents under the tree. She surveyed the room. Nate had been hoping she would lend a "woman's touch" to the place when she moved in, and she had let him down. The furniture—garage sale finds, most of it—belonged to him. A dusty ficus sat in the corner by the bookshelves. She could clean it up and hang a few ornaments on it. "Perfect," she said.

The next morning, Malcolm turned down the corners of his mouth at the sight of the houseplant, decorated with some dangly earrings from her high school days. "What is this? We should at least have some lights or something."

She had made an effort to tidy up the living room, sweeping her piles of books and papers into the bedroom and shutting the door. The dishwasher was loaded with her dirty cups and plates, the rug vacuumed, the kitchen counter relatively clear. If she'd known Malcolm expected evergreen garlands and dancing nutcrackers, she might have rummaged around for some decorations. Unhappy with the dearth of festivity, Malcolm made them spend an hour of Christmas morning taking advantage of the holiday discounts at the store.

They were going to make cinnamon rolls, he announced when they returned. Growing up, he and his mom had always made cinnamon rolls Christmas morning before his dad got out of bed. They'd let them rise while they were opening presents "under an *enormous* tree with *thousands* of ornaments" and then put them in the oven "so the *whole house* smelled like cinnamon."

"Wow," was all she could think to say in response to that.

She couldn't even remember a Christmas with both of her parents together. She and Laura spent Christmas morning with her mom, and went to Denny's for dinner with their dad. The only redeeming feature of the split-household Christmas was that they got to open presents twice in one day.

Once Malcolm had strung a new strand of twinkling lights across the living room, plugged in a little artificial Christmas tree, and set the dough on top of the refrigerator to rise, he was in high spirits. They settled themselves on the floor in front of the little tree to exchange gifts.

Malcolm presented her an unwrapped wooden box. It was about the size of a thick book and sanded smooth.

"It's just a box," he said. "Inside is the present." She opened the lid, took out a tiny square of paper, and unfolded it, revealing a sketch of a little hut with a built-in bench. "I'll build you one this summer in your backyard," he explained. "If you still want one."

"Want one? I'd kill for one."

"Right. Ever since the time you made out with me in that one I built over at Ted's, right?"

Joanna felt her cheeks grow hot. "What are you talking about? We didn't—"

"Oh right. That was later. You lured me upstairs and *then* you jumped on me."

"If that's the way you want to remember it, be my guest."

"Thank you. I will. Okay. My turn." Malcolm reached for the large package she had wrapped the night before. Nate kept what seemed like an entire closet full of wrapping paper and ribbons, and she had spent forty-five minutes making the present appropriately festive. Now she wondered if the glinting foil paper and jaunty crimson bow would create false expectations for the box's contents.

She lunged for it. "Wait. Don't open it."

"It doesn't count if it's not on Christmas." He stared her down. "Give it to me."

Joanna relented and handed him the package. She watched as he untied the bow and then ripped off the paper. For a minute, he just peered into the box, lifting items out and setting them back in.

"Why, thank you, Joanna," Malcolm said. "This stuff will certainly come in handy. I mean, everyone likes coffee. And dental floss."

"It's not just coffee and dental floss, of course. I mean, give me some credit."

"Right. And popcorn—"

"Do you think I'd just gather an assortment of sale items from the grocery store shelves?"

"Well …"

She laughed. "Okay—look. Real coffee—you missed it while you were gone. You said you could only find instant. Natural peanut butter, spices—the food was so bland. You wrote me about it, that you'd give anything for a jar of red pepper flakes—"

"Dental floss?"

"You told me it was available only in the big towns."

"Right."

"I guess it would have made more sense to send this to you in Kazakhstan."

"Nah," he said. "Hey—come here."

She leaned in to hug him, then kissed him on his prickly cheek. It was like kissing a porcupine. "Merry Christmas," she said.

It was dark outside, freezing cold. "Looks like we might have a white Christmas after all." Malcolm's teeth chattered through his words.

"I don't know how you survived two winters in Kazakhstan. It's probably seventy or eighty degrees warmer here than it is there."

He crossed his arms across his body and tucked his hands under his armpits. Neither of them was dressed for such cold weather. It had been drizzly when she woke up that morning, but now they were surrounded by fog. She didn't even own a real coat; she was wearing two sweaters and a wool jacket with a hood. He had his hooded sweatshirt on over a sweater and a long-sleeved shirt. A few hard flakes of snow whirled around them. It didn't seem as if they were falling from the sky as much as following them down the street.

The movie theater greeted them with a blast of hot air. They sat down with a bucket of popcorn between them. When her hand brushed against his, she flinched. Even after almost fifteen minutes of previews, his hands were ice cold. "Malcolm!" she whispered. She took his hand and pressed it between both of hers, trying to get the blood flowing through his bony fingers. He stared straight ahead, absorbed in the opening credits. After a few minutes he lifted the armrest between them and shifted toward her, placing his other hand between hers. They sat like that, all four hands together in a heap, for the entire ninety-two-minute movie.

In the lobby, Joanna took a quick peek at her phone to see if Nate had tried to reach her during the movie. "You can call him if you want," Malcolm said.

"He was just returning my call from earlier. See?" She showed Malcolm the text message Nate had left her.

"'Merry Xmas'? That's what you get? He didn't even type out 'Christmas.'"

She shrugged. "I'll talk to him tomorrow. It's a holiday."

Outside it was snowing, which would have made Joanna delirious with happiness if she had been wearing a real coat and hat. They shuffled back to her place, then stood shivering at the doorstep. "Do you want to come in?"

He put his arms around her and squeezed. "Are you offering to warm me up?"

She gave him a gentle shove. "You'd better go."

That night she kept waking up, teeth chattering, even with every blanket in the house piled on top of her. At seven o'clock in the morning, her breath came out in visible puffs. So this was what orphans endured in Victorian novels. Her body couldn't move under the weight of so many covers. After a half hour of shivering, she wrapped two or three blankets around herself and made her way to the thermostat.

Malcolm's voice sounded groggy when he picked up the

phone.

"My heater is broken! It's forty-six degrees in here!" she informed him.

He told her a story about standing at a bus stop in Kazakhstan when the bottom of his boots had frozen to the street. Then he grumbled and said he'd come to her rescue.

Malcolm tapped on the thermostat, stomped down to the basement, and returned a few minutes later. "You're out of oil."

"What?"

"The oil tank. It's empty."

"So what do we do?"

"You've got to call an oil company and have them fill it back up."

"Okay."

"It's the day after Christmas. And tomorrow's Saturday."

"So?"

"So good luck." He smiled at her. "You can stay with me if you want."

It was still snowing—the entire street was hushed and white. They barely made it to Malcolm's place. "We're going to be snowed in all weekend," he said when they arrived at his doorstep.

His apartment—a large, rectangular room with a kitchen tucked off in one corner—sat on the corner of the first floor of a three-story building, set up off the street so passersby couldn't peek in. She threw herself on the couch and looked out the bank of windows at the snowfall. Snow lined every branch of every tree. When the wind picked up, a flurry of flakes would dart across the sidewalk and collect in a heap along the edges of the building.

"Tea?" Malcolm asked.

Joanna nodded. When Malcolm went back into the kitchen, she dialed Nate's number for the fifth time that day.

He picked up on the first ring. "Joanna! What is this all about?"

"You got my messages?"

"The furnace broke or—"

"We're out of oil. I can't get anyone to come fill up the tank. We're practically snowed in here."

They talked for a bit about the weather, the price of oil. "You at Laura's?"

She paused. "Laura and Ted are in California, remember?"

"Oh yeah. You're not home, are you? It's got to be freezing in there—"

"Well, I called Malcolm when I couldn't get the heat to turn on. So ... well, I guess I'll stay over at his place for a few days."

She didn't hear anything on the other line for a few moments. For a blissful second she thought they'd been cut off. "Good, good," he said at last, in a cheerful tone. "Thank Malcolm for me, okay? We can take care of the oil tank when I get back."

Malcolm walked in, set the cups of tea on the coffee table in front of the couch where she was sitting, listening to Nate, who had started talking about his Christmas. She smiled her thanks to Malcolm as he sat down next to her.

"So my parents ended up inviting her to stay for New Year's," Nate was saying.

"Wait. What?"

"Melissa. She's staying with us for a bit, just so she can get back on her feet again."

"What? How did this happen?"

"It's complicated. It had nothing to do with me. ...

My parents invited her." She'd been there for two nights already—two nights!—and planned to move back to Seattle for good after she sorted a few things out.

"Like what kind of things?" Joanna was having a hard time figuring out why his ex-girlfriend would need to stay with Nate's parents, of all people. What about Melissa's own parents? Didn't she have any friends at all? Relatives?

Unfortunately, Melissa's own parents had already made plans for Christmas they couldn't get out of, Nate explained. Melissa had downplayed how unhappy she was, told them she was going to spend Christmas with some friends from high school. So her parents went ahead and left town without her. That's how Nate's parents came to find Melissa at the supermarket, crying in the dairy aisle. She had gone in there and forgotten how to shop for herself! It had been so long since she had been in control of what she bought at the store. Charles had done all that for her.

Malcolm's eyes widened in alarm as Joanna's voice got louder. "This doesn't make *sense!*" He made a motion to stand up, but she grabbed his arm. He sat back down, and she positioned the phone between them so Malcolm could listen in. Nate was sighing, saying she was being unreasonable. "Say thanks to Malcolm for me," he said for the second time before hanging up the phone.

"Can you believe this?" she asked Malcolm. "His ex-*fiancée?* Meanwhile, he doesn't seem to care that I'm spending the night with you."

"You want to give him something to worry about?" He set his tea down and snaked an arm around her shoulder.

"Come on, Malcolm." She gave a nervous, half-hearted laugh, but then settled into the crook of his arm. "Be serious."

"I can sleep on the couch," she said that night. "I brought

my sleeping bag."

"Don't be ridiculous. You can sleep on the bed."

"I don't want to kick you out of your bed. The couch is fine, really."

"You wouldn't be kicking me out. It's big enough for the two of us."

She laughed. "Right. Nate would love that."

He held up his hands in innocence. "Hey. I can control myself. Now, if *you*, on the other hand, don't feel you could resist—"

"You're forgetting that I have a hot guy—complete with a tan and well-defined ab muscles—coming back for me. You're the one who's all alone."

"Well, if you like that Ken-doll look—"

"I do." When she'd first met Nate, her initial thought was that he was too handsome, almost faultless. He was tall, tan, and his chestnut brown hair waved perfectly over his head. But when he smiled he didn't look quite as perfect anymore. It's not that his teeth were crooked or that his smile was gummy—it's that his mouth was too big for his face. His teeth, too, were oversized, gleaming white. It threw everything off—but in a good way. She didn't trust physical perfection.

Malcolm stripped down to his boxer shorts, pulled back the covers, and hopped into bed. He patted the other side of the bed. "Coming?"

She had deliberately packed her most unbecoming pajamas, so as to not give off the wrong signals. Wearing drawstring sweatpants and an oversized T-shirt, she wondered if she may have taken the idea a bit too far. "Just stay on your side of the bed," she warned, lying down next to him.

"The same goes for you," he said primly, pulling his

covers up to his chin.

She laughed and turned away from him. "Good night."

Her feet were cold, but seeking out another blanket or a pair of socks seemed like too much trouble. She lay there, gazing out at the snow, watching it drift through the glow of the streetlight. Hours later her eyes opened. Her entire body had warmed to a perfect toasty temperature. Malcolm had wrapped his body around hers, his hand rested on her hip. She listened to the steady rhythm of his breath: in and out, in and out.

She should move his hand off her hip. She thought this, agreed with herself that this was what she should do, then closed her eyes again.

6

even dentists have problems

Joanna found a very convenient way to not care about her boyfriend spending Christmas with his ex-fiancée: she just turned off her phone and directed her attention to other things. She and Malcolm hunkered down in his apartment. His street remained unplowed, so no cars could get in or out. They played cards and read books. They tromped outside with broken-down cardboard boxes and sledded down carless streets.

On the second night, they watched a movie, sitting on his bed, sharing popcorn. Then they snuggled under the covers as the snowdrifts outside climbed their way up the sides of the building.

"They say this happens only every ten years or so," Joanna said.

"What happens?"

"All this snow. Not even a foot on the ground and every-thing shuts down for a week."

"We got lucky then."

Even with the T.V. off she could see Malcolm perfectly, his face illuminated by the streetlights reflecting off the snow. "How long do you think we'd survive in here?"

"Well. Forever, I guess. All the stores are still open, so ... "

"I mean, if it got worse. More and more snow, all winter long. The stores shut down and we had to stay here."

"Hm. What would we eat?"

"We'd have to hunt. Set traps outside for raccoons and squirrels."

"I couldn't eat a squirrel," said Malcolm.

"Okay, fine. So we'll have to live on pantry items and melted snow."

"In that case we could make it a few weeks. A month, maybe."

"That's it?"

"It wouldn't be the worst way to go," he said.

She woke up in the middle of the night with her head on his chest, his arms around her. She listened to his heart thumping, slowly at first, then picking up. Her breaths came out in shallow huffs as she tried not to move. And then he pulled her into him. His lips touched her cheek, then her mouth. She felt something drop in her, like an elevator lurching and then sinking to the floor below.

She put her hands on his chest and pushed him away from her. "Malcolm!" she whispered. "What are you *doing*?" He just mumbled, still asleep, and turned away from her. He murmured something she couldn't catch. They woke up late the next morning and made gingerbread pancakes.

Only once did they journey beyond Malcolm's block.

Bundled up in layers, they headed out to the store and were amazed to see that life had been carrying on without them. It was as if they had gone out to buy some groceries and instead found a new civilization with indecipherable customs. Walking back the four blocks from the store, it started to snow again. They burst back into the apartment, shed their extra layers, and returned to their cozy little snowed-in life.

Before they got into bed that night, she announced that they should sleep with a barricade between them. She gathered some throw pillows from the couch and lined them up and down the center of the bed.

"And what is the purpose of this?" he asked, amused.

"No more funny business."

His face revealed nothing. "I have no idea what you're talking about."

She looked down, cleared her throat. "You know." She gestured to herself, then to him, standing on the other side of the bed. "Last night." She paused. "You kissed me."

His eyes widened. "Me? You?"

She hesitated. She couldn't read his expression. "It's not going to happen again!" She turned down the covers, careful not to disturb the line of pillows on top of every-thing. Maybe she should have arranged them *under* the sheets. She got into bed and sat against the headboard with her arms crossed over her chest.

Malcolm got in bed, too, and then turned onto his side and looked up at her. He lowered his voice, so she had to strain to hear him. "Well, you did let me put my hands all over you the night before. And then you inched closer and closer to me, practically forcing me to hold you. So excuse me if maybe I got the *wrong idea*—"

Her mouth fell open. "I thought you were *asleep!*"

He smiled up at her. "Right. We were both 'asleep.' Let's go with that."

"You bastard!" She grabbed one of the pillows and hit him over the head with it.

"Ow." He picked up another pillow and threw it in her general direction. It flew across the bed and landed on the floor.

She saw where this was headed: pillow fight on the bed, both of them screeching, feathers flying through the air, then somehow both of them landing in a heap in the middle of the bed, panting … "I'm going to sleep on the couch," she said. "I'm serious this time."

"No you're not. Come on. Go to sleep. I'll be good, I promise."

The next day she made a big deal about calling Nate. She locked herself in the bathroom for privacy, sat on the edge of the tub, and stared at her phone. She couldn't handle talking to her boyfriend just yet. So, she dialed her sister's number and carried on a hushed conversation for as long as she could sustain it. Then she called Nate. They chatted for a bit, and after five minutes he said he had to go. She turned off the phone and just sat there for a moment, trying to clear her head. She felt completely exhausted all of a sudden. She'd hardly slept the entire weekend. She soaked a washcloth with cold water, wrung it out, and pressed it to her face. Looking in the mirror, her reflection revealed the same worn out face as a moment before—only now it was slightly damp.

She emerged from the bathroom to find Malcolm in the kitchen. "Just in time," he said, pulling a pan from the oven.

"Mmm," she said, breathing in the chocolaty air.

"Brownies."

"From scratch, I'm sure."

"Of course." He took out a spatula, cut her a large square, and placed it on a saucer, presenting it to her with a flourish.

It was so hot she had to pluck a small piece from the edge and blow on it before popping it in her mouth. She jolted awake, as if tasting the blissful combination of sugar, butter, and chocolate for the first time. "Oh my god. So good."

He stood leaning against the counter and studied her as she ate.

She moaned between every bite. "This is the best thing I have ever tasted in my entire life."

When she finished, she finally noticed him staring at her. "Aren't you going to have some?"

He gave a sad little smile and shook his head. "Why don't you just break up with him?"

Joanna froze. "What?" She tried to sound surprised. She and Nate had always said they'd end it before it got bad. But it was never that bad. She wasn't going to dump him for chewing too loudly or leaving his running clothes on the bathroom floor. She was reasonable. Leaving Nate would feel like knitting half a sweater. To spend all that money on yarn, all those hours counting stitches, twisting needles together—only to crumple it all into a shoebox and shove it under the bed—seemed like such a waste. She had logged some solid hours getting to know him. His favorite color: blue. The name of his childhood pet turtle: Shelly. How he liked his coffee: with five packets of sugar, unstirred. And in return, he got to know her, too. He was good about things like that.

"You know you're miserable with him. Do it now. Call him back, tell him it's over." Malcolm came up to her, took the saucer from her and set it on the counter. Then he put his hands on her waist and peered down at her.

She blinked but didn't push him away. "And then what?"

"Then—" Malcolm pulled her closer to him. His voice deepened. "I throw you back on the bed, and—"

She jerked away from him, let his arms fall down to his sides. "What I *mean* is, I'm not going to call up my boyfriend and break up with him. We *live* together. I'm not going to just put two years into something and then throw it all away for some … snowed-in fantasy."

"Fine." Malcolm turned away. "Do what you want."

The city began to emerge from the storm. Just the day before—no, just hours before—she had been suspended in a winter wonderland of sparkling icicles and snowflakes bigger than cotton balls. Now brown slush coated the streets. A cold drizzle of rain replaced the delicate flakes of snow.

"There's maybe one foot of snow on the ground and the whole city shuts down for a week," Nate grumbled. They were waiting in a coffee shop, where they would stay until the oil company filled their tank. They had had to call five companies before someone would agree to arrive that day. Then it would probably take a few hours to heat the house twenty degrees.

"Well, you know they don't have the equipment to deal with storms like these," she said. They'd had this conversation before, probably last winter. "Other cities have major snow storms every year. They have snow plows, people have snow tires on their cars, not to mention proper coats and—"

"I know." He had been in a bad mood since returning late that morning. Part of her wanted to ask about Melissa, but another part was content to sit in the coffee shop eating bagels and drinking tea. Maybe we don't need to talk things through, she thought. Isn't *talking things through* what got couples in so much trouble? Wouldn't we all be happier if we just agreed to overlook certain unpleasant subjects and move on?

"So, I want you to know that I had nothing to do with inviting Melissa to stay with my parents for Christmas," he said.

She sighed. "All right."

He told her the whole story. Melissa had been going through a "rough time." She had been living in Boston with a very controlling and manipulative boyfriend, to whom she was engaged. This boyfriend—Charles was his name— told her she was fat, *even though*, Nate insisted, she had a very trim and petite body due to diligent exercise and good eating habits. Charles wore her down to the point that she developed an eating disorder. "And she's a dentist!" As if *that* was what made it all so incomprehensible. It all ended in a huge fight that involved Charles punching walls and breaking dishes. He broke up with Melissa and pried the ten-thousand-dollar engagement ring off her finger. She packed her bags and flew back to Seattle that very day.

"The good news is, she really seems to be doing much better."

"That's good," Joanna said flatly.

"The thing is," Nate said, "she'll probably be staying with my parents for a bit longer, until she can find a place—"

"She's moving back to Seattle? What about Boston? Didn't she have a dental practice there?"

He shook his head. "She just worked at a clinic. In fact, she's going to be able to transfer to the same one back home."

She took a sip of her tea, which was now cold. The

teabag floated in it, waterlogged. "But I don't understand why she has to stay with your parents."

He hesitated before answering. "It's just … everyone thought … she was doing so much better—"

"But doesn't Melissa have anywhere else to go?" Joanna interrupted. "I mean, she's a dentist. She runs marathons for fun."

Nate shrugged. "Even dentists have problems." Right then his phone rang. He answered it while she waited, studying his face. He looked tired. "Good news," he said. "We have oil."

That night they sat side by side in bed, each ready to sink into a thick book. She nudged closer to him and inter-twined her leg with his. "I missed you." Once she said it, she decided it was true. It was nice just lying next to someone like this, their bare legs touching, without feeling any sort of nervousness or uncontrollable flutters. She could reach over, kiss him, grab him if she wanted to. And she knew that he would respond. And even if he didn't, she wouldn't be offended.

She closed her book with a loud snap and turned to Nate. He looked up at her. Then she was all over him, kissing his face, working her way down his neck, tearing off his shirt, kissing his chest, his tanned and toned stomach. He responded in kind. Surprised, but willing.

Over an hour later, Nate shuffled to the kitchen. This was one problem she had with Nate: the sex seemed to go on forever. Forty-five minutes to an hour and a half. Most women had the opposite problem, she knew. She tried to maintain her interest during the act by running her hands along his arms and chest and neck. She couldn't look at his face, with his eyes clamped shut, as if he were savoring each interminable moment. It's not that his body turned her on so much as she thought it *should*. "He's a beautiful man," her friend Allison had told her when Joanna had first wondered about him. She had seen him around campus, making eyes at her. He wasn't a grad student, but he worked at the university, in admissions. Soon Joanna had what any woman would be lucky to have: a beautiful man who could make love for hours at a time. Maybe something was wrong with her, for not wanting it.

Nate came back into the bedroom, still naked, carrying an armful of snacks. He was always ravenous after sex. He opened a Tupperware container and offered it to Joanna. "Brownie?"

Her face flushed. Malcolm had tossed the container in her suitcase as she was packing up to leave. "Here," he'd said. "Enjoy these with your boyfriend." Joanna shook her head at Nate and pushed the brownies away. She couldn't eat one in front of Nate.

"I don't know what got into you tonight," Nate was saying, crunching down on a potato chip. "But I like it." He smiled and kissed her on the forehead. "It's good to be home." Then he sighed. "I just wish I didn't have to go back in a couple weeks."

She had been leaning into him, holding on to his arm, but she stiffened. "What are you talking about?"

"I promised Melissa I'd help her move. She found an apartment next to the clinic where she'll be working."

"Why didn't you mention this earlier?"

"Is this a problem?"

She stared at him, her mouth hanging open. He infuriated her, the way he did this. He acted nonchalant and unruffled to highlight how unreasonable and neurotic she was behaving. "Yes, it's a problem! Melissa is a grown woman!

I think she can figure out how to move into an apartment without your help!"

"I thought you wanted her out of my parents' house!" He threw up his hands. It was like he was acting out a part in a play or a sitcom. She could almost imagine him rolling his eyes and falling back onto his pillows in an exhausted heap. "Women!" he'd exclaim, cueing the laugh track. "It's not like I'm going up there for fun. It's not a *vacation*. I'm going up there to help her out. She's not in a good place right now—"

"I know that," Joanna said.

"Well, the way you were acting—"

"You're just trying to help. I know."

"Exactly. Listen—I know I've been gone a lot. You could come up with me, if you want."

"To help your ex-girlfriend move?"

"She really wants to meet you."

Nate's parents' house, painted forest green, blended into the hill it stood on. A huge fir tree loomed over it, so close to the house the branches touched the windows and left a cushion of needles on the ground. The whole drive up had been bleak, hurtling through sheets of rain, windshield wipers swiping back and forth. By the time they arrived in Seattle it was almost dark, and the rain had stopped. Seattle air felt colder and saltier than Portland air.

No one greeted them at the door. Inside, the only light came from the gas fireplace glowing at the end of the room. Quiet flames flickered over ceramic aspen logs. Melissa huddled in front of it, her face blinking in and out of the shadows. She could pass for a child, but she was twenty-nine years old. Nate's age. She shivered and pulled a terrible brown and orange afghan closer to herself. She was like a mouse in a children's book.

"Hi Melissa," Nate said in a careful voice, the way you might talk to a patient in a mental institution.

Melissa gave them both a little smile. "Hi guys," she said. The afghan slipped down her shoulders. She was wearing a pair of mint green scrubs. Her hair was all one length, chopped off just below the chin, and light brown, the kind that, in childhood, was probably blonde.

No one talked much during dinner. Nate's mother said, "It was so nice of you to come up, Joanna," but her voice sounded off. Melissa excused herself from the table and went upstairs before dessert.

"She's been resting a lot," Nate's father explained. They all acted as if Melissa was an invalid, too fragile for this world. It was hard to imagine her working as a dentist or even working at all.

Hours after everyone else had gone to sleep, Nate and Joanna brushed their teeth. The upstairs rooms were damp and cold, letting off an odor of cedar and mothballs. The bedroom Nate used to share with his brother had remained unaltered since their childhood: two twin beds with matching plaid bedspreads, a cork bulletin board pinned with track and field ribbons. "Well," Joanna said, sitting down on the brother's bed, "I guess I'll head downstairs." His parents "didn't feel comfortable" with them sharing a room, and Melissa was already occupying the guest room. Joanna had insisted she'd be fine downstairs on the sofa bed. She couldn't kick him out of his own room.

"Rough day," Nate said.

"She's not what I expected."

"What did you expect?"

"I don't know. I thought she'd be blonde, for some reason. Blonde and perky."

Nate shook his head. "You should've seen her a couple weeks ago—she was even worse. Like a cult member. Dead eyes."

"What did he *do* to her?"

Nate's face froze. "I'm not really sure." She thought she saw him hold back tears. "She was so different, back when we were together. Every guy wanted her. Always laughing, really funny. I mean, it used to bug me, how guys were always coming up to her, telling her how hot she was. She had such a cute little—"

"Okay," Joanna said, "I get it."

"Joanna—" Nate came over and put his arm around her. "You're pretty, too." He kissed her on the cheek. "But you know that."

Joanna turned to him, and they kissed. "You're warm," he murmured into her neck. She reached to pull his shirt up over his head, but he stopped her. "Not here," he whispered. He tilted his head toward the other room. "Melissa's right next door."

Joanna sighed.

"You know I want to," Nate said. "But it's weird, right? In my parents' house …"

"Right," Joanna said. She patted him on the leg. "Well, it's just one weekend."

"She'll be gone tomorrow night," he said. "Rain check?"

"Sure."

"We could go out to dinner. Anywhere you want."

"Sounds nice." She smiled up at him, and he ruffled his hands through her hair.

The next day, Nate and Joanna met in the kitchen for breakfast. Joanna dressed without taking a shower, since

Nate had suggested they get an early start. "Where's Melissa?" Joanna said.

Nate's mom, wearing a bathrobe, shuffled in and poured herself a cup of coffee. "You two might want to get started without Melissa," she said.

Joanna looked at Nate, but he wasn't paying any attention to her. She should march upstairs and shake Melissa by the shoulders. *Wake up*, she would shout in that tiny, scared face. *This* is your *life!*

"What's Melissa up to?" Joanna asked, trying to make her voice sound light and conversational.

"She's sleeping," Nate's mom said.

"Oh." So that was that.

Nate and Joanna rented a trailer. They stopped by Melissa's parents' house in Green Lake to pick up her old bedroom furniture. Then they drove all the way to Renton to buy the dresser, coffee table, night stand, and kitchen table Melissa had circled in the IKEA catalog. They put it all on Melissa's credit card. Other than that, Melissa didn't own any more than a couple suitcases, which Joanna imagined were stuffed with scrubs and sweat pants.

It was late in the afternoon before they picked up Melissa to deliver her to her new place. Melissa rode up front to navigate, and Joanna was stuck in the back next to Melissa's bedding and a wiry tangle of hangers. They traversed the city again. The apartment was on the other side of town, over a highway, past downtown Seattle, the Space Needle gleaming in the distance. It wasn't raining. She could see the clouds billowing up over the Puget Sound, the Olympics jagged and blue, dotted with snow. Postcard perfect.

If Malcolm were still in Kazakhstan, she'd stop by a drugstore and buy the best postcard—funny or beautiful, it depended on her mood—and send it. After Malcolm had returned to Portland, the letters had stopped. This struck Joanna as unfair, somehow. They lived in the same city but didn't pour themselves out to each other anymore.

No more letters. But she could text him. She took out her phone. "Why am I here?" she wrote.

A minute passed, but then a message appeared: "Existential crisis?"

"Here, in Seattle. Here, stuck in the back seat of the car like a kid on a road trip," she said.

"Jump out at a stoplight," he wrote.

She wondered what they'd do if she did. Would they even notice? She could slip out, quietly, at a stop sign or red light. They'd keep driving.

They unloaded everything from the trailer and moved Melissa into her new place. Nate looked at his watch. "Okay, we've got to return the trailer before they close tonight." Nate looked over at Joanna. "You know where you want to go to dinner?"

Melissa walked over to the window. "Not much of a view," she said. It was dark, but you could see lights in the apartments across the way.

"First night in your new place," Joanna said to fill the silence.

Melissa let out a fluttery breath. "You guys, I'm so, so grateful for your help today. I mean, my own parents didn't—" She stopped because she was choking back tears. "I just don't know what I would have done—"

Nate went up to Melissa and put his arm around her shoulders. Melissa gave a stoic little smile. "You two have dinner plans."

Nate and Joanna exchanged glances. "We can stay for a little bit, help you get settled," Joanna said.

Melissa nodded.

"I still have to take that trailer back—" Nate said.

"I can stay with her," Joanna said.

Nate promised to return with Thai takeout, leaving Joanna and Melissa alone in the apartment.

Joanna suggested they make up Melissa's bed with the sheets Nate's mother had bought and washed for her. "Thanks for staying with me, Joanna," Melissa said, adjusting the fitted sheet over the mattress.

"You don't have to keep thanking me," Joanna said. "I wanted to come."

"You must think I'm a mess."

Joanna didn't know how to respond. Every time she looked at Melissa, she tried to reconcile the stories Nate had told her with the woman standing before her. The flirtatious college girl who mesmerized every guy she talked to. The heartbreaker who got pregnant with another man's baby and still managed to keep Nate in her thrall. Today Melissa was wearing a pair of patterned scrubs, bright fuchsia, scattered with cartoon molars. This was the woman who made another man so jealous he wouldn't let her leave the house without him. "What *happened* to you?" Joanna asked. As soon as she said it, she regretted it. "Sorry—"

Melissa smoothed the blankets over the bed and sat down on top of it. Joanna sat down, too. "I don't know." She shrugged. "It just happened."

Later that night, after Nate had returned, and they'd stored the leftover takeout containers in the fridge, Melissa asked if they would stay just a little bit longer. "Just until I fall asleep." And Melissa shut the door of the bedroom behind her, leaving Joanna and Nate with nothing to do but assemble her furniture. "We can't leave her like this," Nate whispered, one hour and a completed coffee table later.

"We can't stay here all night!" Joanna whispered back. It wouldn't surprise her if Nate suggested it. They could sleep curled up in boxes like cats, warming themselves with recycled packing materials.

"Let's at least finish the dresser."

It was past midnight by the time Joanna was tucked into the sofa bed at Nate's parents' house. She was exhausted. Before she went to sleep, she sent Malcolm a text: "Am I an idiot for coming on this trip?"

He wrote back almost immediately. "Probably."

"I thought I was being helpful."

"No, you thought you were keeping an eye on him." Joanna wanted to deny it. No, no, she should write back. That wasn't it at all.

"What a romantic weekend in Seattle," she wrote instead.

"You deserve it."

"Look, this isn't working," Nate said, a week after returning home. They'd fought every day after their weekend in Seattle—talking in circles, neither one willing to back down.

"What?"

"We always said we'd end it if we weren't happy."

"You're not happy?"

Nate's face answered her question. "Are you?"

"Do you care if I'm happy?" Now she was mad. "No, Nate, I wasn't *happy*. I spent last weekend helping your ex-girlfriend move. Do you think that made me happy?"

He shrugged. They argued for another hour, and at last they agreed to go to bed, lying side by side without touching. By then she had stopped crying; she was no longer angry or sad.

Her dominant feeling was relief, like stepping out of shoes two sizes too small.

7

the sound of rain

After two weeks of looking for a new place, she finally settled for a small efficiency apartment with industrial carpeting. It was in Southeast Portland, right across the river alongside warehouses and other old cement block buildings. It had two redeeming features: immediate availability and a view of the Portland skyline over the river, once you looked past the tarred rooftop directly below.

The apartment was too small to accommodate more than a bed and an upholstered armchair, which stood awkwardly on the linoleum next to the strip of kitchen where a table and chairs were probably supposed to go. She ate her meals sitting on her bed, looking out at the city. Malcolm had brought over a large jade plant in a heavy glazed ceramic pot for her birthday/housewarming present. It rested on the floor next to the chair, under the window. She spent perhaps a little too much time dusting each smooth, dark green fleshy leaf until it shone and pruning branches with her gardening shears. She kept it on a strict ten-day watering cycle. It did not escape Joanna's notice that she was once again funneling her love and attention to a plant.

Malcolm kept his distance after she moved; she told him she needed time to be on her own. They talked on the phone sometimes. She would lie on her bed and look out at the weird view of the Portland skyline and they would talk until she got too sleepy to form sentences.

She was living in an efficiency; her whole life had become efficient. She ate the same things every day, mostly shelf-stable foods. Instead of feeling pathetic she felt self-reliant. The depressing apartment turned out to be a blessing in disguise. She went out more, stayed longer after work, and joined colleagues for drinks afterwards. She became reacquainted with a few of her old friends from graduate school. She ran into Allison Chalmers at one of the community colleges where Joanna taught Introduction to the College Essay. She and Allison had gone to grad school together. She'd been working toward an MA in English with hopes of applying to PhD programs in postcolonial literature. But there she was, still in Portland, picking up adjunct positions.

"How's it going with Nate?" was the first thing Allison asked Joanna when they met each other at the coffee shop down the street from the community college. Allison had worked with Nate in the admissions office at the university and had, in fact, been the one to introduce Joanna to him in the first place. Allison had out-of-control curly brown hair that stuck out six inches from her head and big, blue eyes that gazed intently as she talked, as if she were concentrating very hard on what Joanna had to say. Her narrow, serious face somehow balanced out the unruly curls. Joanna had waved her hands and smiled. Long story, she'd said. But it's all for the best.

Allison and Joanna—along with Malcolm and three friends from graduate school—made plans to spend spring break on the coast. Over the years Joanna had learned to adjust to the Oregonian mindset, and now she, too, could get excited about bundling up and walking along the shore through a persistent gray cloud. She had to shuffle from the house, up some dunes tufted with grass, and then mime her way towards the loud crashing of waves to get to the ocean.

Elaine and Tracy owned the beach house. They were gourmet cooks and planned to make elaborate meals for everyone all weekend. Malcolm hung out with them in the kitchen, acting as their sous-chef. From Joanna's vantage point in front of the fire, everyone seemed to be having a marvelous time. She'd hear him mumbling something in his low voice, then outraged peals of laughter emit from the two women. More murmurs, then laughter, strident exclamations, and then his voice again, more animated this time.

Joanna was curled up on a couch with a book and a cup of tea, listening to the wind and rain and the crackling of the fire. It was dark outside, the windows rattled. Everything was right in her world at that moment. She could stay in this very spot for hours, for the rest of her life. But eventually her curiosity demanded she stand up and join the others in the kitchen.

Dinner turned into one of those rare occasions when everyone feeds off everyone else's ideas—where conversation manages to be somehow stimulating and self-affirming, as if they were voicing each other's secret thoughts. As they opened a fourth bottle of wine, they vowed they'd return to the coast every year—the six of them.

After dinner, Malcolm and Allison took off to pick up some ice cream for dessert while Joanna and John—a slight, bookish guy she and Allison knew from a Shakespeare seminar—cleaned the kitchen. With the table cleared and the dishwasher purring, they started up a Scrabble game with Elaine and Tracy. Allison and Malcolm still hadn't returned. "Where *are* those two?" murmured Elaine. After an hour they began wondering if they had gotten lost. "Maybe they got in a car accident," offered John.

Ten minutes later, Malcolm and Allison burst through the door, holding up a plastic bag of ice cream like a trophy. "What happened to you guys?" Tracy asked, taking the ice cream into the kitchen and immediately spooning it into bowls. Both Malcolm and Allison insisted that they had no idea they'd been gone for over an hour. They'd just driven to the store, stood by the ice cream case debating the attributes of vanilla over mint chocolate chip, and come right back.

"You spent an hour at the store and got *vanilla*?" The glow Joanna had felt with the beach house crowd during dinner had dimmed with her miserable performance during Scrabble and the prospect of vanilla ice cream for dessert.

Malcolm stood behind Joanna and peered at her letters. "Ouch," he said, eyeing her tray full of vowels—four of which were I's—and a blank.

He put his hands on her shoulders, bending over to get a better look at the Scrabble board, and she shrieked. His hands were freezing, as usual. He just laughed. She shrugged him off.

"Ah, but vanilla is a blank canvas," Allison remarked. "Put hot fudge on it, and you have a hot fudge sundae. Add caramel and pecans, and you have a tin roof—"

"Yeah, but you guys didn't get any toppings," Joanna pointed out. "This is just vanilla."

"Vanilla's good," John said diplomatically.

She pouted. "Not really."

"Hey," Allison said. "Let us play."

Joanna frowned. "We're kind of already in the middle of this game."

Elaine yawned and stood up. "You two can have my letters. I'm heading off to bed."

This was a personal pet peeve of Joanna's: flaky Scrabble players. You knew going into it that it could take all night. To quit after forty-five minutes was ridiculous. She opened her mouth to protest, but Elaine was already shuffling off to bed, and Malcolm and Allison were bending over the same tray of letters, whispering to each other.

It was almost one in the morning before everyone got to bed. Malcolm and John camped out in the living room. Allison and Joanna were sharing the second bedroom, each lying on a twin bed under matching homemade quilts. "So tell me how you know Malcolm again," Allison said in a whisper as soon as they'd turned out the lights.

"He was my brother-in-law's old roommate."

"What's the deal with you two?"

"Allison." Joanna sat up in bed to look over at her friend. It was too dark to make out her expression. "You don't like Malcolm, do you?"

"Why? What's wrong with him?"

"Nothing. Nothing's wrong with him. I just wouldn't have thought he'd be your type."

"You have to admit he's funny," she said. "And there's something weirdly sexy about him, too, don't you think?"

Joanna had not anticipated her two best friends falling for each other. Maybe they would hit it off. They'd date, fall in love, get married, have a brood of big-eyed kids, live happily ever after in a house Malcolm made with his own two hands. Meanwhile, Joanna, philosophically opposed to marriage, would remain single and childless. They'd ask her to tag along to readings held by obscure writers, make her the godmother of their children. They'd call her Aunt Joanna. She'd be knocked over to the periphery of their lives. At least they'd have to credit her with introducing them to each other. They'd owe her that much.

"I was with Nate for the last two years, remember?" Joanna said. "Malcolm and I are friends. You two should go out. You'd be good for him." Allison didn't respond, and Joanna closed her eyes.

She awoke a couple hours later to the sound of rain splattering against the windows. She lay still for a few moments, just listening to it. She wanted to throw the windows open, let in a gust of sweet, wild air. "Allison?" she whispered. Her friend's bed was empty. The room felt unbearably warm; the oxygen had been sucked right out of it. She ran to the window and opened it up. A gust of cool air blew in, and she took in a sharp, greedy breath. She leaned on the windowsill, looking out at the darkness and listening to the rain, until the room was cold.

The next day, Allison and Malcolm were insufferable, nuzzling each other's necks and giggling over the fifteen-egg frittata. Joanna pulled on her rubber boots, buttoned her raincoat over her pajamas, and headed out the door while everyone else was still drinking coffee. She ran through the dunes to the edge of the ocean. The weather hadn't improved since the night before. She plodded through the sand along the shoreline, her face tucked down to fend off the spray of rain and saltwater. She was already soaking wet. The wind had blown her hood back, whipped through her hair. She was all alone—a tragic figure from a Brontë novel, wandering the moors, her eyes dark with pain and longing. Soon she'd fall onto the dunes, too weak to carry on. A handsome stranger on horseback would swoop her up, gallop back to his estate, where she would spend the next two months recovering from a vague and lingering illness.

The sad thing was what appealed to her most about this fantasy was not the handsome man on horseback, but the thought of everyone's reactions back at the beach house. What would they do if she never returned? As night fell they would begin to panic. They'd form a search party. Soon they'd lose all hope at finding her, assuming she'd slipped on a rock and drowned. Little would they know that she was less than a mile away in a magnificent seaside manor, suffering from amnesia.

As she turned around and trudged back toward the beach house, she focused on Malcolm's role in this narrative. He would blame himself for her death. He would never marry, never forgive himself. One day—ten, twenty years later—she would see Malcolm on the streets of Portland. He'd be older, disheveled, wild-eyed. But seeing him would unlock something inside her. Her memory would flood back in an instant, and she'd call to him. He would cry tears of joy. But unfortunately for him, he would learn that she had married that man who had rescued her on the dunes all those years before. Malcolm would spend the rest of his days alone with his regrets.

She arrived back at the beach house, so overcome by her own imagination that she was not only wet and shivering, but sobbing. Inside, no one appeared to have lost a moment's relaxation with worry over her whereabouts. John and Allison had started another game of Scrabble at the table while Elaine and Tracy puttered around the kitchen. Malcolm was tending the fire. He looked up when she came in and a smile crept up on his face. She unzipped her coat and swept the wet tendrils of hair from her cheeks, counting on the rain to disguise her tears. She stood in a puddle of water in the tiled entryway, like a wet dog.

"What possessed you to take a walk in this weather?" he asked. "Stop!" As she made a move to enter the living room, he gestured for her not to step onto the carpet. He darted into the hall and returned with a towel. "You'll get the whole house wet."

He peeled off her coat, shook it twice, and hung it on a hook. Lifting the towel to her face, he began dabbing away her tears and rain. She stood still for a moment, looking up at him. He was concentrating on the act of drying her, pressing the towel to her hands, her hair. Then he handed her the towel. She took it silently and walked down the hall to the bathroom.

Back in Portland, the land of puffball pink cherry trees and chirping birds, she sat alone in her apartment. At this very moment, Malcolm and Allison were out on the town, taking in a dinner and a movie. Joanna had more or less arranged the whole thing. It was the first Friday night of spring term. After a boring dinner of cheese melted on a piece of whole wheat bread, Joanna turned on the light over her bed and gazed out at the city as she went over her syllabi, devising ways to interest her students in the dreaded ten-page research paper.

She fell asleep sitting up, surrounded by papers and open books. A knock at her door, just a persistent tapping, jostled her awake. She looked at the clock—a quarter to midnight. She stood up, letting papers flutter to the floor, and shuffled over to the door. Two huge dark eyes blinked at her through the peephole. She unlocked the door, opened it, and flopped back on her bed.

Malcolm let himself in. "Oh, were you asleep?" He walked over to her bed and began gathering up her books and papers.

"Hey—" she started, but then stopped. She'd have to go through it all tomorrow anyway.

He sat down on the edge of her bed, forcing her to scoot over to make room for him. He flung his arm around her shoulder.

"How was the big date?" she asked, inching away from him. She closed her eyes, feigning tiredness and boredom.

"Good," he said.

"Okay. So I take it you like Allison now."

"Do you want me to like Allison?"

She opened her eyes to glare at him. "What do you mean?"

He shrugged. "Nothing. Yeah. I like her. She's funny."

"That's what she said about you."

"Hey, Joanna?" He nudged himself closer to her.

"What?"

"You can be our bridesmaid if we get married."

She punched him in the arm. "No thanks."

"I love it when you're *jealous*," he said, kissing her temple.

She pushed him away from her, angry now. "Is that why you're with Allison now? To make me jealous? Why? I mean, what's the point?"

"Come on, Joanna. That's not how it was."

"Allison is a good friend of mine. If I had known you were going to just *use* her like this—"

Malcolm was shaking his head at her. "You practically set me up with her. Now you're mad?"

"I just—" She felt a tingling sensation in her nose. She

took a deep breath, staving off the urge to burst into tears. She didn't continue her thought, left her words hanging.

They were silent for several minutes. She turned away from him and climbed under the covers. "Are you staying here?" she said.

She heard him get up, take off his coat and shoes. He lay down next to her and wrapped his arms around her waist. She held still and closed her eyes. After a few minutes, he skimmed his hand down her thigh, then back up again. Up and down, gently, almost lulling her to sleep. Then his hand strayed from its course, reached between her legs. She stopped him—laced her fingers between his and settled their hands in the warmth of her stomach. Then she fell asleep.

8

yesterday's clothes

Joanna sat on the swings at the playground, kicking cedar mulch around with her foot. She'd been waiting for Laura to meet her for ten minutes. Finally, her sister opened the doors at the back of the elementary school where she taught sixth grade. She walked across the blacktop, around the rainbow-colored playground equipment, and sat on a swing next to Joanna, giving an exaggerated sigh of relief. "Conferences," Laura said. "Sorry I couldn't meet you until now." It was almost five o'clock and the sky was darkening.

"You're the one who wanted to meet," said Joanna.

Laura wasn't looking at her—she was peering out over the soccer field as if she were searching for someone. No one was around. Joanna shivered. Perhaps Laura wanted to announce a pregnancy—what else could be so urgent, require a secret meeting on a swing set at sundown? But Laura didn't look as if she were bursting with good news.

"Okay, Joanna, I'm just going to say it. I am not sure if this is even going to bother you or not, but I figured you might hear about it from someone else, and I didn't want that to happen."

"Just say it," Joanna said, trying not to panic at the sight of Laura wringing her hands and biting her bottom lip. An absurd thought entered her head: Laura had killed someone and needed Joanna to help her hide the body.

"Okay, so Ted stopped by the store last night, and he ran into Nate."

She laughed. "Is that what this is all about? Laura, really—"

Laura held up a hand, silencing her. "So they get to talking, and Ted's just making small talk, but then Nate tells him that he's selling the house, moving back to Seattle."

"Really?" This was unexpected, but she could hardly claim to care. She hadn't even seen Nate since they'd broken up three months earlier.

"And, uh—" Laura said, "he told Ted that he's getting married."

"Married? Well—what a surprise."

"I'm sorry," Laura said.

"Why? I think it's great. Nate and I are friends. Why would it bother me if one of my friends got married?" Nate would probably not qualify as a "friend" under the loosest of definitions. The last night she had spent in his house, a couple days after they had officially split, he had suggested they have "break-up sex" for "closure." After he had collapsed on top of her, panting with loud, ragged breaths, he had asked her if they could still be friends. She saw now that she'd agreed just so she could get him off of her. And out of her.

Laura appeared skeptical.

Joanna was gazing down at her feet, still kicking mulch. The top layer was dry, but as she dug her toe into the ground, she unearthed some darker, dirtier wood chips, wet from old rain. She could even smell it—rain, dirt, and decomposing wood.

She felt fine. Calm, even. "Thanks for telling me," she said. "I'll have to send him a crystal vase or a toaster." Joanna pushed off on the swing, pumping a few times until she was high enough to jump out, then landed in front of Laura. "Okay, I've got to go now." She crossed the soccer field at an unnaturally brisk pace, her sister calling after her.

For several blocks she simply walked with no destination. She didn't want to go home. The soles of her shoes hit the pavement with angry slaps. She didn't know what her problem was. She certainly didn't care if Nate got married.

After walking four or five more blocks, she found herself at Malcolm's apartment. The windows were dark. She looked up and down the street, as if she expected him to emerge from the shadows. "Malcolm," she whispered into her phone, "call me as soon as you get this. It's urgent." She sat on the steps outside his apartment building for a few minutes, tapping her foot on the cement. Then she went home.

She took off her coat and scarf and tossed them on the floor upon entering her apartment. When Malcolm still didn't pick up his phone, she called Allison. Joanna had been avoiding both of them since the night he came over to her place a few weeks ago. As soon as Allison picked up, Joanna rushed in with her story about Nate. "He must be marrying Melissa. He must be."

"Oh my god," Allison said. "I feel terrible that I ever introduced the two of you."

"It's not your fault."

"You know what you should do?" her friend asked.

"What?"

"Call him."

"I have no desire to ever speak to him again."

"Don't you want to know what he was thinking? Don't you want to just … tell him off?"

Allison was right. Joanna ended the call and dialed Nate's number before losing her nerve. She pressed her hand to her chest. He answered on the first ring.

"Hey," he said. "It's been a while."

"Yeah." Her voice was low, steady. "So, I heard you ran into Ted."

"Yeah," said Nate.

"And he said you were moving."

"If I can sell this place."

"Moving back to Seattle?"

"Listen, Joanna." She could hear some uneasiness in Nate's voice. "Maybe I could come over? I could explain everything."

"I want to hear it now."

"Okay," he said, but then didn't elaborate.

"So you're getting married?" She felt too keyed-up to sit down. Instead she paced back and forth in front of the strip of kitchen.

"Listen, Joanna, I didn't tell you because I wasn't sure you'd find out anyway. What was the point? But yeah …"

"Who's the lucky girl?" She attempted a light-hearted lilt to her voice but knew it came out bitter-sounding. On the other end of the line, he sighed.

"I don't expect you to be happy about this. But Melissa and I—"

"How did this even happen? We broke up at the end of *January!*"

Nate was silent for so long that Joanna thought the connection had broken. For the second time that day she had a prescient flash of insight right before she heard confirmation. "Well, last Christmas—"

"Christmas!" Joanna screamed into the phone. She was shaking. Until those last few miserable weeks with Nate, they'd rarely argued. They had never been passionate enough about anything to raise their voices in anger at each other. There was no yelling, swearing, or dish-throwing in their household, no matter how annoyed they might have been with each other.

Nate tried to explain how it had "just happened" when he went home for Christmas and found Melissa staying at his house. Seeing each other made them understand that they had never fallen out of love. Breaking up and moving away hadn't changed anything. "Except it wasn't so simple," Nate said. "I had you. I told her I couldn't just leave you like that."

"Oh, thanks."

Nate ignored her. "So, we decided to put our feelings on hold. I said I was going to go back to you, see if I could make things work. She made me promise to come back in a month no matter what, to help her move. Well, then you and I weren't getting along at all and I was sure that I'd go back to Seattle for good—and then you ended up going back there with me—"

"Because you *asked* me to. Nate, why didn't you just break up with me? That was the plan, right? Whatever happened to ending it before it got messy?"

"I don't know," he said. She could picture him exactly, sitting on the floor of the living room in the house they used to share. Surrounded by boxes and Star Wars figurines, a dumb, helpless expression on his too-handsome Ken-doll face.

"Just tell me one thing." She stopped pacing and sat

down on her bed, deflated. "Did you have sex with Melissa? While we were together I mean."

His hesitation answered her question. She hung up before she could hear his response and then threw her phone across the room. She needed to do something.

When was the last time she had vacuumed? It had probably been over a month. It seemed so futile to run a vacuum over such a small patch of carpet. The color was a strange mauve shade that hid all sorts of crumbs and fragments, providing little motivation to keep it clean. She wrestled the vacuum cleaner out of the closet, plugged it in, and ran it over the rug. Then she used one of the attachments to vacuum the covers on her bed and the upholstery on her chair. She felt like a demented housewife. If only she had on an apron and high heels. Maybe a string of pearls.

After rearranging her spice rack, polishing each jar with a sudsy cloth, Joanna went to call Malcolm again and saw that he'd already tried to call her back sometime during the cleaning spree. "Where have you been?" she said into the phone, so relieved to hear his voice at last that she almost started crying. Tears welled up in her eyes, but she willed them back.

"Work," he said. "What's this urgent news you had to tell me?"

After listening to her hysterical rant for a few minutes, he interrupted her. "I'll come get you," he said. "Don't do anything desperate."

He arrived to find her sitting in a heap in the middle of her bed, tears streaming down her face, cutting up photographs of Nate into tiny pieces.

"What happened to you?" Malcolm said when he saw her blotchy, red face. He sat on the edge of her bed and extended a hand to her. She took it and let him pull her over next to him. He handed her a tissue and she blew her nose. "I mean, you don't want to be with him anymore, right?"

"No."

"And you never thought you were going to marry the guy."

"So, you're saying I shouldn't be upset? That because I didn't marry Nate—or want to marry Nate—that was like a free pass for him to shit all over our relationship?" Malcolm held up his hands in defense. She was no longer crying. "Look, we'd been in 100 percent agreement about how it would end, and this was *not* how it was supposed to go. It was like the two years of my life with this guy were a joke. He didn't respect me. He *lied*."

Malcolm stayed quiet for a moment, and then he gave her leg a little pat. "Come on. Wash your face. I'll take you out to dinner."

She hadn't eaten a thing since lunch. When she thought back at herself at lunchtime, eating that peanut butter and honey sandwich on whole wheat bread, it was like glimpsing into the distant past—a past in which she didn't know what Nate had been up to since their breakup and didn't care. She was starving.

In the bathroom she saw that Malcolm had understated the awfulness of her appearance. Her whole face was hot and red, her eyes puffy and swollen. Her junior year of college had been a weepy one, necessitating elaborate rituals involving frozen spoons and hot washcloths. She no longer kept spoons in the freezer—a washcloth would have to suffice. She soaked one with hot water, wrung it out, almost burning her hands, and unfolded it over her face. She breathed in, deeply, inhaling the warm, clean scent, and pressed down on her eyeballs with the heels of her hands. She repeated the procedure three times, ending with cold water.

Malcolm was still sitting on the edge of the bed, engrossed in one of her composition textbooks. He looked up when the bathroom door opened. "Much better," he said.

The night was clear, warmer than usual for April, and people were walking along the sidewalks, darting into bars and restaurants, laughing and talking. She had one of those moments in which she realized that her problems were just that—her own. Life went on whether Nate was marrying Melissa or not. He had wronged her. No one cared but her.

Malcolm put his arm around her shoulders as they walked along the street in search of a restaurant. He led her into a dark wine bar that served elaborate appetizers and desserts. Sinking into a soft velvet chair, she let him order a cheese plate and a bottle of wine. She had already attacked the breadbasket, devouring what must have been an entire baguette.

"Look, Joanna," he started as she stuffed a huge hunk of bread in her mouth and chewed. "Nate is obviously an asshole." She was still chewing, so he continued. "This is the best thing that could have possibly happened. He's moving to Seattle—you'll never have to see him again. And now—hey—you'll never be tempted to get back together with him." She started shaking her head, but she was still working on the chunk of bread she'd stuffed in her mouth. She wanted to say that she had never considered getting back together with him in the first place.

She swallowed her bread and took a large gulp of wine. Then she went ahead and polished off the glass. He narrowed his eyes at her. "Feel better? Hey—that's enough for you."

She offered him a weak smile. "I don't know why I'm so upset."

Malcolm nodded slowly. "Yes you do."

He led her to his apartment after dinner. She hadn't been back there since they were snowed in together last Christmas. They sat on Malcolm's bed to watch a movie in the dark. Joanna wormed her way under the covers and leaned against his arm. An hour into the movie, the tears started streaming down her face again. "Maybe we should have gotten a comedy," she said.

"This is a comedy." There was nothing intrinsically sad about the story, but she was suffering right along with the characters as they bumbled their way around the television screen. He turned towards her, wiped away her tears with the sleeve of his shirt. "Joanna," he said, "come on."

"You know what the worst part is?" she asked, and then didn't wait for an answer. "It's not that he cheated. Or that he's marrying her—his *ex*-fiancée! That kind of thing happens all the time."

"Well, still—"

"It's that I went to *Seattle* with him." Joanna's tears had stopped flowing. She wiped them off her face with the back of her hand. "I helped her move. I spent hours assembling her *dresser*." Joanna shook her head in disgust, then flung herself on the bed and bent into fetal position. "I'm such an idiot."

Malcolm curled up behind her and patted her thigh. "You should have asked me—I would have told you how stupid it was to go over there with him."

Joanna managed a rueful little smile. "Thanks."

"Happy to help." After several minutes, Malcolm's hand went from petting to caressing.

"Why do we always end up like this?" Joanna said, and he inched closer.

"Mmm." His hand traveled over her clothes, up to her breasts—where they lingered for a few moments—then back down to her hips.

She took in a sharp breath when his lips brushed against the back of her neck.

"Turn around," he said, his voice low. And she did.

He took her face in his hands and kissed her. They pressed their bodies against each other, parted only long enough to undo buttons—"*so* many buttons," he muttered—or toss unwanted clothing onto the floor. She wrapped her arms around him and he brought her close to him, until his bare skin touched hers. For once his hands felt warm, right down to his fingertips.

The next morning Joanna woke up alone in his bed under a tangle of crumpled covers. She squinted in the daylight until she could make out Malcolm sitting next to an open window. He was watching her. She couldn't read his expression. He had his usual rolled-out-of bed look with his dark eyes and unshaven face. He was fully dressed in jeans and a dark brown sweater she had never seen before.

"I'll make you breakfast if you want," he said tonelessly.

"Okay."

She waited until she heard the pots and pans clanging around the kitchen before reaching for her clothes, doing her best to smooth out the wrinkles with her hands, while he made scrambled eggs and toast. They ate in silence. She wished she could take a shower, brush her teeth, find something else to wear. She wanted to touch him again—or she wanted him to touch her. He reached for the salt and sprinkled it over his eggs, his hair falling over his eyes. If only they had stayed in bed a little longer, with the curtains closed, clinging together in the dark. Instead she had to teach a class in an hour wearing yesterday's clothes.

9

the jade plant
needed competition

Joanna began to resent the jade plant Malcolm had given her for her birthday last January. New, tender leaves kept popping from its branches. It expanded in all directions. She had to drag the heavy pot a few inches from the wall because it had started looking cramped. Its branches twisted and twirled, reached for the light, as if they were on stage, dancing.

"Cool plant," Allison said upon entering Joanna's apartment. When Allison approached it, the plant looked even bigger—it was wider than she was and almost as tall.

"I hate that thing," Joanna said. Sure, she kept it on its ten-day watering cycle, fed it special succulent fertilizer, and dusted off its leaves until they shone like emeralds. But she detested these small chores. While Joanna was barely keeping it together, trudging around town to teach beginning-level English classes, making a cup of tea on the dented electric burner in the efficiency kitchen, and falling asleep on her cold, hard bed, that plant was *flourishing*.

The only thing keeping Joanna going was the fact that she was moving to her new house at the end of June. She'd done some research and discovered that—on paper anyway—it looked like she made a decent salary. Five classes added up. Right away she figured out that buying a house by herself was an exercise in lowering expectations. She had at first envisioned herself in one of the darling Craftsman bungalows around Hawthorne Boulevard. But she could barely afford to buy a house within Portland city limits, let alone a bungalow in the Hawthorne district. After looking at a 400-square-foot "rustic cabin" and a few bank-owned houses—one of which appeared to have a small animal decomposing on the carpet—she was about to give up.

She finally placed an offer on an old house with a big, open backyard surrounded by a chain-link fence after looking it over for less than ten minutes. If she wanted to plant a garden, she needed to act fast. So what if the yard was really just a field of mowed-down weeds? She was going to rip everything out, start from scratch. As soon as she had the keys, she'd go straight to the backyard and put in a vegetable garden, some decorative grasses, sunflowers, dahlias, fruit trees, raspberry bushes, bamboo—anything, everything! The jade plant needed competition.

Allison had come over to grade papers. They did this sometimes, though working with Allison made Joanna insecure about her own teaching skills. Allison always arrived with color-coded folders and an assortment of pens suitable for marking up papers. She zipped through four papers while Joanna still mulled over one, struggling to figure out what to say, attempting that perfect blend of encouragement and criticism.

Allison, it turned out, had been very busy lately. "I've

been *dating*," she said, recording a grade down in her notebook.

"Dating, huh? As in, multiple guys?"

A large smile lit up Allison's tiny face. "Yes. I went out on three dates last weekend. This is a record for me. My last date before that was—well, I guess it was that one with Malcolm. If that counts as a date."

"Why wouldn't it count?" Joanna felt herself turning red. She looked down, shuffled through some papers. She had tried—but never managed—to tell Allison about her own dalliance with Malcolm.

Allison shrugged. "Malcolm's cool. But you were right. Not my type."

"So how are you finding all of these eligible young bachelors?"

"Online. I signed up last week. I got like fifteen messages within twenty-four hours of posting my profile."

"Wow."

"Yeah. It slows down after that. It's just, when you first get on there, you're like fresh meat."

"Sounds delightful."

"Well, it beats sitting around waiting for someone to show up. After college, how do you even meet people? Everyone has a boyfriend or a girlfriend already—or they start marrying off. I'm almost thirty. How else am I going to find these guys?"

Joanna had heard all of these arguments before. Everyone making lists of what they do and don't want in a future mate—then matching those lists up with other people's lists. It was like applying for a job that required endless interviews. "I always pictured you crashing into an African lit expert in a library. But you know, the Internet is just as romantic."

Allison laughed. "But I need to keep myself busy while I'm waiting around for that guy, right? That's the point: there's always someone else. You know when you used to just stick with the same old guy for months, just because you thought you needed to give him a chance? Because there was no one better around? You don't need to do that anymore."

"Oh. Well, good."

"You should do it too, Joanna. Seriously."

"I don't think so."

"Come on. Why not? You could meet the man you are going to marry. Think about it: somewhere out there is the perfect guy for you—but there is no way you'll meet him otherwise. You run in different circles. Live in different parts of town. Go to different—"

"I thought the point was to date as many guys as possible."

"The point is not to waste time with the wrong guy so that you can find the right guy. Anyway, have you got any better ideas? You should get out there. It'll be good for you." And so, Allison talked Joanna into developing an online profile. "Okay, so describe yourself," Allison said. She was sprawled out on the bed with Joanna's laptop, ready to take dictation. She had already culled through Joanna's photos and uploaded the most fetching ones to dazzle potential suitors.

Joanna sat in her upholstered chair and frowned at the jade plant, which seemed to be reaching for her. She brushed it off, snapping a leaf in the process. Serves you right, she thought. "Well," she answered. "How would I describe myself? I'm a nihilist. And a misanthrope. I don't get along with anyone at all." She would just never activate the account. Allison would go home, bug her about it for a few weeks, and then give up.

"Misanthrope pretty much says it all," said her friend, tapping on the keyboard.

"What did you write?"

"Just that you have a sarcastic sense of humor. Okay, how do you prefer to get around? Bike, walk, bus?"

"That's a question on there?"

"Just a bunch of random things. Here—I think I know the answer to most of these." Allison spent a few minutes clicking around.

"You know, I don't even want a boyfriend right now," Joanna said.

Allison pointed to the computer screen. "Not a problem. You will be a dream come true for these guys."

She made Allison save the profile without posting it. "I want to look it over first," she said.

Allison frowned. "What are you afraid of?"

"I'm afraid of breaking hearts left and right. I can't have that hanging over my head."

"Very funny. Think of it this way: online dating is about taking control. Not leaving everything up to chance. It's liberating."

"I'm kind of busy right now," Joanna said, and Allison rolled her eyes. "We still need to wrap up the semester."

Essays were pored over and marked, the grades were in the mail. She could wipe her hands clean of the last term and enjoy the first party of the season. She had always envied people with late spring or summer birthdays. The lawns were all lush and green from the early spring rains. Bright red poppies, bigger than baby heads, flanked the walkway up to Ted and Laura's house.

Before Joanna could reach the door, Laura popped out, shutting the front door behind her. "Joanna," she said, "I've got to tell you something. Hey—you look nice. And we said no presents!"

Joanna had worn a dress for the occasion. Her hair, brushed smooth, fell down past her shoulders—an impossible feat when it was raining, as her hair frizzed into a tangled halo around her head. "This is just a joke," she said, holding the wrapped box up.

Her sister didn't appear to be listening. She kept looking back at the house like a character in a horror movie, waiting for a ghost to flutter out from the edges of the closed door. "Seriously, Joanna—"

"What?"

"Malcolm's here."

Joanna paused. "He's back?" She shook her head. "Well, that makes sense. It's Ted's party."

"Yeah, but—"

"Laura!" Three women clomped up the stairs to the porch. Joanna recognized them as teachers from Laura's school. They chattered all at once, overflowing with energy now that school was out and three whole months of summer loomed ahead of them. Joanna made her way to the door, ignoring Laura's silent pleading.

She wove through crowds of people, looking for somewhere to set down the present. How did Ted and Laura have so many friends? There must be twenty people standing around, snacking on sushi and salad rolls, and the party had just begun.

Then she saw Malcolm, standing in the kitchen. He looked different. For one thing, his hair was shorter. Instead of hanging down over his eyes, it was sticking out in every direction. And he was wearing a narrow, red plaid shirt with pearlescent snaps. The kind cowboys wear—or the kind of thing you put on to indicate a well-developed sense of irony and nostalgia. He never used to wear shirts like that.

It had been over a month since she had last seen him, glowering at her in his apartment. A week later, he'd left her a message on her phone. He'd found some contracting work in Alaska. He didn't know when he'd be back. Her sister had tried to talk Joanna into calling Malcolm and sorting it all out—she was convinced it was all some terrible mix-up, a misunderstanding. Laura had a point. But the thing was, she didn't want to call him and ask him what was going on; she didn't want to hear his answer.

She had gone over and over her night with him, trying to pinpoint where it had gone wrong. He had kissed *her*; she was sure of that. And later, lying beneath him, her hands on his back, the way he looked at her unnerved her so much that she had snapped her eyes shut, hid her face in his neck. But this was what she kept returning to: it wasn't all just a mistake, a ditch they'd stumbled into. Afterwards, lying next to each other in the dark, he had stroked her arm. He smelled good, like clean skin. *Holy shit, Joanna*, he had said. At the time she thought he was marveling at what had just happened, that he felt exactly the same way she did. Now she wondered if he had meant something else entirely.

Malcolm looked up. They locked eyes for a fraction of a second, and then he turned around. Someone had called his name. A beautiful, tall, slender girl sidled next to him, put her arms around his waist. She smiled up at him, her shiny dark hair cascading down her back.

Joanna was rooted to the floor, clutching Ted's birthday present. She wanted to drop the box and run, but she couldn't move. "Hey, you made it!" Ted said.

She smiled hugely and shoved the present at him. "You

can open it later. It's just a joke." Ted was wearing a blue plaid shirt similar to Malcolm's. And they both had on boots. Had she somehow missed a cowboy theme? Laura had been wearing jeans and a sheer cotton top that hadn't struck Joanna as particularly country and western. She scanned the room. No one else had arrived in cowboy hats, chaps, or Wranglers.

"Did you meet Nina?" Ted asked Joanna, pulling her towards Malcolm and the girl hanging all over him.

Laura materialized at Joanna's side and stood right next to her so their arms were touching. "I need some help with … uh, the drinks," Laura announced.

"They met in Alaska," Ted said with a laugh. "Can you believe that?"

Laura nudged Joanna. They didn't look at each other, but she understood the gesture. She knew she was supposed to introduce herself to Nina, who was smiling at her. "Hi," was all she managed.

"You must be Joanna." Nina's lip gloss sparkled.

Malcolm wasn't saying anything, but he was trying to catch Joanna's eye. She kept her gaze on Nina, ignoring him. "So … you're from Alaska?"

"I live here. It was the funniest coincidence.… " Nina still had her arms around Malcolm, and she squeezed him closer. She was obviously about to embark on the wonderful, romantic story about how she wooed Malcolm in some igloo out on the frozen tundra. Joanna didn't want to hear it. She stepped on Laura's toe, gently.

"Sorry," Laura said. "I really need my sister's help with something."

"No wait, you've got to hear this!" Ted was saying as Laura led Joanna by the hand, away from the happy couple.

The sisters huddled in the corner by the bookshelves.

"Thanks for not telling Ted about me and Malcolm," Joanna said.

"I promised I wouldn't."

Joanna tilted her head toward the kitchen. "So she's his girlfriend, I take it? That was quick!"

"I know." There was real heartache in Laura's voice. She was taking this worse than Joanna.

"I guess I should have expected something like this."

"*What?* He goes to Alaska for three weeks or whatever it was and comes back with a *girlfriend?*" Laura shook her head in disgust.

"How did they even meet anyway?"

"I don't know. I think she's a geologist or something. She was up there the same time he was and they met in a bar. Then they found out they both live in Portland."

"A *geologist?*"

"It's so obvious why he went for her."

Joanna laughed. "Why, because of that body?"

"Because she looks exactly like you! Who else is tall, thin, with long dark brown hair … ring any bells?"

"She's wearing a *cargo skirt.*"

"You could be sisters," Laura said.

"No thanks." She smiled at her pale blonde sister. Laura smiled back.

Joanna sighed. "This seems to be happening to me a lot lately."

Laura shook her head sadly.

"Allison wants me to do online dating," Joanna said.

"You should!" Laura clapped her hands in excitement. "That's how I met Ted!"

"I know."

On that positive note, Joanna sent Laura off to "enjoy Ted's party." Joanna promised to stuff her face with sushi and start mingling. Who knew? Maybe Ted had some other charming friend she could meet and make out with. This seemed to satisfy Laura, who left Joanna alone by the bookshelves.

Two pounds of sushi and three vodka tonics later, she was waiting in the hall for her turn at the upstairs bathroom when she heard his voice. "Joanna." She turned to find Malcolm peering down at her, his eyes dark and serious. She didn't even bother answering him. She turned her head towards the bathroom door and willed whoever was in there to come out. "Can we talk for a minute?"

She was horrified to feel tears welling up in her eyes. Her nose tingled. If he said even one more word, she would break into uncontrollable sobs. She took a slow, deep breath. The tingling subsided. She didn't trust herself to speak, so she just shook her head. She tapped her foot against the floor. Maybe someone had gone into the bathroom and passed out. Certainly she'd been standing there for an hour, at least.

"Come on," Malcolm said. He took her by the arm and led her down the hall into Ted and Laura's bedroom. It was quiet in there, peaceful. Laura had painted it sky blue. Everything matched, everything was orderly and in its place. A breeze was blowing the sheer white curtains out into the room. They billowed out, then shrunk back in, like they were sighing. He shut the door and leaned against it, so she couldn't get back out. He was still hanging on to her arm. "I want to explain," he said.

"There's no need to explain. I'm pretty sure I get it." She reached for the doorknob but he blocked it. "Let go of me."

"Look, I'm sorry."

"Sorry for what?" She, for one, was not sorry, no matter what trouble it ended up causing them. If only it had been awful, if they'd stumbled around together, maybe they both could have laughed it off and proceeded as normal.

His voice was quiet. "I fucked everything up. I know that."

"You went to *Alaska*. I had to hear that from my sister. And then, if that wasn't bad enough …" She let that sentence dangle. She didn't want to fill in the blank. *You brought back a girlfriend.* That was really the most unbeliev-able part of all. How did he manage to find a girlfriend—in Alaska of all places—in a matter of weeks? She tried to push him out of her way. "Let me out."

He wore a sad, droopy-eyed expression, but he stepped aside. She burst back into the hall. The bathroom door was open, finally. She locked herself in, sat down on the edge of the bathtub, and took ten deep breaths. Then, without saying goodbye to anyone, she left the party.

When she got home she was greeted by the monstrous jade plant. She wanted to open the window and push it out, where it would land on the rooftop below with a satisfying thud, its branches breaking off, dirt spewing everywhere.

But of course she didn't do that. It was too heavy to lift. And anyway, it was just a plant.

10

they made pioneering
seem so easy

It would be a lot easier to get over Malcolm if he weren't always hanging around. At the end of June, Joanna finally got the keys to her new house. Ted, Laura, *and* Malcolm all arrived to help her move. As they drove from southeast to northeast Portland in a borrowed pickup, Joanna looked back and saw her jade plant waving in the wind. The huge ceramic pot teetered whenever they turned a corner, dirt sifting out onto her boxes. Soon the whole scaly brown trunk would snap and the top of the plant would take flight, land on the street, get trampled under the wheels of passing cars. Joanna knew it, she had a sixth sense about it—she was experiencing a rare moment of prescience.

Ted was driving, Joanna crammed between Laura and Malcolm. The entire side of her body was touching his. He didn't seem to mind at all. She would even say he was enjoying it, one arm stretched out the open window, a smile on his face, his other arm slung across the back of the seat.

"Good moving day," he said. They all murmured in agreement.

The image of the splattered plant was so vivid in her mind that she was surprised to find the plant intact at the end of the short drive. So much for prescience. She fingered one of its leaves, polishing it until it glowed. "Sorry," she whispered to it. Malcolm carried it into the living room and set it in front of the window. She vowed to be kinder to the plant. It's a plant, she reminded herself. A *plant*.

"I'll pick Mom up at the airport tonight and bring her over to your place first thing tomorrow morning," Laura said. "Apparently she wants to help you settle in."

"Great," Joanna said.

"I can help, too, if you want," Malcolm said.

"Not necessary," Joanna said.

"She said she has something important to tell us," Laura said.

Joanna went pale. "What? Did she say what it was?"

"No, she said she wanted to tell us in person."

"Wait—tell me exactly what she said."

"I'm sure it's nothing."

"If it was nothing, why would she fly out here to make an announcement?"

"Well, what could it possibly be? Maybe she got a promotion or something."

"I'll bet she's getting married. She's been with Jeremy for almost a year, right? And remember what she said at your wedding?"

"I really doubt it, Joanna." Laura laughed. "But good for her—"

"It's not funny! It's not really something to joke about. Oh, crazy Tess! Getting married to some underage cowboy!"

"I think he's in his forties. Anyway, she deserves to find someone."

Joanna shook her head. "Believe me, this is not going to turn out well."

The next morning, Laura took Joanna aside after dropping their mother off, reminding her to "act like a grown-up," which put Joanna in a bad mood from the very beginning.

"Did she tell you what it was?" Joanna had asked her. "Her big announcement?"

"She wants to tell you herself," Laura said. But all day, Tess didn't say a word.

"I'm here to help you settle in," her mom said. "Anything you want—just say the word."

"The garden. We need to start there."

"I thought maybe we could go get you some furniture? A table and chairs, maybe?" Joanna's sole piece of furniture in the front room was her upholstered chair propped in front of the fireplace. A dusty old chandelier dangled down the middle of the ceiling off the kitchen, but there was no table to put underneath it. They stood in the empty living room, their voices echoing.

"You just said you'd help me do whatever I want. I want to plant the garden. Planting season is practically over. It's *June*."

"But there's nowhere to sit. Don't you want to get some furniture?"

"Furniture? *Furniture*?" She tried not to panic. "Mom, I need to get a garden in *today*." She took in a deep breath, trying to calm herself. She knew she was acting like a petulant teenager; Tess seemed to inspire this kind of behavior in her.

Half-crazed, Joanna dragged her mother into gardening stores, nurseries, and supermarkets, throwing bags of compost, garden tools, and plant starts into the car. It was past noon before they unloaded everything and stood outside with brand new shovels. Joanna had lent her mother some jeans and a T-shirt, and they both snapped on bright green gardening gloves. The sun beat down on them as they surveyed the plot of land.

"Okay," Joanna said. "You dig over there. I'll start here." The plan was to rip up a layer of grass and weeds, making two 4x10-foot plots for her vegetable garden. The starts sat wilting in the sunlight, cowering from the argument Joanna and Tess had had over them earlier that day. Her mother had suggested saving money by buying packets of seeds instead of shelling out four dollars for established plants, and Joanna had lashed out. "We don't have *time* for seeds, Mom! Don't you understand?"

They lifted their shovels, broke into hard clay. A half hour later, they slumped over the handles, wiped the dust from their faces. At this rate they'd be working until nine o'clock at night before clearing this small patch of land. "Argh!" Joanna cried out. She flung her shovel off to the side and crumpled down on the weed-infested lawn. Her mother stared down at her, breathing heavily through her mouth.

In one of the *Little House and the Prairie* books, Pa had built a cabin out of his own two hands while the family had lived in a dugout in the side of a hill. When a plague of locusts had descended upon their crops and landed on their food, their skin, their hair, even two-year-old Carrie was too stoic to cry about it. They made pioneering seem so easy.

"You two look exhausted!" Joanna looked up and squinted. Malcolm's girlfriend was smiling down at them, the sun forming a golden aura around her head.

"Nina wanted to drop by," Malcolm said, stepping up

behind her. He tried to shoot Joanna an apologetic look, but she pretended not to see.

Tess beamed. "Malcolm! It's great to see you. We've worn ourselves out working on the garden." Everyone looked out at the yard, which looked exactly like it did before, except now it featured two large mounds of dirt. Joanna stayed slumped on the ground, too dispirited to stand up for her unannounced visitors.

"I wanted the grand tour," Nina explained.

"Okay," Joanna said carefully.

"I tried calling but no one answered," Malcolm said. "So we decided to come over."

Why, Joanna wanted to ask. Why are you *always* coming over—and now with your girlfriend?

"Why don't you two stay for a bit?" Joanna heard her mother say. "We could have a barbecue!"

"Oh, I don't think—" Malcolm said.

"We'd love to!" Nina responded.

"Mom, I don't have a grill."

"No problem," Nina said. "We'll get pizza. Malcolm and I will go get it. Our treat."

"Sounds like a plan," Tess said.

"Mom, we still have to get all the starts in, remember? We were just taking a break…."

"They could come back in a couple hours," Tess said. "Six o'clock?"

Joanna had to agree that there was nothing preventing this plan from taking shape.

Joanna was feeling better about everything—the plants were in. Now she just had to water them and pray the weather would hold. She'd also taken a hot shower, soaking up the water and steam, digging the dirt out from under her nails. She had spent an embarrassing amount of time deliberating over her outfit. What articles of clothing would most convincingly convey her irritation with Malcolm, while still managing to dazzle him with what he'd tossed aside? She settled on jeans and an olive green T-shirt, an ensemble that managed to say absolutely nothing at all.

"We got you a housewarming present," Nina said, handing Joanna an aloe vera plant in a blue ceramic pot as she walked through the front door. When Nina smiled, Joanna could see her two front teeth overlapped a bit. Malcolm probably found it adorable.

"Oh, thanks," Joanna said. She set it on the mantle and stepped back to admire it. "Now my jade tree has a friend." When she turned around she saw Malcolm observing her, his eyes dark, and the corners of his mouth downturned.

"Friendship is important," Malcolm said, staring at Joanna. He was standing in the middle of the empty room, holding two pizza boxes. They locked eyes for a split second. Then Joanna broke the connection and looked down. She brushed some imaginary dirt from her pants.

"I'm starving," Tess said, coming in to the front room from the hallway.

"Well, let's eat then. Please, have a seat." Joanna gestured toward the floor.

"Here?" Tess said.

"Nowhere else to go," Joanna answered. Her mom sat down and Malcolm set the pizzas in front of her. Joanna went back into the kitchen to gather the plates and silverware.

"Thanks for having us over. I just really wanted to see your place." Nina had followed Joanna into the kitchen.

"Okay," Joanna responded after a pause. She started pulling glasses out of a cardboard box, freeing them from their newspaper cocoons. She let the newspaper drop to the floor, set the glasses on the counter.

Nina picked a wrapped glass out of the box and followed suit. "I feel like we have so much to talk about. You know?"

"We do?" This sounded ruder than she intended. "I mean, I guess I don't know much about rocks."

"Well, I mostly do geotechnical investigations, soil and groundwater sampling, stuff like that," Nina said.

"Oh. Well, I know even less about … that."

"I really hope we can hang out more." Nina unwrapped another glass.

Wow, Joanna wanted to reply. That's pretty much the opposite of *my* hope. Instead, she pushed a box of plates between them. She was beginning to intuit Nina's motives. She was keeping her enemies close, trying to stuff Joanna into that less attractive, quirky "guy's best friend" mold so that she, Nina, could emerge as the triumphant beautiful girlfriend. Well, Joanna had no intention of playing Eponine to Nina's Cosette!

When Joanna didn't respond, Nina continued. "And I really hope you and Mal stay good friends." *Mal?* "You know, I can't even think of the last time I picked up a novel. Probably freshman English? I know you two loved to talk about *literature.* He told me all about you guys."

"He did?" Joanna tried to keep her voice neutral. So that's how Malcolm had described their relationship to Nina: A meeting of the minds. Chaste hours of silent sustained reading. Earnest conversations about Russian Formalism in coffee shops.

"It was just so cute the way you used to send each other secret messages in books." Nina smiled.

Joanna stared blankly at Nina. "What?"

"You know, when he was in the Peace Corps …"

Nina had the story about the books all wrong. Joanna had sent Malcolm a few old classics she'd had in a graduate school lit class, since he was always short on reading material in Kazakhstan—but she'd forgotten to remove the Post-it notes she had stuck on the pages. Mostly she was just marking important passages, jotting down quotations she might use in a paper. Malcolm had pulled the notes from the pages, chained them together in order, added his own commentary, and mailed them back to her. In this way they had conversations about all the texts she studied in class. These little dialogues added to her enjoyment of the books more than her classes had—not that their musings were especially insightful. About "The Chrysanthemums" she'd written, "The flowers symbolize Elisa's self-worth," after which Malcolm had scrawled, "Duh."

Joanna couldn't look at Nina. "We'd better bring in the dishes," she said. "The pizzas are probably getting cold." She took the stack of plates and brought them into the living room, where Malcolm and her mother seemed to be having some sort of intense discussion about Willamette River run-off. Apparently this was a topic dear to Nina's heart, because she jumped right in, offering up her opinions on storm drains and bioswales.

Joanna didn't have any opinions on storm drains and bioswales. She sat down on the floor and took a slice of pizza from the box. After a while, she began to tune them out.

Joanna couldn't get to sleep that night. It was too hot in

the room; the sheets, clammy and lumpy, stuck to her skin. Opening the window didn't help—only brought in the noise from the street, black clouds of exhaust. She flung the covers off and went into the kitchen. If she couldn't sleep, she could at least get something done. Under the sickly tint of a single fluorescent light bulb, she freed the remainder of her dishes from their newspaper casings and placed them in the cupboards, sticky with layer after layer of paint. She'd had vague plans of refinishing them before unpacking. Oh well. Too late now.

"Can't sleep?" her mother said. Tess stood in the doorway wearing a short robe.

"Just unpacking."

Tess stepped into the kitchen and opened a box and stared into it as if flummoxed by the contents. "I like hanging out with your friends," she said, lifting out a half-empty box of rigatoni, then setting it back inside.

"They're not really my friends," Joanna said.

"What do you mean?"

"It's complicated."

"Complicated how?"

"Never mind."

"Did something happen?"

"Mom, I said, never mind."

Her mom's eyes narrowed, then she began to nod slowly as if she'd suddenly had some deep epiphany about the mysteries of life. "I get it," Tess said. "Believe me, Joanna, I know what you're going through."

Now neither of them even pretended to unpack. Joanna's hands went suddenly cold; they felt detached from the rest of her body. "I doubt that, Mom," she managed to say.

"I know what it's like when you can't get the one you want."

"That's not what's happening."

Tess nodded. "You want him. It's obvious."

"Mom—" Joanna stopped. She didn't have the energy to deny it.

"I went through it myself, you know. With your dad."

Joanna had never known—nor had she wanted to know, exactly—why her parents split. They had always seemed so happy together—their dad goggle-eyed at their charming mother, blonde hair swishing as she threw her arms around him and kissed him in the kitchen. Their dad would dip her down to the ground, and Joanna and Laura would squeal and clap. Their father adored their mother back in those days.

Tess went over to the sink and turned on the tap. She filled a mug with water and drank it before turning back to Joanna again. "I left your dad, you know. And then when I tried to get him back, he wouldn't take me. Worst time of my life. One of them, anyway."

"Why did you leave if you still loved him?"

"We outgrew each other, I guess."

As much as she had feared hearing some dramatic secret that would warp her opinion of one—or both—of her parents forever, she also did not want to hear that the marriage was so flimsy, so easily cast aside. "It's a marriage, not an old coat," she remarked.

Tess laughed. "You know, it just seems so simple when you fall in love with someone. It always seems like you're both going in the same direction, you both want the same things. But really you're just going like this." Tess held her two index fingers together, then shot them out in opposite directions, until her arms were spread wide. "And there's no coming back from that. Your father is a very practical man. When we first moved to Reno it was supposed to be for a year, maybe two. Then we were going to sell everything, go on a road trip across the U.S. I had this dream of running a ranch out in Eastern Nevada. We could spend all day riding horses in the mountains, live off the land. We hadn't figured it all out, but that's what I was counting on. And the thing was, he was happy where we were. And eventually—what? Fifteen years later? It finally dawned on me that we were never going to do any of the things we used to talk about. I just couldn't stand that thought—that this was it. This was all there was."

Joanna was silent. When she was ten and Laura was thirteen, their parents sent them to Colorado to visit their grandparents for two weeks. They returned to two apartments, four toothbrushes, two night-lights, four identical bedspreads on four different beds. Aren't you girls lucky? Two houses, two families! And oh yes, we're getting divorced. Sometimes she wondered if she missed the house more than her parents' marriage. She had loved that place, loved staring out at the shadows the clouds made over the mountains. One morning she'd woken up early to find eleven wild horses roaming right in their yard. She schemed up ways to fence them in, tame them, but by the time her parents and sister got up, they were gone.

Tess now lived in a two-bedroom townhouse, mere miles from the house she'd spent her marriage in. Oh, the townhouse was nice—certainly a big improvement over the apartment where Tess and Joanna had lived together all those years. And the men Tess had dated, one after the other—guys she'd met in the diner or out grocery shopping at all hours of the night, men wearing cowboy hats to disguise their thinning hair—couldn't have been any more worldly than her father, the high school teacher.

Tess was staring off into the corner of the kitchen.

"Mom—" Joanna hated seeing this childlike, hurt expression on her mother's beautiful, aging face. "Mom, I thought you were coming up here to tell me something. Me and Laura. She said you had an announcement." Joanna took in a deep breath and braced herself for bad news. As the day went on and on, through the gardening and the awkward pizza party, Joanna had convinced herself that it was worse than she'd originally imagined. Maybe Tess had cancer, or a rare incurable disease of some kind.

"I didn't want to tell you over the phone," Tess said.

"Just tell me."

Her mother's chin began to tremble, and Joanna stopped breathing altogether.

"Jeremy and I—"

"Oh no …"

"We broke up."

Joanna felt herself exhaling in relief. Then she quickly tried to look sympathetic instead of elated by the news. "Oh, Mom. I'm sorry. I know you really liked this one."

Tess shrugged. "It wasn't meant to be, I guess."

"So this was your big news? I mean, you dated him for less than a year. I thought you were *dying*."

"Oh, Jo-Jo. Don't be silly. I came to help you settle in, remember?"

"So you're handling this okay?"

"Don't worry about me."

"I can't help it."

"I'll get through it okay. I always do. Sooner or later."

"Look, maybe this is a good thing! For both of us. Where would I be today if I were still with Nate? Look at what we've done on our own! Think of all the time and energy we put into these guys we could be putting into better things, more interesting things. We don't need men around—"

"But I like having them around."

"We should just be done with men. Don't you think?"

Tess yawned. "If you say so, Jo-Jo."

Joanna went back to bed. Her eyes stung and her entire body ached from attacking her backyard with that shovel. The air coming in through the window felt cooler now. She pulled the top sheet over herself and closed her eyes. She drifted into a formless dream. No people or images—only tapping, like fingers on a typewriter. The tapping grew louder and louder, forcing her into consciousness. Someone was knocking at the door. She considered staying in bed, but after a minute the tapping became so annoying that she jumped off the bed and walked to the front of the house to peek through the window. She pulled back the dusty, gauzy curtains and flicked on the porch light, revealing Malcolm standing at the door. She opened the door but didn't let him in. "You're the only one who invites himself over at all hours of the night."

"It's midnight," Malcolm responded, as if this were a very reasonable hour for an impromptu visit. "Can I come in?"

She went out to join him on the porch, closing the door behind her. The night was still warm, but she shivered. She crossed her arms over herself, aware that she was wearing a sheer—most likely completely see-through—tank top and cotton pajama bottoms.

"What do you want?" she asked, flashing with anger. "Why are you *always* hanging around?"

"Because I want to see you." He was leaning against the porch railing, bathed in streetlight. The yellowing light made the shadows under his eyes more pronounced. He turned away and looked out at the street below. A car passed by, its sound whooshing over them, then receding.

She felt the sudden impulse to put a hand on his face, to touch his prickly cheek. Another shiver rushed through her; she kept her arms crossed tightly over her chest.

"Joanna," he said. "I don't want you to hate me."

After a moment, she sighed. "I don't hate you."

"Good."

"All right. Good. Well, thanks for stopping by. Next time, try the phone." Joanna whirled around, prepared to march back in the house, but Malcolm grabbed her arm and pulled her back.

He stared down at her. She looked into his eyes, then tilted her chin up. His grip tightened around her arm, and he drew her closer. She would let him kiss her; she wanted him to. She wanted him to grab her and kiss her so hard their bodies would go flying, hitting the side of the house with a *thwack*. She would let this happen, let herself enjoy it, even, biting his lips, sinking her fingers into his skin—and then she would push him away, both hands thumping hard against his chest. Push him so hard he'd go sailing over the porch railing, where he'd land in a bramble of blackberry thorns.

But then he averted his gaze and it was over; the moment fluttered away, nothing more than a piece of dust floating around in her imagination.

"What are you trying to *do* to me?" She wanted to sound angry, but the words came out soft, deflated.

Malcolm took his hand from her arm and stepped back. He didn't answer—just kept looking at her, his eyes dark and gloomy. He opened his mouth to say something and then closed it again.

Joanna was horrified to find tears building up behind her eyes. She took in a sharp breath and shook her head. She could only hope she managed to appear annoyed rather than just … sad.

After a moment he turned away from her.

Joanna stood on the porch and watched him walk away. When she turned back toward the house, she noticed for the first time that the exterior paint was coming off in flakes larger than leaves.

11

in fact, she preferred
it this way

"So you're a teacher?"

"Freshman composition, mostly."

"Oh, a college professor!"

"Just an adjunct."

"So, you like teaching?"

"I do. I do."

Joanna couldn't believe how badly this was going. The guy sitting across from her in the dimly-lit bar wasn't bad looking—maybe even interesting looking, with black horn-rimmed glasses and curly straw-colored hair. And he wasn't pompous or obnoxious; in fact, Joanna could see that he was kind—doing his best to draw her out. He would ask her a question, and she'd come up with an answer, but that was it. They weren't really having a conversation so much as ticking off the boxes on some sort of "getting to know you" form.

She should have come prepared. Why oh why didn't she have Allison or Laura—or even Ted!—quiz her on hot conversation starters? They could have done some role-playing to hone her dating skills. Reading those women's fashion and lifestyle magazines as a teenager had been a complete waste of time. All of those tips for flirting, satisfying a man in bed, finding a man in the first place—

"So what about *you*?" she asked her bespectacled companion. A magazine tip floated up from the recesses of her brain: let him talk about himself. Men like to talk about themselves. Ask him questions. Compliment him.

And so the date was salvaged. They even made plans to go out for dinner and a movie later in the week. But she went home and flopped onto her bed; one date had sucked all the life out of her. Still, she picked up the phone. She had promised to call Allison and tell her every excruciating detail.

"How did it go?" her friend asked, not bothering to say hello.

"It was awful. I really don't know how you can go on more than one date a month. It's just so … draining."

"It gets easier. So this guy—which one was he again?" Allison had been thrilled when Joanna told her she was considering activating her online dating account. She had even combed through all of the eligible bachelors in Portland, trying to find the perfect man for Joanna. *Avoid this one*, she would warn, pointing to someone's tiny picture on the computer screen. What if they ended up dating all the same people? Joanna had asked. That's how it goes, Allison had replied.

"The blond guy with the glasses."

"Oh yeah. 'PDX Journalist.' His username is somewhat uninspired."

"It was painful, sitting there, quizzing each other on the banalities of our lives."

"Okay, well, move on! Line up the next date."

"I'm going out with him again on Friday."

"Friday? Really? Well, he must like you."

"I'm already dreading it."

Joanna told herself she was too busy to be dating right now. She canceled her date for Friday with the excuse that she just wasn't "cut out for online dating." She imagined he must be relieved that he didn't need to suffer another boring Q&A session over glasses of wine and baskets of bread.

Anyway, she *was* busy. She had an entire backyard to attend to. What she had initially thought of as a blank slate, open with possibility, now stood before her as a vast, unknowable field. The grass—what there was of it—had turned brown. The weeds flourished. Foot-high dandelions! She hadn't seen the likes of these before moving to Oregon. And of course they kept shooting up, higher and higher, then blossoming, drying into soft gray puffballs, and then finally falling apart and sprinkling all over the ground and sprouting into a brand new, more persistent generation of weeds.

She stood out by the vegetable patch, pulling out any errant growths. At the very least, she could keep this small section of the yard tamed. The starts were doing well— nothing had withered up and died. The pepper plants hadn't grown even one centimeter, and some of their lower leaves had turned pale yellow and fallen off. How could she possibly go out on dates with strangers when, in her very own backyard, seeds were struggling to burst from their shells, shoots were yearning to break through the crust of earth, reaching for a scrap of sunlight? Only to spend the rest of their lives kicking earwigs off their roots and aphids from their tender buds, begging for water, for worms to loosen the soil around them….

"I can handle this," she said out loud, her hands on her hips. She surveyed the yard, this time with determination. She would take control, turn this weed garden into a lush lawn with winding flagstone paths, bordered by tall ornamental grasses and flowers. And she would start now.

At the garden store, she stood in a warehouse with a tin roof, just as overwhelmed as she had been at home. Bag after bag of fertilizers, herbicides, insecticides, soils, soil amendments—if only she could only find the right combination and sprinkle it all over her grass like fairy dust, it would magically transform her landscape. "Can I help you find something?"

She turned around to face a guy about her age wearing a green apron. She looked at his nametag. Charlie Wu. "I have this huge backyard," she said. "It's just a field of weeds. I need to get rid of all the weeds and make it nice and green again."

Charlie shook his head. "No you don't."

"Excuse me?"

"You don't want to do that. What do you need a lush lawn for? You plan to host croquet tournaments back there?"

"Well, I mean, now there are just a bunch of dandelions. I just thought if I could get it back the way it was… " she trailed off. Charlie had his arms crossed. He was upset with her; she could tell by the way he was scrutinizing her. "Do I know you from somewhere?" he asked.

"I don't think so," Joanna said. "I mean, I've been coming in here a lot. I bought a house. With a yard."

"That's not it. You just look really familiar to me."

"Well … I'm pretty sure I don't recognize you." Joanna could be certain of this, because she would have remembered him. He didn't look like the other employees at the nursery, who tended towards soft, worn jeans, tattered wool sweaters, and scraggly facial hair. Charlie, in spite of the green apron, managed to come off as stylish in crisp, dark jeans, an ironed cotton button-down shirt, and brand new striped athletic shoes.

"I'll figure it out in a minute," Charlie said. He led her out of the warehouse area and into the main part of the store where they sold gardening tools, books, and seeds. In the corner was an unattended customer help desk. Charlie went over to the desk and started sketching something on a piece of paper. "Okay, look. What you want to do is get rid of most of that lawn. Put in a border around the edges—like this. Plant trees, bushes, whatever. You could even turn some of that grass into an edible landscape, make it useful—"

"I *do* have a vegetable garden," Joanna interrupted. "It was all kind of slapdash, but—"

Charlie smiled and pointed at Joanna. "I know who you are! You're 'The Gardener.'" He emitted a short laugh. "Am I right?"

Joanna felt her face turn hot. "The Gardener" was the ridiculous user name she had chosen for herself on the online dating site. Allison had suggested going with something catchier—"Calendula" or "Marigold," maybe—but Joanna had stayed firm. "The Gardener" conjured up images of an eighty-year-old man, white legs sticking out of shorts, pruning hedges. Because Joanna hadn't really planned on activating her account, she enjoyed playing around with Allison, who had eventually muttered, "Okay, The Gardener it is."

Now, in the garden shop, Joanna just stammered at Charlie: "But I've never seen you before!"

"You only date tall dudes. I get it."

Joanna's blush turned an even deeper shade of red.

"Hey, no worries. I remember looking at your profile,

thinking you were pretty cute, but you don't date guys under five foot eight, so I figured—"

"My friend filled that out for me!" This came out sounding so false and ridiculous she couldn't help but laugh. "I'm serious."

"Right," said Charlie, amused. "Hey, I'll take a look at your yard sometime. If you want."

As soon as Joanna got home, she logged on to her dating account, curious to find out why she had never seen Charlie's profile. Allison had combed through the prospects for her—perhaps she had narrowed the search criteria too much? She opened up the search to include men of any height, race, age, religion, transportation preference, dietary lifestyle, and so on. He popped up on the thirty-third page of results.

She sent him a message right away. Then she called Allison to tell her how online dating had, in a roundabout way, paid off.

"So have you ever dated an older woman before?" Joanna asked Charlie when he came over to redesign her lawn. She immediately wished she could take it back; she didn't mean to imply that this was a date. He was just giving her some landscaping advice. Maybe he was even here on a professional capacity—Joanna hadn't considered that. Should she offer to *pay* him?

"What are you—twenty-six?" Charlie asked.

"Twenty-seven."

"That's just three years' difference." Charlie looked up from his sketch of her backyard to smile at her. "Yeah, I've dated plenty of older women."

Joanna didn't reply, not sure if he was joking or not. They stood in silence for several minutes as he sketched out a plan, scribbling furious notes.

"Okay," he said in an official voice. "Here's what you need to do. See this? Where we're standing now?" They were at the back of the house perching on a patch of weedy grass. "You could make a patio or a deck here. Then group some plantings around it. You could do raised beds next year, make some brick pathways between them. And that leaves just a manageable patch of grass here." With a flourish, Charlie made a circle in the middle of the sketch.

"Wow." Joanna was truly impressed. "Okay, so what do I do first?" She looked at him eagerly, as if she expected him to hand her a checklist, a detailed list of step-by-step instructions she could then follow by the letter.

"Well, it's up to you. This is like a multi-year plan."

"Multi-year?" Joanna frowned and surveyed her plot of land. It gaped open, a huge, hungry mouth. She'd fill it. Fill it with dirt, with seeds, with plants, with water. And it would swallow everything whole.

At the end of August, Joanna and Charlie lay sprawled out on her bed, on top of the covers, in their underwear. An electric fan whirred at the end of the bed. They had to lie with deathlike stillness to keep it from dropping off the edge. Every once in a while it would crash down to the floor, and one of them would have to position it again. It was ninety degrees inside the house and 103 outside. She had shut all the windows and curtains, trying to trap the heat outdoors. Now the air inside was stale and hot. They took turns spraying each other with water from a spray bottle. The mist and the air from the fan made the heat almost bearable.

"We should go to a movie," Charlie said.

"It's too hot to walk to the car." They didn't talk for ten more minutes. "It's supposed to cool down for the weekend," she said after spraying herself in the face with the spray bottle. She opened her mouth, letting the mist land on her tongue. "It better, or my party will be ruined."

"Yeah, it's supposed to be ninety-five by Friday," Charlie said. "On Saturday it will be in the high eighties, low nineties." They had been obsessively checking the weather forecast ever since the heat wave rolled in at the beginning of the week.

Joanna was too hot to respond.

Charlie turned toward Joanna on the bed. "Listen, Joanna, something came up. So I'm not going to make it to the party after all. Sorry."

Joanna propped herself up and tried to focus on Charlie's face. "But you were going to meet my sister, my friends." She had been throwing herself into party planning for weeks, even though (as her sister pointed out) the backyard now featured a four-foot cardboard border along the fence. She and Charlie had spent hours—in coffee shops, in fancy restaurants and bars, in bed—dreaming up plans for her garden. By now they had envisioned a wonderland of bamboo, water features (a pond *and* a fountain), a raspberry patch, fig and pear and blossoming cherry trees, ferns and fuchsias. It all started with cardboard weighted down by bricks.

"I'm sure I'll get another chance to meet everybody."

"Do you have to work?"

"Ah … well, actually, I got the chance to go camping."

"Camping?"

Charlie swung his legs over the side of the bed, pulled on his jeans, and buttoned up his shirt. Even in 100-plus weather, he would not wear shorts. "Yeah. Normally I would turn it down—because of your party—but it's in the Gorge with views of this lake...."

"But ... what about the party?"

"I'm sure I'll really be missing out. It's just, this *opportunity*—"

"Whoever heard of an 'opportunity' to go camping? You can go camping whenever you want! Have you ever even *been* camping before?"

"Not since I was a kid. Once," he said.

"Who are you going with?"

Charlie paused. "You don't know her."

"Is she like ... a date?"

"Well, I guess you could say we're dating. It's nothing serious."

She reached for her clothes, too, suddenly aware that he was fully clothed, standing over her bed, and she was wearing an old bra and underwear that didn't match and squirting water all over herself. The fan crashed to the floor. Its blades spun around uselessly, blowing air up to the ceiling. Charlie picked it up and set it on the bed again, pointing it at Joanna.

"Listen, Joanna. We're just having fun, right? I mean, neither of us ever took down our profiles."

It took Joanna a second to figure out that Charlie was talking about their online dating profiles. She hadn't given it a second thought. She would get a message from someone on the site every now and then, but she just ignored them. It hadn't occurred to her that taking down the profile was the next logical progression in their relationship. They hadn't even met online!

Charlie walked over to Joanna's side of the bed and took her chin in his hand. She suppressed an overwhelming desire to flinch, to scramble across the bed—anything to free her face from his grasp. "I'll call you next week?"

"Maybe not," Joanna said. He dropped his hand. She sat up straight, struggling to assert some dignity despite the stifling heat, her damp and wrinkled clothes.

So this was how it was supposed to go. She should thank Charlie for his honesty, for cutting things off and moving on. She would still throw her first party on Saturday, and it would be a smashing success. Instead of showing off her landscape architect boyfriend, she would just have to dazzle everyone with her spirit of independence, her gutsy determination. She was enjoying thinking of herself as forty, fifty, sixty years old—never married, no children. She would instead devote herself to some great cause, travel around the world in crisp wool suits and shiny shoes, winning worldwide admiration, fame, and a few prestigious awards. The Nobel Peace Prize and the Pulitzer Prize, for example. Maybe a MacArthur Genius Grant.

With this newly acquired gutsy determination, she set about surviving the heat wave alone. Who needed a man? She could pick up her own fan off the floor. She could hoist the warped, paint-flecked double-hung windows up by herself, letting a hot breeze whoosh in like a hairdryer blasting directly on her face. She could tromp out back to the garden wearing an old tank top and a flimsy cotton skirt and pick tomatoes, parsley, and cucumbers. Without consulting a recipe, she would throw everything in the blender and, voila, out would come gazpacho. She would eat dinner alone, but it wouldn't bother her a bit. In fact, she preferred it this way.

The day of the party, the temperature had dropped to a

respectable eighty-five degrees. Laura said that she knew of a store with unbeatable prices on cheese where they could go to pick up all their party supplies. "There are four stores within walking distance of my house," Joanna said. Laura argued that this store was worth the trek. They'd save so much money that she truly had to insist that they go there. "I go there before all of my parties," she said. "To stock up." Laura seemed to be relishing her role of party planner, even if she had originally tried to talk Joanna out of hosting a party in an unfurnished house with a cardboard-covered backyard.

Laura drove all over town, got on a highway, then took a bridge over the river. "Laura, where are we going? We're in *Washington*. We'll have to pay sales tax!" She was regretting asking her sister for help, although she admitted that her original idea of handing her guests a bowl and letting them tromp out to the garden to pick their own vegetables—kind of like the ultimate salad bar—hadn't been exactly practical. But now they were spending half the day cheese shopping.

"I don't think they tax cheese," Laura said. "Here, you navigate." She handed Joanna a printed sheet of instructions. "I don't really know my way around Vancouver." By the time they loaded up with cheese and crackers and crossed the river back to Portland, two hours had transpired. It took Laura another two and a half hours to zigzag all over town for other sundry items—wine, brandy, citrus fruits, citronella candles, biodegradable paper plates made from recycled materials, a new table cloth, some tiki torches, a box of tiny cocktail umbrellas. When they finally rolled up to the curb by the house, Joanna jumped out before the car had come to a complete stop.

"Calm down, Joanna," Laura said.

Allison was waiting at the front porch, wearing a

turquoise sundress. "You're early," Joanna said. She unlocked the front door.

"I thought I'd help out."

In the kitchen, Joanna unloaded their wares on the counter. "*Thank* you," she said to Allison, directing a pointed look at her sister. "Laura took us across state lines to buy eight pounds of cheese and now we're running behind schedule. I'm going to go out and pick some more carrots for the vegetable platter—"

"I'll get them!" Laura almost shouted. "Just—carrots?" She took off to the back of the house.

"So I finally get to meet the elusive Charlie Wu," Allison said.

"No," Joanna said. "You don't."

Allison stopped unwrapping the Gouda. "What happened?"

"He's going camping. With another girl."

"Huh."

"Well, I'll always have the memories."

Allison looked skeptical. "You aren't upset?"

Before she could answer, Laura came back holding a bunch of carrots by the leaves. "Okay, everything's ready. Come out and look."

Joanna took the carrots and ran them under water. "I'm busy."

Laura reached over and took the carrots out of Joanna's hand, tossing them into the colander with the green beans and cherry tomatoes. "Just come and look at how we've set things up."

Joanna narrowed her eyes at Laura, then Allison. "What's going on?"

Laura led her through the house to the sliding glass door. When she opened the door, at first all she noticed were Ted, Malcolm, and Nina standing in a row, as if they'd been waiting for her appearance. "What are they doing here?" she mumbled to Allison. In the spirit of forgiveness and open-heartedness, Joanna had decided to invite Malcolm and Nina to her party. Or maybe it wasn't the spirit of open-heartedness, exactly, but the spirit of reprisal. Of course she knew she was only inviting Malcolm to show off Charlie. She had moved on; what was wrong with demonstrating that? When things had ended with Charlie, she could hardly retract the invitation, but she hadn't expected them to show up *early*.

"It's not six o'clock—" She stepped down into the yard, then stopped. Joanna put her hand to her mouth. In the corner of her yard stood a structure, exactly as Malcolm had drawn it for her last Christmas: a deep covered bench made of rust-colored wood, topped with a corrugated tin roof. A bench-hut. She took a cautious step toward it. "I can't believe it," she said to no one in particular. It was beautiful, better than she'd imagined, smelling strongly of new cedar.

"Merry Christmas," Malcolm said. Fine shavings of wood coated his hair, his clothes, his skin. He was squinting at her, unsmiling.

She looked back at him, trying to read his expression. "I didn't think you remembered," she said.

"I said I'd build you one."

Joanna was suddenly aware that everyone was listening to their conversation. Ted—also grimy with sawdust and dirt—had an arm slung around Laura's shoulders. Allison was watching her with curiosity. Even Nina had a strange little smile on her face.

"I love it," Joanna said in a stilted, public voice. She clapped her hands and gazed up at the hut, already adjusting her vision of the backyard to showcase it. She caught

Malcolm looking at her. Their eyes locked for a moment. She blinked hard, and turned back to admire the hut.

Over the next hour, more guests trickled in, many of them bearing food and drink. By eight o'clock it was almost dark—summer was coming to an end. A cool breeze rustled the tops of the neighbors' trees, ushering out the last of the heat wave. She could almost taste the air, sweet and metallic, hinting of rain.

Joanna fixed herself a glass of sangria and walked back to the bench hut. All evening, her guests had oohed and aahed over it, scrambled inside it, trying it out. She hadn't had a chance to sit in it herself, so she climbed in. The bench was so deep she had to clamber up and almost crawl to the back. When she sat down, her legs stretched out in front of her.

"I'll get you a cushion for this," Malcolm said, patting the bench. He stood at the edge of the hut and peered in at Joanna. "I didn't have time for the finishing touches."

"I could sleep out here," Joanna said. "Or even *live* in here."

Malcolm stepped inside and sat down beside her. They looked out at the party, not speaking. Laura and Ted had set out the tiki torches. The plants in the garden cast strange shadows over the rest of the yard. Ten or twelve of her friends—or Ted and Laura's friends—were roaming about, grazing the food table, ladling sangria from the punchbowl into their glasses. "This is how we met," Joanna said, breaking the silence.

Malcolm shook his head. "Nah. We met inside. I remember. By the bookshelves."

"I know. But it was that same night."

Malcolm turned his face toward her, then nudged her so their arms were touching. They sat like that for a few minutes, not saying anything. He cleared his throat. "Okay," he said. "Well, I'd better go find Nina."

Malcolm started to leave, but Joanna put a hand on his sleeve. He looked back at her, but she didn't have anything to say, really. "Never mind," she said.

He opened his arms and she wrapped her arms around him, burying her face into his shoulder. With her fingertips, she felt along the bones in his back. Then they broke free from the embrace, and she hopped off the bench with a thud. She made her way over the lawn—a tangled assortment of weeds and grasses—and through the flickering shadows to rejoin the party.

12

the house was coming undone at the seams

The first week of October, Joanna plucked all the tomatoes from their vines and spread them out on the counter in the kitchen. She picked the last of the beans and peppers but left the carrots in the ground to be sweetened by the upcoming frost. This was unusually early in the year for Portland to freeze over. Last year the tomatoes came in until Thanksgiving. She worked in the dark, pulling out plants, cutting them up with gardening shears, and dumping the tattered stems and leaves into the compost heap. The beds should get covered with straw for the winter, but her hands could barely function in the cold.

She opened the sliding glass door and stepped into the back room, kicking off her gardening shoes. She would make herself some tea and warm her hands on the mug. She walked through the house in the dark and snapped on the light in the kitchen. It took her eyes a moment to adjust, but then Joanna noticed, for the first time since she had moved in over three months ago, that she lived in a dump. The once white kitchen cabinets were grimy with grease and fingerprints. The vinyl floor curled up at the edges, creating a gathering place for crumbs and spills and little odds and ends like rubber bands and twist ties.

She walked into the living room, holding her mug of tea with both hands. The room was empty except for the jade plant by the window, the aloe vera plant on the mantle, and books on the built-in bookshelves on either side of the fireplace. Not a stick of furniture. If she wanted to sit down, she could sit in the chair in her room, or on her bed. She took her meals sitting up in bed, leaning against the wall.

But the fact that the room was unfurnished wasn't the only problem—the house was coming undone at the seams. The ceiling had a series of concentric gray rings at two different spots, one over the fireplace, one by the chandelier where a dining table might go. The window sashes had been painted white, but the sun had baked the paint into hard, curling flakes, exposing the soft, worn wood underneath. And the wall opposite the fireplace could serve as a museum to the history of wallpaper: five layers of faded patterns were peeling off the walls, as if the previous owners had attempted to tear the sheets off with their bare hands and then given up after a few hours.

How was she going to survive the winter in this ramshackle place? Soon—very soon—it would rain and maybe even snow, and she would be trapped in a cold, empty house. She could almost hear the wind whistling under the cracks in the door, whooshing down the hall, rattling the lights.

Malcolm tapped on the window. She had been expecting him. Malcolm had called earlier that day, asking Joanna if he could crash at her place for a few nights. "It's freezing out here." Malcolm let himself in, bringing with him a cold gust of air. "It's not much better inside."

"I haven't turned the heat on yet," Joanna said.

"Why not?"

"I was outside."

"You're inside now."

Joanna turned the thermostat up three degrees. A clinking sound, then a couple clunks, and soon warm air was blowing through the vents. The scent of burnt rubber and dust wafted through the room. "The heater works. Good to know." Part of her terrified vision of living in this house through the winter involved a broken furnace. She didn't even have any furniture to use as kindling for the fireplace—that's how dire her situation had become. It was comforting to know that at least one thing functioned as it should.

Malcolm stood in the middle of the living room and dropped his suitcase to the floor. His hair looked dull and matted, and he had dark circles under his eyes. He took off his coat, unwound his scarf, and dropped those on the floor, too. "Joanna," he said, "this place is a disaster."

"It's not that bad. Maybe I could get a couch or a chair or something."

"That would be a start."

"I just haven't gotten around to it yet," she said. "I've been so busy with the garden."

"But where do you *sit*?"

"In my room. Here—" Joanna picked up his coat and scarf and hung them in the closet in the short hallway. "Go in there and sit down."

Her mug was now cold. She put the kettle back on, took two tea bags from a box, and waited for the water to boil. She carried the hot tea into her room and handed Malcolm a mug. He was sitting against the wall, his legs crossed at the ankle. "God, Malcolm," Joanna said, "What happened? You look horrible."

He frowned into his mug. "What have you heard?"

She sat at the foot of the bed, across from him. "I haven't heard anything."

"Well, that contractor I've been working for basically told me he didn't have any more work for me, so I've been out of a job for the last few weeks. I had to move out of my apartment, so I'm keeping my stuff in Ted and Laura's garage. I stayed with them for a couple days. They didn't tell you?"

Joanna shook her head.

"Since then I've been staying at my friend Scott's house." He shuddered dramatically. "There are like five guys living there. I wake up stuck to the floor, covered in crumbs."

"Right." Joanna laughed, but Malcolm didn't appear to be in a joking mood. "So why don't you stay with Nina?"

He looked up at her, surprised. "I thought Laura would have told you."

"I said I hadn't heard anything."

"Well, it's over." Malcolm set his mug on the T.V. tray Joanna used as a bedside table. Then he put his head in his hands.

"Poor Malcolm." Joanna crawled across the bed and sat beside him. She tousled his hair with her fingers. "Wow, you weren't kidding. Your hair is coated in … something."

"Probably beer and potato chips."

"You should have come here sooner."

Malcolm offered up a pathetic little grin. "I didn't know if you would want me here." A lump forming in Joanna's throat prevented her from answering. "And who would blame you—" Malcolm's phone rang. He took it out of his pocket and stared at it. "It's Nina."

"You should answer it." Joanna hopped off the bed and walked to the door. "Answer it!"

The ringing stopped as she shut the door behind her. Fifteen minutes later, he came out and joined her in the kitchen, where she had been passing time arranging tomatoes and peppers on plates. "How did it go?" she asked. He frowned in response. "That bad, huh?" She hesitated, then put a hand on his arm. "Come on Malcolm, it's going to be okay."

"Why are you being so nice to me?"

"Because we're friends," she said. "Right?"

"I hope so."

She pushed him away, sensing her eyes about to well up again. "You need to take a shower before you can stay in my guest room, though."

"Oh yeah," he said. "I'd hate to bring the place down."

While Malcolm showered, Joanna set up the camping mattress in the back room. The mattress popped into shape in under a minute with a loud hiss of air. When it finished, she heard the sound of angry knocking. In the living room, she peeked out the window and saw Nina standing on the porch, her arms crossed in front of her. Nina stomped inside as soon as Joanna opened the door. "Where is he?" she demanded.

Joanna was too surprised to answer.

"Nina?" Malcolm walked in wearing a clean T-shirt and pajama bottoms, his hair wet. "What are you doing here?"

Nina's chest was heaving up and down. She looked right past Joanna, her eyes flashing at Malcolm. "We need to talk." Her face was pale, her eyes dry, but puffy. And she was wearing lipstick. Lipstick, all by itself like that, at eleven o'clock at night, sent an unexpected pang of sympathy through Joanna.

Malcolm and Nina disappeared into Joanna's room. Joanna didn't know what to do with herself. What had she done to deserve this? Nina was shrill; Joanna couldn't help but make out some of her complaints: *of all places, just to spite me, are you fucking serious.* Malcolm's voice was low, his words unintelligible.

Great. Malcolm had left her for Nina, and now she was trapped in her own house, forced to listen to their lovers' quarrel.

She was pacing around the living room when Nina burst out of the bedroom and tore past. She flung the door open wide, letting in a rush of cold air. Then she pointed right at Joanna. "He's all yours, *bitch*," Nina spat out, slamming the door behind her.

Joanna turned to Malcolm, her eyes wide. "Whoa," she said. "What was that all about?" Malcolm appeared to be frozen in place. "What did I ever do to her?"

"Nothing."

"She seemed mad at me."

"She is. But don't worry about it."

Joanna said she would make them more tea and he could tell her the whole story. "Okay," she said, back in her room. "Spill it."

"Let's just say Nina found out I was staying with you, and she wasn't too happy about it."

"Why not? What did you tell her? About us, I mean."

Malcolm peered into his cup. Then he gave Joanna a sheepish look. "I didn't lie to her. But I may have given her a false impression of the timeline. ... Anyway, back when I started making that bench hut for you, she really lost it. I told her I'd promised you earlier, but she wouldn't hear it. And then she got the idea that we were making out in there at your party—"

"How did she get *that* impression?"

"She said she saw it with her own eyes."

"But it was completely dark out."

"I know."

"And we weren't making out."

"I know." Malcolm and Joanna smiled at each other for a moment. "But that wasn't the only thing we were fighting about," he said. "Her number one complaint was probably that I never told her I loved her."

Joanna was silent for a moment. "Didn't you?" she asked. "Love her, I mean?"

Malcolm shrugged. "I told her not to take it personally— I've never told anyone."

"You've never been in love?" When he still didn't answer, she pressed on. "Not even when you were like fifteen or sixteen—I mean, what about that girl in college—"

Malcolm shook his head. "I just don't think it's something I'm going to go around saying to every girl I date."

"Not every girl you date. But the ones you stay with— don't you think, after a while, it becomes an issue? How long can you stay with someone like that? Six months? A year? What—you're going to get married, not say it? Fifty years go by and—"

"Don't be ridiculous," Malcolm said.

"Who's being ridiculous?"

And so Malcolm confessed that he would not declare his love to anyone but his future wife. Joanna studied his face, searched for some sort of smirk or glimmer in his eye that would reveal this all to be a joke. But he just leaned back against the wall, his hands clasped around the empty mug. Then he looked up at the ceiling and a little smile appeared on his face. Dreaming, Joanna could only imagine, of his wedding day. Lifting the veil from his bride's head, looking deep into her eyes, and then, in a deep and steady voice, saying, "I love you." This image amused Joanna so much that she laughed out loud.

"You shouldn't laugh at me," Malcolm turned to her. "I'm going through a rough time."

"I'm sorry. I just never in a million years would have known you were a man of such romantic notions." She gathered their empty mugs and carried them to the kitchen, leaving them in the sink.

She showed him to the back room with the inflated camp mattress resting in the middle of the floor. "Did you bring a sleeping bag?" she asked. "Sorry I don't have any sheets."

"It wouldn't kill you to buy a few things," he said. "But I came prepared."

"You know—" she started, then cut herself off.

"What?"

"Nothing."

"No. Go ahead. What?"

"It's just … aren't you potentially sabotaging relationships with this little philosophy of yours? I mean, I think it's pretty normal to know if you love someone after—I don't know—a month. Or six weeks. Or surely, if you haven't said it in *six months* … well, you see where that got you."

Malcolm did not answer. Instead, he left the room and came back with his suitcase. He opened it up and pulled out a complete set of carefully folded sheets. Joanna watched him as he made up the camp bed. "I probably do have an extra blanket around here somewhere," she said, making no move to look for one. "Or you could use my sleeping bag as a blanket."

"Aren't you the one who doesn't believe in love, anyway?" Malcolm asked, smoothing the sheets over the mattress.

"What! I never said that."

"Yeah you did."

Joanna shook her head.

"Well, you must have misunderstood," she said, "because I never said that. It's just that I know it's fleeting. I think I'd like to have a series of meaningful relationships, you know? They last a few years, then they're over. What I don't get is marrying someone, thinking it will bind you together forever. Most of the time, it won't work out that way."

"But sooner or later, you're going to want a baby," Malcolm said, looking up at her. His gaze was so disconcerting that she turned around, started rummaging through the closet, making a show of opening boxes, peering in them, and closing them up again.

"Where is my sleeping bag?" she wondered out loud. Into a box: "A *baby*? Who said anything about—"

"So you just have a kid with whatever guy you 'love' at the time, then you move on? Pop out another kid? What kind of life is that?"

"It happens all the time." Joanna turned back around and looked back down at Malcolm, who was now lying on the mattress. She had suddenly lost the thread of the conversation. What was she arguing about?

"Well, of course. But to plan it that way?"

"You've put a lot of thought into this, for someone who never wants to have children."

Malcolm looked up at Joanna, squinting at the overhead light. "What makes you say that?"

"You told me!"

"I did?"

"It was practically the first thing you said to me. That you had no desire to sire children. Those were your exact words."

Malcolm laughed. "Oh, right."

Joanna flipped the light off. "I'm going to bed." As she

was walking back to her room, she heard Malcolm yell for a blanket. She dug her sleeping bag out of the hall closet and threw it back into the room where Malcolm was staying.

"Hey!" she heard him say when it landed on the floor. "Thanks."

The next morning, Joanna awoke to the smell of coffee. Since she didn't even own a coffee maker, this was an unusual occurrence. She found Malcolm in the kitchen, whisking eggs in a bowl. "How do you want your eggs?" he asked. The circles had disappeared from under his eyes; he was smiling.

"Over easy."

"I'm making scrambled."

"Okay."

"Coffee?"

"Please." Joanna watched Malcolm with curiosity as he poured her coffee from a French press he must have brought over in his suitcase. He tossed butter on the skillet, then poured in the eggs, whistling softly. He made a production out of it—rushing around for the proper utensils, shaking the pan on the burner, then flipping everything in the air and catching it all again for no purpose that Joanna could discern. He scooped some eggs out of the pan and placed them on a plate exactly when the toast popped up from the toaster.

"Impressive," she said. "What is this all about?"

He hopped on the counter next to her, and they ate side by side. "You need a table," Malcolm said.

"I know."

"I know how you could get a table," he said.

"Buy one?"

"For free."

"How?"

"Let me move in with you. I have furniture."

"Move in? You mean, indefinitely?"

"Sure. Why not? I need a place to stay. You need furniture. Plus—" Malcolm raised his fork in the air, "I can help you fix this place up. We can work out a deal."

"I don't know...."

"Joanna. Look around you. We're sitting on a counter. You moved in three months ago, and you've done nothing to this place—"

"That's not true! I—"

"Yes, I know. You worked on the yard. But sweetheart, have you ever stopped to notice the *inside* of this house before?"

"Well, nothing really needs to be done right away. So there are five layers of wallpaper peeling off in the living room—that's really just a cosmetic issue. And the floors in the kitchen and bathroom are kind of old and curling up, but I can deal with that." Joanna stopped, lacking the enthusiasm to enumerate the many projects she didn't mind leaving undone.

"The roof," Malcolm said. "You need to get that done before it starts raining all the time. You should have done that as soon as you moved in."

"So you're saying if I let you move in, you'll re-roof my house?"

"No. I'll take care of it for you, though."

"Not that this isn't a very tempting offer, but do you really think it's a good idea? A month ago we were barely speaking to each other. And last night your ex-girlfriend came over and screamed at me. What if you got back together? Don't you see how completely *horrible* that would be?"

Malcolm set his plate down next to him on the counter and turned toward her. "Listen, Joanna. I promise I will never get back together with Nina. And she won't come by here again."

"You can't guarantee that."

"Okay, if she comes over, I won't let her in."

"Nice."

"I mean, if she's desperate to talk to me for some reason, I'll talk to her. But not in your house. I promise."

"So you'd be like my … manservant?"

"If that's what you're into," Malcolm said.

Joanna thought about it for a minute, then shrugged. "Okay," she said, extending her hand for him to shake.

Malcolm held up both hands, as if fending her off. "Actually, on second thought, I think I prefer to be called the house boy."

"Hm. All right." They shook hands, unsmiling. Then they stopped shaking hands, but Malcolm didn't loosen his grip.

Laura was already seated in the corner of the teahouse when Joanna arrived. It was six o'clock and it was already dark outside. Inside, the teahouse was overheated, steamy. It smelled like spices, flowers, and an unfamiliar, earthy aroma. Mung beans, perhaps. Joanna ran her hands over her hair, trying to smooth it down. After darting through the rain to get to the teahouse on time, her hair had morphed into a frizzy halo sparkling with mist.

Laura had called Joanna to the teahouse after work for

an "emergency meeting." Despite the putative urgency of the meeting, Laura waited patiently as Joanna examined each page of the menu, reading the elaborate descriptions of all the teas. Laura was always prepared for every type of weather. She owned matching umbrellas, hats, and hooded jackets that contributed to her fresh, polished appearance. Her hair was smooth, as if she had just combed it. No one could ever describe her sister as "frazzled," "disheveled," or "ill-kempt;" three adjectives that Joanna might use to describe herself at this moment.

"I never knew the difference between green tea and white tea before," Joanna said. Laura just poured herself a tiny cup of tea from a blue ceramic pot. "Maybe I'll just get chai. They have really good chai here."

"You always order it," her sister said.

"That's true." The teahouse was located right next to Laura's school. It was peaceful inside, surrounded by pots and cups, hanging plants and brown wicker furniture. She ordered the Hundred Mile Chai.

"Okay, Joanna. You know why I wanted to talk to you, right?"

"Why?"

"We heard."

"What?" Joanna looked up innocently.

"You and Malcolm. He's moving in with you?"

Joanna nodded. "Yep. That's right."

"Are you sure this is a wise idea?"

"He said he'd help me fix the place up. I didn't really notice when I first bought it, but it really needs some work. The roof, for instance, is going to cave in at any moment."

"And the only way to prevent this from happening is to have Malcolm move in?"

"He said he'd take care of it."

"Joanna." Joanna could see Laura searching for the right words. "Need I remind you of what Malcolm put you through just a few short months ago? Alaska? Nina?"

Joanna's tea arrived in its own dark blue ceramic teapot, with its own little cup. She poured herself some, then leaned over her cup to smell the cardamom and cinnamon. "That was then. This is now."

"Okay. So you're over him? Or what? You want him back?"

"No!" Joanna said, flinging her hands out for emphasis, accidentally hitting the wicker table. Laura's teapot trembled on its tray. "It's just—different now. We're sort of … well, it's hard to explain. "But we're friends again."

"And Malcolm feels the same way?"

Joanna took a sip of tea before answering. "If Malcolm wanted to be with me, he could have been with me last spring. Instead, he left. Then he came back with someone else. So I think he made his intentions toward me pretty clear."

"But maybe there was a reason!"

"What could possibly explain it? I've been over and over it. He wasn't ready for a commitment? He came back from Alaska with a brand new girlfriend—and he stayed with her for six months!"

"Well, why don't you *ask* him?"

Joanna poured herself more tea. She didn't want to ask him; she'd be more likely to ask for a slap in the face. "Anyway," she said, "I don't want to be with him, either. Like I said, this is a new phase in our friendship. I don't want to ruin it again."

"So you're just friends, then."

"You say that like it's nothing!" she burst out. She lowered her voice. "I've known Malcolm practically as long as you've known Ted. Well, I hate to break it to you, but more than half of marriages end in divorce. There's no guarantee for you guys. So five, ten, fifty years from now when you and Ted are signing divorce papers, Malcolm and I will still have our friendship." Immediately, Joanna regretted her outburst. She liked Laura and Ted together; she didn't want them to get divorced. But Laura just laughed.

"But I don't want to be 'friends' with Ted! And I don't believe for a second that you want to be friends with Malcolm—"

"You don't know the first thing about it."

"All right." Laura threw up her hands. "Fine. Well, since your friendship with Malcolm is just too special to sully with romance, maybe you should date other guys."

"Maybe I will."

"Are you still doing online dating? You could open your account back up, you know. Find some other guys. You barely even tried it—"

"I did try it! It was horrible."

"But you can't say that after—what? One bad date?"

"Why are you so invested in this?" Joanna asked. "Who cares if I go on more anonymous dates? Can't we just let things *happen* anymore? Does everything have to be orchestrated by us? Do we have to order our dates now, like we order shoes, or groceries?"

"We just think—"

"We? *We?* So you and Ted have this all planned out?"

"Fine. *I* think you should keep your options open."

"My options are open. Wide open."

Her sister gave her a serious look. "Promise me you'll go out with other people."

Joanna laughed. "I'm not going to promise you anything!" She took a prim sip of her chai. "But I will consider it."

She came home from work on a Monday evening and set her bag on the couch. Yes, there was a couch in the living room now. There was also a rug, a coffee table, and a television set. She now spent hours curled up under blankets, staring out the window at the street below. Nothing much happened outside. Every once in a while a car or bike would zoom by, or she would see a mother pushing a stroller or teenagers walking to or from school. People going places, walking in and out of their houses—she had missed all this, simply because she hadn't had anything to sit on before. How she had underestimated the desirability of furniture!

She cast a nervous glance around to make sure she was alone, then picked up her laptop and logged on to her online dating account. Five new messages. At first she chalked up her secrecy to embarrassment. Yes, everyone did it—Laura met Ted this way!—but there was still something less than ideal about finding someone to go out with on a computer instead of, say, wandering the streets of Paris or crashing into each other in Central Park.

Then she wondered if what she felt every time she sneaked around, scrolling down the screen reading various profiles and typing out flirtatious messages, was more guilt than embarrassment. But why should she feel guilty about finding someone suitable for her while Malcolm puttered around the house hammering things? Wasn't he the one who abandoned her all those months ago, making it pretty clear where he stood on the whole matter? She told Allison all about her online dating exploits. She should tell Malcolm, too. Maybe she would get him to jump on the bandwagon as well. They could go out on dates, come home late at night, sit on the couch, and give each other

relationship advice. Yes. Their friendship had taken a circu-
itous route, only to end up at this very place: best friends,
the kind of friends who talk about everything, especially
their love lives.

With this new course of their friendship mapped out
so clearly in her mind, Joanna typed out three messages
to three different guys in quick succession. It was time to
meet them in person, get the ball rolling. Who knew? One
of them might end up being the love of her life—or one
of the loves of her life. He and Malcolm would become
fast friends, too. Maybe they'd build things together. Or
fix up her house for her, together. The three of them would
sit around the kitchen table, celebrating holidays and
birthdays.

Joanna shut down her laptop and snapped it closed,
and went to check on Malcolm's progress. She found him
pacing around the kitchen, pen in hand, his notebook open.
"What are you doing?" she asked.

"Hey." He jotted something down in the notebook. "I
was just going to get you," he said after a moment. "Now
that the roof is taken care of, I've made a list of all the
things I could work on in here."

Joanna took the notebook from him and started reading.
She flipped through three pages with growing horror. He
had organized the list by room and included the yard,
exterior, garage, and "other" as additional categories. Under
each category he had listed at least five projects of varying
complexity and expense. "'Bathroom:'" Joanna read from
the list. "'Remove tub, sink, and toilet. Tear down closet.
Reconfigure plumbing. Tear out vinyl flooring, install tile
floor. Tear out beadboard. New drywall + tile? New ceiling,
light fixtures, towel rack, etc. Paint. Install new tub, sink,
and toilet.'"

"I was just trying to be thorough."

"I didn't think the bathroom was that bad!"

"Well, we don't have to start with the bathroom," Malcolm said. "These are just *suggestions*."

Joanna handed him back his notebook. "It's just … the list is so long."

"Well, we don't have to tackle it all at once. Just pick a room! The kitchen?"

"Okay," Joanna said, relieved that someone had made a decision. "So, do you even know how to do all this other stuff?" She flipped through the list again. "Rewiring the whole house? Drywall?"

Malcolm shrugged. "Sure. How hard can it be?" He laughed at her skeptical expression. "Yeah, I know how to do it. Don't worry about it."

"I'm not worried."

A couple days later, Joanna found Malcolm scrubbing the doors of the cabinets. "Looking good," she said, although actually, the entire kitchen, empty and gutted, was a disaster area.

Malcolm glanced up. "Where are you going?"

She was dressed up; she even had lip gloss on. "How do I look?"

Malcolm studied her for a moment, narrowing his eyes. "Good," he said at last. "What's the occasion?"

"I'm going on a date."

"A date? It's Wednesday."

"So?"

"Are you sure you want to go out on a date in that?"

"You said it looked good!"

"That's before you told me you were going on a date."

"What's wrong with what I'm wearing?"

"Nothing! Like I said, you look good. But I'm not sure

that's the message you want to be sending out on a first—it is the first, right?—date."

"Exactly what kind of message am I sending out?" She looked down at her outfit, a black knitted top with three-quarter length sleeves, a skirt, and boots. She had worn the same ensemble to teach her classes; it hardly qualified as come-hither wear, especially considering how cold it was outside. Once she bundled up for the elements she'd be swaddled in three inches of fabric.

"That shirt is kind of form-fitting. That's all," Malcolm said.

"Okay. Well, I think I'm going to risk it. I hope he doesn't dissolve into a frenzy of lust at the sight of me."

"So who is this guy, anyway?"

"His name is Gunther."

"Gunther? What kind of name is that?"

"It's a German name."

"I know … I meant—never mind. Have fun."

"Thank you. I will." She left him standing in the kitchen, a wet rag in his hand, attacking the cabinet doors with renewed vigor.

13

like peppermint

Joanna and James had planned to meet at a new bar for their second date but found it was packed full of loud drunks dressed in tooth fairy and sexy witch costumes. It was the designated evening for the over-twenty-one crowd to celebrate Halloween. They tried another place, a dive bar popular with both hipsters and old men, but it, too, was packed. They sallied forth, the night getting colder, finding sanctuary in a grocery store. They walked up and down the aisles just to warm themselves up, and ended up rifling through costumes on the sales rack. "Check this out," Joanna said, holding up a barmaid costume.

James found a pirate costume, which came with a black curly-haired wig, an eye patch, and an oversized ruffled shirt. "I guess you're on your own for pants," Joanna said.

"Pirates can wear jeans, right?"

"On weekends, maybe." She pulled the barmaid costume on over the clothes she was wearing. Her plaid skirt hung down about five inches below the frilly skirt, and her black fitted sweater worked hard to negate the sexiness of the low-cut blouse. "How do I look?" she asked, adjusting the blonde wig on top of her head.

"Lusty," he said, pulling her towards him. He leaned down and kissed her. It happened so quickly that she didn't have time to respond. Her arms hung down at her sides. She made a start to move them, to put her arms around him, but then it was over. It was their first kiss. He stepped back and examined the plastic package of the costume. "They're on sale," he said.

Again they headed out in the cold, wearing the costumes over their clothes, under their coats. James flung his arm around her. She looked up at him and smiled, but he was staring straight ahead. He was quite good-looking, Joanna decided. She wasn't sure if he was her type. He had thick, dark hair and wore black-framed glasses. Both of his arms were covered in tattoos: the left arm with vegetables (they shared a passion for backyard gardening), the right with books (and recreational reading). She decided to take the tattoos as a good sign.

They walked over the sidewalk, past big buildings closed for the night. During the day these buildings housed mortgage lenders, banks, chain coffee shops. "It's dead here," Joanna said.

Neither of them could remember why they had started out in this direction. They stopped, looking up and down the deserted streets. Joanna hopped up and down, trying to get warm. This sent a dull pain through each of her feet, so she stopped and hugged herself.

"Where's your car?" he asked.

"At home. I took the bus."

"Me too."

"I think we're by the Max. Or we could go back to MLK

and catch a bus back to my house," Joanna suggested. "It's warm there."

"What about our costumes?"

"What about them?"

"You know. Free cover charges."

"Forget it," Joanna said. She wondered as they sat on the bus, surrounded by costumed revelers, if it was unwise to invite someone over on the second date. Maybe she should have tried to think of somewhere else to go, somewhere public. A wine bar perhaps, one of those places with burgundy walls where rowdy college kids in costumes wouldn't want to go.

Inside, her house was warm. She took James's coat and hung it in the closet next to her own. "Malcolm!" she yelled toward the back of the house. "It's too *hot* in here." She adjusted the thermostat. "Don't you even care about the environment?"

"Who's Malcolm?" James asked, sitting down on the couch.

"Oh, just a friend of mine. I mean, he lives here. He's my housemate, I guess you could say." Now that she was out of the cold, she began to feel the blood circulating inside of her. She felt happy all of a sudden, almost giddy. She sat down on the couch next to James. "Nice wig." She reached over to pull one of the shiny black ringlets.

Malcolm walked into the living room and surveyed Joanna and James on the couch. If he was surprised to see her with a blonde wig and a barmaid outfit on over her clothes, seated next to a hipster pirate, he didn't indicate it. He nodded at James, who gave a half-hearted little salute in exchange. Malcolm turned around to view the thermostat, re-adjusted it, and retreated back to the kitchen. Joanna and James heard boards landing on the ground with a clatter, then the loud, grinding whine of a table saw.

"He's remodeling," Joanna said. She stood up, smoothed down the costume. "Come on—it's quieter in my room."

"Is your housemate always so—"

"Yeah," said Joanna.

They sat on her bed, facing each other. James took her by the wrists and pulled her toward him. He was smiling, about to place his lips on hers when they were interrupted by the screech of a table saw. Joanna pulled away. "I'll go make us some drinks. Wait here."

In the kitchen, Malcolm was busy slicing up some boards.

When Joanna walked in, Malcolm stopped sawing and lifted his goggles up to his head. He was sweating, dirty, wearing a thin white T-shirt and old jeans with holes in the knees. He wiped his forehead with his arm. "Where's Captain Hook?" he asked.

"James? He's still here. I'm making us some drinks. Want one?"

"What are you making?"

"Something appropriate for the holiday." On the counter she had lined up the results of her fall harvest: five small sugar pumpkins, three butternut squashes, and a Danish acorn squash, now covered in a layer of sawdust. She had just picked them, their leaves shriveled and powdery blue with mildew. Earlier in the day, when Malcolm had been at the hardware store, she had steamed one of the pumpkins according to her sister's instructions, scraped the orange flesh from the skin, and pureed it all in the blender. It had taken hours. And after it was all done, she had no real plan for the pumpkin puree. She took out a glass jar of neon orange puree from the fridge, struck with a sudden inspiration.

"What is that?" Malcolm asked.

"I think I'll make pumpkin drops. Or—'pumpkin pies.' Like, a new drink," Joanna said.

Malcolm's eyes narrowed. "I'll pass."

Joanna took out two lowball glasses. Now that Malcolm lived with her, she had an entire shelf full of barware. She spooned a dollop of puree in each glass while Malcolm looked on with a fascinated expression. "You don't have to stand here and watch me," Joanna said.

"Oh, but I want to."

Joanna shook her head and added some spices, shaking each glass spice jar vigorously into the cup: nutmeg, cinnamon, ginger, allspice, and cardamom. Then about a tablespoon of sugar. "What else?"

"Milk?" Malcolm suggested. "It's in pumpkin pie. Either sweetened condensed milk or regular milk."

"We don't have sweetened condensed milk." She went back to the fridge and filled the glasses halfway with 2%. "Okay, now alcohol. What goes with all this stuff?"

Malcolm backed away as Joanna searched the cupboards. She pulled out a bottle with a waxy red cap. "Hey, that's my Maker's Mark." He took the bottle from her. "No way are you wasting it on this—ah—recipe."

"Fine. How about … brandy. Does that go?"

"Oh yeah," Malcolm said. "Totally." Joanna topped each glass off with brandy, stirred each drink carefully, then took one in each hand. "Aren't you going to taste it first?" Malcolm asked. She gave a little shrug and headed back into her room.

"Here you go," she said grandly, handing James a drink and shutting the door behind her. "It's a pumpkin pie. I invented it."

He eyed the thick, orange drink. "Is there really pumpkin in here?"

"I grew it myself. In my garden."

"Impressive."

"I thought you'd like that." James had caught her eye because of his list of favorite authors: Ann Beattie, Raymond Carver, Amy Hempel. On their first date they'd talked about writers and writing. James had been an English major in college, too. Of course now he was a graphic designer, "Like half of Portland." He asked if she was an aspiring writer, and she had answered truthfully. No, she didn't write. This set her apart from almost all the other adjuncts who taught composition. "I just wanted to teach," she explained to James. "I'm a teacher."

Lately, though, she had been wondering where, exactly, her "career" was headed. No one went to graduate school with the distinct *ambition* to be an adjunct at community colleges. But that's precisely what Joanna had done. They talked about that, too—the way they saw life while in college, where they ended up, not knowing where they'd be five, ten years from now, but how that was okay. They weren't their parents. They could be in their thirties, maybe even forties, before figuring it all out.

She looked into James's eyes and smiled as she took a sip of her pumpkin cocktail. "Ack!" She shuddered. "This is *awful!*"

James laughed, then raised the glass to his lips. "No!" she cried. She reached across the bed, trying to grab the drink from him. He held onto his glass, jerked it in toward his chest. Some thick orange sludge splashed onto his pirate shirt. They both dissolved into laughter. "Seriously, James. It's terrible. I should have tasted it before I—"

"I'm going to do it," James said, holding the glass in one hand and raising a finger with the other. He took a sip, then nodded thoughtfully, licking his lips. "Cardamom?"

"Among other things," she said. "I don't know *why* it's bad. It's homemade pumpkin puree."

"It's not bad." He took another sip and gazed up thoughtfully, as if he were sampling a fine wine.

Joanna tried some more. The taste wasn't so offensive, really. It was the texture—thick and gritty. She could feel a fibrous string of pumpkin between her teeth.

"We should down them," James said. "On the count of three."

"No way."

"Scared?"

After several false starts, punctuated with laughter, they did it. She finished hers in five gulps. She closed her eyes and grimaced.

James took their glasses and placed them on the floor. Then he kissed her, coaxing her onto her back. "You taste like pumpkin pie," he said when he came up for air.

She pulled the ridiculous wig off of his head. "So do you."

The table saw whirred in the background. For a few paranoid minutes, Joanna was sure that the blade of the saw began to spin every time her lips touched James's. She stopped him and half sat up in the bed.

"What's wrong?" James had his hand up her real skirt and her barmaid skirt.

"I can't do this," she said. She tilted her head toward the kitchen. "Not with my housemate chopping up boards in the kitchen."

Five minutes later, James was out the door, insisting he'd catch a bus home. Joanna went into the kitchen to make herself some tea. She wasn't tired at all. She was shaky, keyed-up. She rummaged through the cupboards in search of nourishment, finally settling on cheddar cheese and crackers she didn't remember buying. Maybe they were Malcolm's.

Malcolm walked in. "Hey," he said.

"Hey," she responded. Only then did she notice the change in the kitchen. While she'd been in her room, he'd finished the table and benches he'd been working on for the kitchen nook. She went over to admire his work, running her hands over the smooth, sanded surface of the cherry wood. "It's beautiful."

Malcolm didn't answer, but he leaned against the wall, watching her.

She set her plate of crackers and cheese on the table and sat on a bench. She could still smell the varnish, the scent of wood shavings. Malcolm took a seat across from her. Joanna's mouth was dry, filled with crackers. She pointed to the plate and raised her eyebrows.

"No thanks." Malcolm grabbed the edge of the table, examining his work. "Yeah, it works much better this way. It'll be good to have that table out of the kitchen." His face sagged. The kitchen was still a mess—curls of sawdust coating the floor, little cans of paint and stains stacked up on the stove, the cupboard doors still off their hinges, stacked up against a wall. "Where's Captain Hook?"

"You mean James?"

"Like James Cook?"

"What?"

"Never mind."

"He left."

"Oh."

"Why? Would you care if he stayed?" Joanna asked. She truly wanted to know. Ever since Malcolm had moved in with her, she had imagined what it would be like if he brought a girl over. Would she mind? Joanna decided that she would be fine with it. They were friends now. Whatever had happened in the past was just that—in the past. Eventually each of them would find someone else. They would date other people, stay up late and gossip about it right here in this kitchen nook, under the 1920s-style pendant light. She could start right now! Tell him about the kiss, get some advice, the male perspective—

Malcolm shrugged. "No," he said.

How far they had come! Joanna marveled. Just a few months ago, she would barely speak to Malcolm. She smiled at him, her dear friend. "All right then," she said. "Well, good night."

"Night."

Joanna shuffled into the bathroom, brushed her teeth, splashed water on her face. When she focused on her reflection in the mirror, a bleary-eyed barmaid stared back at her. Her fingers struggled to untie the bodice. She had abandoned her boots and the wig hours ago, but now she pulled off her tights, too, and threw them in the hamper. In her room, she pulled on a tank top and some flannel pants. It was still so hot inside the house she could sleep naked on top of the covers. She should turn down the thermostat. Instead she slipped under her sheets and pulled the blankets up to her chin.

Hours later, she woke up in a sweat. Grumbling, she flung off the covers and threw her legs over the side of the bed. Without bothering to open her eyes completely or turn on any lights, she stumbled down the hall to the thermostat. She could barely make out the numbers in the dark. Seventy-two degrees! She should make Malcolm pay her utility bills for the entire winter for his profligate ways. She turned the dial all the way to the left. She'd freeze him out!

As she shuffled back to her room, she bumped into

something. She was standing on Malcolm's foot. "Hey, watch it!" he whispered.

Her eyes opened and she squinted at him. "Sorry." She tried to move past him, but he was standing in her way. She put her hands up to push him aside, but he wouldn't budge. She looked up again and muttered his name, saw through her half-closed eyes that he was looking down at her. Then he took her face in both of his hands, bent down, and kissed her. He smelled like peppermint and sawdust. When he released her she took in a gulp of air, as if she were emerging from underwater. And then he was gone, the bathroom door clicking shut behind him.

14

her mind blank, an open sky

She smelled pancakes. In the kitchen, there was Malcolm, making her breakfast. He was already fully dressed in dark jeans and a white T-shirt, but he looked rumpled. He hadn't shaved in a few days and his eyes drooped. Joanna filled the kettle with water and put it on the stove to boil. Making the coffee in Malcolm's French press had become her job, and she did it well, measuring out those spoonsful of coffee with precision. As usual, Malcolm cooked with gusto, using far more gestures than required—whisking the batter, his elbows sticking out, flicking water onto the hot pan to watch it sizzle, pouring the batter from the bowl onto the skillet from three feet in the air.

He set two plates of pancakes on the new nook table. Joanna pressed down the nozzle of the French press and poured them each a cup. She tucked one piece of butter underneath the top pancake and then nudged it toward Malcolm. With a teaspoon, she drizzled maple syrup over the cakes. Malcolm cleared his throat. "So," he said, "let me know the next time you want to bring someone over." He took a bite of pancakes, plain, and chewed them, staring at her without expression.

Joanna stopped eating. She froze with her fork in midair. "You know I didn't *plan* to bring him over. Everyone was celebrating Halloween...." Why was she explaining this?

"Well, if you're going to be giggling in your room all night, just give me some fair warning next time," he said.

"What's your problem?" She should be annoyed, but she wasn't. She almost hated to admit it to herself: she was flattered. "It's not like I was *doing him* in there. We were talking. Get over it."

"Right, well, it's just embarrassing. I don't need to hear it."

"Okay." Joanna smiled. "I will definitely let you know the next time I have a gentleman caller stop by for a chat."

"Thank you," Malcolm said primly.

They both ate their pancakes, took sips from their coffee. "So ... last night?" Joanna started. "After James left?"

"What?" His face vacant, he looked at her across the nook table, which was so small their plates were touching. Was it possible that he had forgotten? It was the middle of the night. Maybe he had been sleepwalking, or maybe he was acting coy. She could never tell with Malcolm. She would chalk it up to temporary jealousy and forget about it. She was grateful to Allison—and her sister—for encouraging her to see other people. It put things into perspective. She didn't need to sit around examining Malcolm's motives anymore. It simply didn't matter that much. They finished their pancakes, and Malcolm gathered up their plates to put them in the sink. "Hey," he said, "what are you doing today?"

"Nothing."

"We can finish the kitchen today if you help me."

"Really?" The place was a wreck.

"First we have to go buy some paint. Have you thought about colors you want for the walls?" They were currently peach-colored, smudged with fingerprints and grease.

"Not really."

"We'll find something."

Joanna chose a bright green color called "Crisp Apple." Malcolm had talked her down a few shades, telling her it would look much brighter on the wall than on the little swatch in the store. But first they had to move the table saw and sweep up the floors. Joanna could barely lift her side of the table saw, so they agreed to slide it into the living room until they could talk someone else into helping him move it into the garage. "Maybe Captain Hook can do it," Malcolm said.

"He is *very* strong," Joanna said.

"Yeah, I'll bet," Malcolm said. "You found yourself a real man."

Joanna just smiled. They spent the next few hours working. Malcolm reattached the cupboard doors, which he had painted white. He replaced the chipped chrome hardware with polished nickel knobs. Joanna swept the floors, stacked Malcolm's various tools and supplies in the living room, and wiped down the counters. Then she turned to Malcolm for guidance.

"Haven't you painted before?" he asked.

"We repainted my mom's apartment once. She did the whole thing in shades of blue. It was depressing. Don't we need to tape everything?"

"No." Malcolm threw two huge plastic tarps over the floors. "I'll show you how to do the edges. Tape is for hacks."

"I think we established that I am a hack."

"See this?" He pointed to the brush in his hand. "This is an edging brush." He dipped it in the paint, then dragged it along the edge of the entry way, making a perfect line without getting green on the white moldings. "Here you go. Give it a try."

Joanna dipped the brush in the paint. "Not that much!" Malcolm warned her. "Okay," he said. "Now go." It was easier than she had expected. "Good," he said. "Now do all the edges."

"I've *got* it," Joanna said, pushing him away.

The two of them worked in silence for a half hour at least, listening to the rain hit the windows as they worked. Joanna was having a good time. Painting edges was fun; it reminded her of childhood hours spent filling in pictures in coloring books with crayons.

"Is your boyfriend coming over tonight?" Malcolm asked her, bending down to inspect her work. She was almost done with the bottom edge of the wall. They had moved the stove and fridge out. Joanna had been a little disgusted at what they had found—gray clouds of dust, dried-up bits of food adhered to the linoleum. But now it was clean, and she was blotting out any remaining smudges with a nice, new coat of paint.

"He is *not* my boyfriend. *You* seem pretty obsessed with him, though. Maybe you two should hang out. You want his number?"

"I don't socialize with people who wear pirate costumes. What is it with Portland and pirates?"

"It was for Halloween, Malcolm. He's not one of those … semi-professional pirates."

"Just let me know next time he comes over. I'll be sure to stay clear."

Joanna concentrated on painting a nice, straight line.

"Fine."

"It's just—I don't want to be around to hear it. Giggling. Moaning and groaning."

"Oh come on, Malcolm. I was not moaning and groaning!"

"It's just embarrassing. I mean, I'm embarrassed for you."

"Right."

"I just don't want to hear it—"

"Okay, Malcolm! I get it!" Joanna stopped painting and glared up at Malcolm, who wasn't even working, just leaning back against the counter, his hair flopping in his face. His mouth was twisted up, his eyes narrowed. He was angry! This was ridiculous. "I'm sorry if that bothered you. It's just—I was so *into* it, you know? When James is wearing that pirate wig, I just go *crazy*. It's unbelievable—"

Malcolm's mouth softened, though he didn't smile. "Touché," he said.

"Let me tell you something." Her pulse quickened. "I didn't exactly like it when you brought a supermodel geologist to my brother-in-law's birthday party, but you know what? I dealt with it!" His expression had relaxed now, but Joanna kept going. "I thought we were over all this." Her nose tingled, tears beginning to well up, threatening to spill out onto her cheeks. She blinked hard a few times and they receded.

Malcolm leaned down, his hand extended, as if trying to coax a scared cat out of hiding. "Hey," he said, softly. She set the brush down on the paint can, placed her hand in his, and allowed him to pull her to standing. She looked up at him, opened her mouth to say something, but no words came out. Her mind blank, an open sky. Then he was drawing her close, his lips hitting the side of her lips, his rough cheek scratching hers. He kissed her again and she closed her eyes, pressed herself into him. His hands went up, under her shirt, touching her bare skin.

They broke apart, took in sharp breaths. "What are you *doing*?" she said into his chest, pushing him back. She wormed her way out of his arms, whirled around and darted into her room, her heart pounding.

"I need to take a break!" she yelled out. "Papers to grade!" Folders of student essays, pens and textbooks—she dumped them all in a canvas shopping bag, threw on her coat, and escaped out the door.

She darted through the rain to a nearby coffee shop she rarely visited. The espresso was always weak, burnt-tasting, the wall art bad—1980s travel posters in cheap acrylic frames. The entire place was empty except for the gray-haired barista, a woman wearing rhinestone glasses on a chain around her neck. When she finished making Joanna's drink, she unfolded the glasses, put them on, and went back to reading the newspaper spread out on the counter.

Joanna attempted to smooth her hair with her fingers and breathed in and out, trying not to sound like she was panting. She then took a good ten minutes organizing her papers into piles, pouring all of her concentration into this task. She was a competent, highly-organized teacher! There was simply no room left in her evenings or in her life in general for anything but her work, her students, their words. She would tackle the descriptive essay first: *What specific place has the strongest associations of "home" to you? A favorite chair? A tree house? The kitchen table? Explain this place to the reader in detail, summoning the memories and emotions associated with it. Remember that this essay still needs a point—you aren't just describing the contents of your garage for five pages, you're talking about what that garage means—why it is home to you.*

Pen in hand, Joanna studied each student's paper, underlining insightful lines, putting question marks in the margins by confusing passages. She composed long, detailed comments, complimenting the students on their strengths and formulating thoughtful suggestions for revision.

After two hours hunched over student essays in paint-splattered clothes, tattered jeans, and an old button-down shirt of Malcolm's, she leafed through three-year-old magazines until the old woman cleared her throat and turned the Open sign around. Out on the sidewalk, Joanna looked up and down the dark street. She couldn't go home. She pulled the hood of her raincoat over her head and took off in the opposite direction. With nothing to grab hold of her attention, her mind wandered to the place she'd been avoiding for the last few hours: his lips on hers, his hands under her shirt, her hands—

Her face went hot; she tilted it up to the sky, letting the mist cool her cheeks. She took in deep breaths as she walked, inhaling the dark-green, earthy scent of wet leaves, grass, and moss. She loved this smell, so different from her childhood smells of sagebrush and pine—which she adored, too, but in a different way completely.

She walked and walked and walked, trying to parse out the events of the last several months—years. Malcolm was obviously jealous and acting out accordingly. The thing was, she couldn't stay strong forever. Eventually they'd wind up in bed; that seemed inevitable. Maybe they'd even make it work for a while. They'd sleep together, be happy for a tiny sliver of time, and then they'd break up, like every other couple in the world.

Once she made her way back to her neighborhood, she knew what she needed to do; she simply needed Malcolm to agree to it. Her pulse thrummed at a steady rate. The meandering journey through the neighborhood had exhausted her and calmed her all at once. She wore a serene smile. It had stopped raining.

From the street, she could see the kitchen light still glowing, the outline of Malcolm's thin frame. Joanna entered the house, let her eyes adjust to the light. She stepped out of her wet shoes and into a pair of slippers she had by the door. Rather than fling her wet coat over the arm of the couch, she arranged it on a hanger, hung it up in the closet. She smiled to herself: a model of tidy, efficient habits. *This* is how she should live her life!

In the kitchen, she leaned against the counter and watched Malcolm as he worked. He whistled while he pushed the broom back and forth over the floor, without a dustpan. A caricature of sweeping. "You were busy," she said.

Malcolm looked up. "Oh yeah. It's coming along." While Joanna had been grading papers and wandering the streets of Portland, Malcolm had pieced the kitchen back together. The cabinet doors, clean and white with a new coat of paint, rested back in their hinges. The paint cans, brushes, and drop cloths had all disappeared.

She went over to the stove, now pushed back against the wall where it belonged, to fetch the teakettle. She could see her reflection in it—the smudges and water deposits buffed off and shined up.

"Tea?" she asked.

Malcolm nodded. He'd stopped working now that she'd taken over, watched as she filled the kettle. "We have some cookies or something around here?" Joanna asked, and Malcolm reached into a cupboard and handed her a package of fig bars. She arranged four on a plate, finished up the ritual of pouring water into two cups. Malcolm was watching her, his eyebrows raised slightly. "We need to talk," she said, placing everything on the nook table and gesturing for him to sit down across from her.

Joanna dunked her tea bag in and out of the water. Malcolm took a fig bar from the plate and bit into the corner, tasting a tiny crumb. She cleared her throat. "Okay, I've been doing some thinking," she began. "This can't keep happening."

"What can't keep happening?" he asked, smiling slightly.

She looked down, trying to avoid fixating on his mouth. "You know very well what I'm talking about," she said into her teacup. "Grabbing me in the middle of the night. Attacking me in the kitchen. That kind of thing."

"'Attacking' wouldn't be the way I'd put it." Malcolm leaned forward and looked into her eyes. "And you kissed me back. Both times."

"That's neither here nor there," she said vaguely. "The point is—we can't keep doing it. It's not healthy."

"All right," Malcolm said, raising his hands in innocence. "Trust me. It won't happen again."

She shook her head. "That's not what I meant. I'm not explaining this very well—"

"Explaining what?"

"I mean, if we're going to do this, we need to do it. Commit to it. You know what I mean?"

"Uh—no."

"I think we should sleep together. I think that would be the most logical thing to do in this situation." Malcolm sat back in his seat and nodded slightly. She kept talking. "I've really been over and over this, Malcolm. It's obvious that—well, that there's something left between us, some-thing unresolved. But here's the thing: I can't lose you again. You know, what happened last March—we didn't talk for *months.* We can't let history repeat itself. If we just fall into that again, we won't survive it. We just won't. One minute you'll be kissing me in the hallway, then we'll fall into bed, then you'll run off or I'll run off or something will happen, and it will be *over.* You know?"

"But it would be logical to sleep together again?"

"Exactly. But see, the difference would be that we'd go into it consciously. We'd be doing it to preserve our friendship."

"That does sound logical." Malcolm did not sound convinced.

"Think about it. There's this obvious—I don't know— let's say attraction here." Joanna gestured between herself and Malcolm. "It seems like, if we were going to be together in any sort of traditional sense, it would have happened by now. But we're way beyond that at this point. We're friends. And when everyone else is breaking up and getting divorced, we'll still have each other. You know?"

"I'm not sure I'm following."

"It's this thing between us—this attraction, for lack of a better word—that could ruin everything! It almost did, last time. So what we need to do is deal with it, with our eyes open."

"And sleeping together once is going to do that."

Joanna waved her hands with impatience. "Once, twice, however many times it takes. We've got to use each other up, get each other out of our systems, see? Then we'll stop before it starts going downhill. The moment before that. And then we'll go back to being friends. The feelings will be gone, used up, dealt with."

Malcolm nodded. "Sounds reasonable." He knocked the table: meeting adjourned. His tea trembled in its cup. He eased himself out of the nook. "Thanks for the tea," he said, heading out the kitchen and back into his room. She heard the door shut behind him.

Joanna sat on the bench sipping her tea, which was now lukewarm.

15

shucked-off and abandoned like this

Somehow, Joanna had thought the words "we should sleep together" would have a greater effect on Malcolm. An immediate effect—taking her hand, knocking teacups from the table, ravishing her in the kitchen nook. Or lifting her up, carrying her into the bedroom, and throwing her on the mattress. Or—okay, at the very least—a mischievous grin, a twinkle in his eye. But this, this non-reaction, unmoored her.

She spent the next six days in a state of agitation. Was he going to do something? Or at least tell her, flat out, that he preferred the challenge of the somnambulant kiss to the "open" sign flashing above her head? He didn't act as though anything had changed. He still looked happy to see her when she walked in the room. If they were both up at the same time in the morning, he made her breakfast. In the evenings he sat on the couch reading and patted the space next to him so that she could sit by his side with her own book or a stack of papers to grade. She would plop down on the couch and sprawl out, affecting supreme casualness. These hours on the couch were torture. She couldn't remember how she had done it before. When she leaned against the arm of the couch, her feet inching toward Malcolm at the other end, she couldn't stop *thinking* about her feet. What if she became so absorbed in a book that they took on a mind of their own, finding their way into Malcolm's lap?

What was Malcolm trying to do to her? Did he think they could just live like this, brushing by each other in the halls, their hands accidentally touching across the table as they reached for the French press every morning?

Malcolm had secured some independent contractor work, so he was out of the house more than usual. She observed him smiling to himself, whistling softly as he padded around the house pounding protruding nails back into the floorboards or repainting the trim on her windows. He'd moved on, she guessed. He'd forgotten their conversation or dismissed it as a joke. Or—another possibility—he was ignoring it. This was his way of letting her down easy.

She came home to a quiet house one Friday evening after teaching all day. Malcolm was holed away in his room; she could see the light coming from under his door. She sighed with relief. No awkward conversation in the living room, no casual suggestion that they should go to the movies or out to eat that would leave Joanna exhausted from the effort of "acting natural."

In her own room, with the door shut firmly behind her, she snuggled under her covers with her laptop. Online, a smorgasbord of ready and willing guys awaited her. She should find someone. Not any of the guys she'd been out with over the last few weeks (James or Tim or Daniel or, or, or)—just some anonymous stranger to have sex with.

She could get rid of this pesky tension taking over her life, return calm and carefree, ready to be a good friend to Malcolm again. After forty-five minutes of clicking through profile after profile, she gave up. No one matched her criteria for an anonymous sex partner: tall, dark-haired, thin, scraggly, brooding. Cold, calloused hands, smelling of wood shavings.

This was pathetic—hiding away in her own house, trolling around for a one-night stand. With a sudden sense of purpose, she threw the covers off and jumped onto the floor to make her bed, tightening up the sheets and shoving the edges under the mattress. She tugged at the duvet, eradicated lumps and wrinkles with a firm hand. Most mornings her bed remained unmade, cluttered with cold, crumpled sheets. Now it was eight o'clock at night and the act felt necessary, important.

With the bed meeting her newly-developed home-making standards, she directed her attention to her own appearance. In the bathroom, she ran a brush over her hair, made her lips shiny with lip gloss. She flashed herself a determined look in the mirror.

It was silent in the hallway. Perhaps Malcolm wasn't home after all. He wasn't prone to leaving the lights on, but maybe just this once he had forgotten. ... She turned to go back into her own room, then pivoted and delivered three firm knocks to his door. "Malcolm?" She let herself in without waiting for a reply.

He was sitting on his bed, reading, his legs stretched out before him. She walked over to the foot of his bed and stood there, her hands on her hips. He glanced up from his book. Seeing him right in front of her—his hair wet from the shower, wearing jeans and a new white T-shirt— strengthened her resolve. Without taking her eyes from his face, she lifted her shirt over her head and dropped it on the floor. His expression did change then, almost imperceptibly. He widened his eyes, but didn't put down the book.

Panic kept her glued to her spot on the floor. She hadn't planned beyond this moment. Removing the shirt should have been enough, should have ignited a spark of interest in him, prompted him to action, made him throw down the book and leap from the bed. Perhaps he required more assurance. Trembling, she reached behind her back and unclasped her bra, then let it fall to the floor. If he laughed at her, she would never speak to him again. She resisted the temptation to cover her breasts with her hands and let her arms dangle uselessly at her sides.

She went over to him, but still, he didn't reach for her. He just held on to that book with both hands, marking his place. It was too late to back out gracefully—hide her chest with her shirt and slink out the door, pretend it was all a joke. He was watching her, waiting to see what she was going to do next. "Put your book down," she said. She climbed on top of him, facing him. He didn't react. In his bed, topless, straddling him! Was he planning on sitting there, mute, a bewildered expression plastered on his face, while she had her way with him? Joanna plucked the book from his hands and dropped it over the side of the bed. It landed with a loud thump on the wood floor.

"Hey!" he said, though he didn't sound the least bit upset.

She took him by the shoulders and shook him. "What are you doing to me?" Her voice broke. She made a move to leave, at once determined to march half-naked out of the room if she had to, refusing to humiliate herself further.

Malcolm latched onto her arm and drew her back to him.

"Ow," she said.

He loosened his grip but didn't let go. "Don't go."

"Why not?"

"It's working."

"What is?"

"This."

She tried to shake his hold on her arm, but he tightened his grip again, then pulled her in until their foreheads met. He ran his other hand down her bare back.

For a moment they just looked at each other. She could barely breathe, bracing herself for the possibility he would break the spell, jump up, grab her clothes, and run out the door.

"Now what?" he said.

She let a nervous laugh escape her. "I can't do this."

"Do what?"

"Can't we just … do this? Like normal people?"

He smiled at her then, his hair falling over his eyes. He pushed her back on the bed, positioning himself on top of her. "Like normal people, huh?" He lowered his head down to hers, so close she could smell his skin. He touched the tip of his nose to hers. She stopped breathing. Then, finally, he brought his mouth down to hers and kissed her, slowly. "Like that?"

She tilted up her chin so he'd kiss her again, but Malcolm was already reaching under her skirt, tugging at the edges of her underpants. She lifted her hips to help him pull them off. "Like this?" he said, scrunching up the fabric in his hand and throwing her underwear across the room.

She took hold of him by the shirt and dragged him back up to her. "I think you're getting the idea."

And then their hands and mouths were all over each other, she was pulling him closer, clothes flying, sheets crumpling.

Afterwards, she lay under a tangle of covers, her hand on his chest, her head nestled in the crook of his arm. She could stay this way for hours, all night, days. Malcolm circled his arms around her and sighed into her hair. "Mm. Your hair smells good." He took a strand and held it up to his nose. "How do you make it smell like this? Do you spray perfume all over it?"

"Why would I spray perfume all over my hair?"

"I don't know. Part of your seduction plan or something."

She laughed. "Right."

Malcolm drew her in and squeezed. "God," he said, "Why haven't we been doing this all along?"

She froze at the words; the warm feelings from the moment before flew out the cracks in the windows, carried out by a sudden draft. She twisted her body to free herself from his arms. "Well, I'd better get dressed. We can't stay here all night." She couldn't look at him as she sat up, securing a blanket around herself. "Thanks," she said as she slipped off the edge of the bed. "It was nice."

In her room, she slipped into a pair of yoga pants and a tank top, shaking her head and mumbling responses to Malcolm's comment. She headed into the kitchen. She would make tea; she needed to calm herself down. What would she do without tea, without this fifteen-minute ritual? Her accomplice in procrastination and avoidance.

Why weren't we doing this all along? I don't know, genius. Maybe because you screwed everything up last time. The kettle began to rattle on the stove, louder and louder, until finally it erupted with steam bursting through the whistle. She let it reach a full piercing wail before lifting it off the burner.

Joanna shook her head again, loosening the thoughts from her head. What was she doing? She and Malcolm were forging new ground here. She couldn't get hung up on the past. That's what this was all about, right? Getting each other out of their systems.

Malcolm sauntered in, jeans on, loose under his hip bones. He brushed his hair away from his eyes. He seemed to have an infuriating way of knowing exactly what effect this gesture had on her. Joanna got a cup out for him and placed it beside her own.

"Are you going to tell me what I did?" He was looking at her with slight amusement. He touched her cheek, lightly.

She concentrated on pouring boiling water into the cups. "Nothing, really. Forget it."

"I mean, one minute you're screaming out my name, then you're storming out on me ..."

"I said forget it. *I* already have. And I wasn't *screaming*."

Malcolm put a finger under her chin, forced her to look up at him. "Well, maybe I need to try harder next time," he said.

This coaxed a true smile out of her. She wrapped her arms around his waist and lifted her face so he would kiss her. He did.

"I made you tea," she said.

The next day she found her shucked-off and abandoned clothes, washed and folded, at the end of her perfectly made bed.

16

a different life on the inside

They had been spending the nights in his room. It was bigger, for one thing—an addition to the back of the house sometime in the 1950s, with light coming in from three sides. It had a sliding glass door that went out to the back. Technically, the room didn't count as a bedroom when Joanna bought the house, with no real closet or heater vents, so she had settled herself in the one official bedroom when she first moved in.

But now she preferred this room. Malcolm had taken the iron bars off the windows and refinished the floors himself. With his bed, desk, plants, and books—and a space heater—he'd made it the best part of the house. Joanna crept out from under the covers, shivering as her bare skin came into contact with the chilly fall air. Wrapped in a blanket, she curled up on a chair under a window, watching raindrops hit the glass and slide down. She turned back to the bluish light of the room and watched Malcolm sleep.

"Hey," he murmured, half-opening his eyes. "What are

you doing up? Come back here." He opened up the covers, inviting her in.

She climbed back into bed. Malcolm tightened his arms around her, and she burrowed into him, trying to siphon off his warmth. "Mm," he said. His eyes were closed again.

"I was just thinking." She nudged him and waited until he mumbled something to prove he was awake, listening. "If we're going to keep doing this, shouldn't we set some ground rules?"

Malcolm groaned. He opened his eyes. "No." Then he kissed her and she kissed him back and then he made her forget why that had seemed like such a great idea in the dark of a rainy morning.

She supposed they were doing just fine without rules, without a plan. The last couple weeks stretched out; it felt like they'd been this way forever. As soon as they walked in the door, they sought each other out, dropped everything to cling together, press their faces against each other, tear off their clothes and fall into bed—where they would stay until one of them would have to leave again, looking up at the clock with surprise, never quite sure what time of day it was—just suddenly realizing one of them or both of them needed to be somewhere, that they had some sort of hazy obligation out there, in the outside world.

And a few times they ventured out there, together—they walked around the neighborhood or ate out at a restaurant or attended a matinee on a drizzly weekend afternoon. By some unspoken agreement, they didn't touch each other on those outings. It felt like an elaborate ruse, a trick they were playing on everyone, strangers. The people they passed by on their walks, the restaurant-goers, the teenagers sitting next to them in the movie theater—no one had any idea that Malcolm and Joanna led a different life on the inside.

The two of them walked side by side, an inch or more of space between them, they sat across from each other at the restaurant table. Exercises in restraint—a game.

As soon as they crossed the threshold, locked the door safely behind them, inside again, they turned to each other, fumbled with zippers, with boots and hats, left trails of clothes in wet heaps, clung to each other as if they'd just survived a flood.

Malcolm had just drizzled honey on her nipples when the blindfold slipped and she caught a glimpse of the clock on the kitchen wall. She tore off the blindfold, which, up until this afternoon, served as a red-checked cloth napkin. "We're late!" she cried.

Now that her vision had been restored, she could see Malcolm eyeing her chest with dread. "Too sticky," he said. "Too sweet."

"You don't have time to lick it off me anyway," Joanna said, trying to catch the excess drips with her hands. "Ugh! What a mess."

They both took a dispirited look around the kitchen. They'd spread an old shower curtain out on the floor, but still, it was difficult staying neat while licking jam, whipped cream and strawberries, and chocolate pudding off each other's bodies—especially while blindfolded.

"We can cross this one off the list," Malcolm said. He took her by the hand and helped her to standing.

"Way off."

The List had started as a joke. It still *was* a joke almost two weeks later—probably. Now Joanna was not quite so sure. Come here, Joanna had said to him that first morning they woke up next to each other. I still haven't gotten you out of my system. After that, lying in bed or on the floor, tangled up in blankets, they would look at each other and laugh, and say, that as wonderful as that was, it hadn't been enough. They still needed more of each other. So what would it take, exactly, to fill them up? What could they do to exhaust themselves of each other? Or were they stuck wanting each other like this, frantic and desperate, eyes glazed over, mouths frothing?

We could lock ourselves in for a week, Joanna suggested, and do nothing but have sex. No television, no talking. What about eating and sleeping? Malcolm had asked. Joanna thought about it. Only water and protein bars. Four hours' sleep a night. No, that wouldn't be the way to do it, Malcolm decided. Locked in the house was no good—they needed to get out. Sex in a public bathroom, for example. Or in an airplane.

And somehow during these conversations the List became real. They had actually taken out a piece of paper and began working on it, absentmindedly, both drawing or writing in the margins until it looked like a note you'd pass back and forth during a junior high math class. Tiny writing, doodles, no attention to the ruled lines of the paper. Scratched out, re-written.

The joke was that they would work their way through the list until they were sick of each other: lock themselves up for a week, have sex in a public bathroom and in an airplane, spray whipped cream on each other *9 ½ Weeks'* style, do it in an elevator, on a bridge, in a tree, in a field, in a snow cave, in a movie theater, in the teahouse at the Chinese Gardens.

The list was growing so big there was no way they could complete it. This thought nagged at Joanna, but then she dismissed it. The List was obviously make-believe. A fantasy. Maybe this was how to do it, how to get each other out of their systems, to imagine it unfolding like this. They were never going to make love on a bed of moss at the end of a rainbow.

"Let's get you into the shower. Hose you down," Malcolm said. Twenty-five minutes later they were seated at the corner of a square table in the middle of a restaurant in the Mount Tabor neighborhood. The restaurant was dark, the periwinkle walls adorned with gilded mirrors and large-faced clocks. Joanna kept losing the thread of the conversation, so intent was she on ignoring Malcolm, his hair falling in front of his eyes in that way she had always found so charming. She watched him as she sipped her drink—some mouth-puckering concoction of chili-infused vodka, coconuts, and lemongrass—and waited for him to lift up a hand, sweep the hair out of his eyes as he always did. "Don't you think so, Joanna?" her sister was saying.

"What?" Joanna tried to focus on her sister and Ted, sitting across from them, staring at Joanna expectantly. Apples—they'd been discussing apples for the last several minutes. It had been an excellent apple season, and there were so many different local varieties. Joanna started nodding with enthusiasm. "Yes," she said. "I am in love with Honeycrisps!"

Her sister frowned. Laura had been shooting Joanna quizzical looks since they arrived. And she and Ted had been acting strangely, bowing their heads together and whispering. They were on to Malcolm and Joanna!—they must be. Malcolm kicked her under the table.

"We were talking about the bark beetle infestation," Ted said. He put his arm around Laura, as if to protect his wife from a descending swarm.

"Bark beetles?" Her mind went blank. She had absolutely nothing to say about bark beetles.

But she was saved by the arrival of menus. Laura and Ted were now huddled together over a single menu, murmuring inaudibly. This was the type of behavior that married couples often exhibited that had a way of making single people feel especially sad and alone. This time, however, Joanna was not bothered by it. Ted and Laura could have their mumbled conversations, inside jokes, and flirtatious looks. She had recently figured something out: it was all just an act. Married people had this desperate need to broadcast their choice to the rest of the world. Everyone knew they were bored, unhappy—yet, perversely, they had a sadistic desire to pull all the sexually liberated singles in to join their ranks, as if to validate their own dubious death-do-us-part decision making.

"Everyone ready to order?" the server asked after reciting the specials and bringing another round of oddly-flavored drinks. The server was perhaps thirty, with straightened, blunt-cut bangs and an extremely tight shirt. She leaned in to hear Joanna place her order, making every effort to afford Malcolm an excellent view of her ample cleavage. She turned to Ted and Laura, and Ted ordered for the two of them, explaining that they would split the smoked trout salad and also share the panko-crusted chicken.

"Maybe you should order a large drink with that," Joanna said. "Two straws."

Everyone ignored her. The server was laughing at something Malcolm was saying. She touched his shoulder as she headed back to the kitchen.

Joanna caught Malcolm's eye and Malcolm shrugged, then suppressed a smile. He tapped the side of his head, above his ear, and Joanna's hand went up to the same spot on her own head. She pulled a strawberry leaf from her hair and discreetly hid it under her napkin.

Joanna leaned in so Malcolm could hear her above the noise of the restaurant. "Do you know her?"

"Who?"

"Our waitress."

"No. Why would I?"

Joanna's foot found Malcolm's under the table. "She was into you," Joanna whispered, so Ted and Laura couldn't hear. They were still huddled together, anyway, lost in their conversation. "She wanted you."

"Hmm," Malcolm said. "I hadn't noticed."

Joanna excused herself to go to the restroom at the end of a narrow hallway. She straightened her hair in the mirror, then washed her hands, splashed her face with cold water, slapped her cheeks to get the color going in them. All this sex over the last couple weeks had created a rather frazzled effect on her—her eyes glassy, her hair tousled, face pale, as if she hadn't been exposed to daylight, locked away in a vampire's den. She dried her face with a paper towel and applied some lip gloss.

Malcolm was standing outside, waiting for her. "I had to go to the bathroom, too," he said. He pressed her up against the wall and leaned down to kiss her. "You taste like jam."

She towed him in by his shirt. His hand traveled up her back, reached behind her and unclasped her bra with one hand. His other hand slipped under her top, crept up to her bare chest.

Laughing, she pushed him off her and cast a swift look around to make sure no one had seen them. With some difficulty, she refastened her bra and then tucked in her shirt, rearranged her hair. "What was that, some high school party trick?" Her head shook in mock disapproval.

"More like sixth grade." He leaned in for one more kiss.

She squinted up at him and swept his hair out of his eyes, then ran her thumb over his lips. "We can't go back there wearing the same lip gloss." She smoothed the wrinkles in her skirt with her hands and she walked back down the stairs to talk about apples, or bark beetles, or whatever the topic had become.

The next week was Thanksgiving. The alarm went off at five, when it was still dark. Their bodies had drifted from each other in the night, but at the sound of the alarm, they found each other under the covers and promptly dropped back to sleep, listening to the sound of rain on the roof. When Joanna woke up she was alone and the sky was gray, crowded with rainclouds. She wrapped a blanket around her and stumbled into the kitchen. The kitchen was bright and warm, already smelling of toast and coffee and cinnamon.

Malcolm was rolling out dough. He had ambitions to make three different kinds of pie. Half a pie per person! But he was determined. She watched him for a moment before pouring herself a cup of coffee. "I can't be expected to help make pies at five in the morning without caffeine." She rested her head against his arm and watched his hands piece together scraps of dough.

"Well, it's nine-thirty." He kissed the top of her head. "But I'm on schedule." She took that as permission to arrange herself in the nook, to read a book and drink coffee while he worked.

Joanna's phone rang as they were stepping out the door. "That was Ted," she announced a moment later.

"Thanksgiving is canceled." She set her tray of vegetables and a pumpkin pie with a pecan crumble topping on the coffee table and perched on the arm of the couch.

Malcolm was balancing a French apple pie in one hand, a cranberry cheesecake in the other. "What? Why?"

Joanna shook her head. "Laura isn't feeling well. This doesn't sound like her at all. She would have to be almost *dead* to cancel Thanksgiving. You know what I think it is? She's onto us. She's punishing me now."

"Yeah, I'll bet that's it."

"They were acting kind of strange at the restaurant, didn't you think?"

"No stranger than usual."

"We should go over there anyway. They're probably having Thanksgiving dinner without us."

"Why would they do that?"

"They're onto us!"

Malcolm set his pies next to the vegetable tray. "Maybe she really is sick."

"I'm calling her." She let it ring and ring until it clicked over to voicemail. "She knows about us!" Joanna unbuttoned her coat and threw it on the ground. "I knew it!"

"I doubt that's it," Malcolm said.

"You're being naïve."

He laughed then. "I don't think so."

Joanna narrowed her eyes. "All right. You know something, don't you?

"I just doubt she's sick, that's all."

"What do you mean?"

"Nothing. Just something I figured out, I guess you could say."

"Okay … What?"

"I'll bet she's pregnant."

"Pregnant!"

Malcolm nodded. "Sure. It makes sense."

"It does?"

"I could be wrong."

"Do pregnant women usually refrain from hosting Thanksgiving dinner? This is Laura we're talking about. I can't believe she'd leave us out on the streets."

"We're hardly out on the streets. And we have the most important part of the meal: the pies."

"You mean the veggie tray."

"Right."

They soon had a roaring fire going and a tablecloth spread out on the floor. They sat cross-legged in front of the fire in their good clothes, two pies, the cheesecake, and the crudités between them. The silver vegetable tray glinted in the firelight. Joanna had taken out their best cups and saucers—the ones without chips, whose handles hadn't cracked off—and made them cups of tea.

Several minutes passed with only the sounds of the crackling fire, forks clicking against tin pie pans. "Is making love on the floor in front of a roaring fire on the List?" Joanna asked.

"It *was*," he said. Their eyes met and then they laughed. "Oh yeah."

"Must not have been very memorable," he said.

"Oh, it was memorable all right. I just didn't know if it was on the List, or if it was—what do you call it?—extracurricular."

"Having sex on a tray of vegetables is not on the List."

"That's probably for the best." Joanna took a bite of cranberry cheesecake right out of the spring form pan and then took a careful sip of lukewarm tea. "So," she said, "what makes you think Laura is pregnant?"

"Just a few careful observations. She didn't order a drink at dinner, for one thing."

"Maybe she just didn't want to drink. I don't always order a drink when we go out."

"Yes you do."

"Okay, but does Laura?"

"Usually. *And* Laura's bra size had probably doubled since we last saw her."

"Good to know you're keeping tabs on my sister's bra size." Joanna watched the flames flicker over Malcolm's face. He gave her a small, mischievous smile. "Well—"

"I guess I've always known you find her so much more beautiful than me...."

"Where did you get *that* idea?"

"You said it! The very first night we met."

"I said that? And you still made out with me?"

Joanna shrugged. "I admired your candor."

"It's not true. Please forgive me." He ran a finger along the side of her face. "I'm not even into blondes."

"I wasn't offended."

"You should have been. Let me make it up to you." Malcolm moved the half-eaten pies and the withered vegetables onto the coffee table and turned to Joanna. She let him take her into his arms and kiss her.

She settled into his arms and watched the sparks crackle off the burning logs in the fireplace. He stroked her hair and her eyes closed. "I'm not sure abstaining from alcohol and expanding boobs mean my sister is having a baby," she said drowsily.

"Well ... that, and Ted told me."

"*What?*" Joanna's eyes shot open and she whirled around to face him. "Why didn't you tell me? Why didn't *Laura* tell me?"

"He made me promise not to say anything. They wanted to make some sort of big announcement when she got to twelve weeks."

"How long have you known?"

"Only two days! He let it slip out when I went over there to pick up that sanding belt." Malcolm put his arm around Joanna, trying to draw her back to him. "I think they wanted to make some sort of big announcement at the restaurant last weekend, but they chickened out for some reason."

"I can't believe this. My own sister. I'm going to call her." She patted the floor in search of her phone.

"Don't do that," he said. "You should be thanking your sister."

"Thanking her? Why?" The fire was getting low—one black log sent out a ribbon of smoke.

"For leaving us to fend for ourselves on Thanksgiving. A vegetable platter and three pies. What more could we possibly need or want?"

Joanna frowned, considering the question. Then she threw another log onto the fire, sending a spray of ash flying out onto the hearth.

17

nothing but flickering lights scattered over the foothills

"It's just for a few weeks. A month at the most."

"I know."

"I am coming back, you know."

"I know." Joanna sighed. She turned on her side to face him, and he reached over to readjust the blankets over her shoulders. What she couldn't explain to him was that she was sad—not because she didn't think he should go to California for this job, which was just too good to pass up, and not because she didn't think he would return, because she had no doubt that he would—but because this was the end. It was the perfect time to do it. She didn't want to; she didn't feel ready to end it, but it had to be done. His leaving town would give them both time to step back and reorient themselves to life without each other. And then, when he returned, they'd go back to their old life—as friends.

She made a point to be extra kind to Malcolm as he neared his departure date. One morning she attempted to serve him breakfast in bed. Her endeavor to prepare over-easy eggs led to a mess on the frying pan, and she forgot to put the bread in the toaster until the eggs had finished and cooled on a plate, but he had appeared to appreciate the gesture.

Joanna imagined that their time apart would allow them to reflect. He would be in California, sitting under a palm tree, listening to the ocean waves slap the shore. She would be home in Nevada, wandering through a field of sagebrush. When they met up again after the new year, they would share a platonic embrace. Instead of feeling sadness for what they had lost, they'd rejoice, knowing they had overcome their desires and saved their friendship. Years would go by, and no matter what happened—no matter how many boyfriends or girlfriends or husbands or wives passed through their lives—they'd always have each other.

He left on a Saturday morning before the sun rose. Joanna got up with him, stood shivering at the front door. "You realize you're just walking fifteen feet down to your car," she joked. He had bundled up for the journey, with a puffy vest over a thick hoodie, a stocking cap on his head. Joanna was still in her pajamas, wearing one of Malcolm's scratchy old sweaters to stay warm in the unheated house.

"It's good to be prepared," he said. He'd packed a grocery store paper bag with sandwiches, six apples, a thermos of coffee, and about twenty energy bars. As if he was driving through Antarctica instead of California. "Well. See you in a few weeks." She wrapped her arms around him and let her head sink into the pillowy layers of his clothes. "I'll call you," he said.

"Don't bother." It came out sounding flatter, meaner than she intended. She looked up at him then, registered his surprise. The rings under his eyes dark with sleepiness. "Write me instead," she blurted out. As soon as the words left her mouth, she recognized the brilliance of this idea: writing old-fashioned letters would take them back to the first couple years of their friendship, when things were simpler. No phone calls, no texts or emails—they could keep a safe distance from each other. Not get wrapped up in hours of conversation each night as if he'd never left.

She watched him drive away. He looked up and waved. Malcolm was not particularly broken up about leaving her. Why would he be? As he said, he was coming right back. Still, it made sense that *she* was on the verge of becoming an emotional wreck. She wasn't made of stone. She and Malcolm were intertwined now, more deeply connected, like two carrots spiraling around each other underground, fusing together in the dirt.

She continued standing at the window even after he pulled away. The neighbor across the street had his lights on. She watched him shuffling around, getting breakfast. Every day, while she slept, other people were waking up, making their beds, eating food, accomplishing things. Today was just another ordinary morning for that old man with the white mustache and brown cardigans who waved at her from across the street when he saw her out on her porch, taking her mail from the mailbox. Five o'clock in the morning, in Joanna's world, was a time reserved for catching a plane, for leaving, for saying goodbye.

Maybe it was time for a change. Why, since she was up anyway, think of what she could do before the shops and restaurants started to open! Clean the whole house from top to bottom, make a vat of soup to feast on for the entire week, go outside in the mud and throw some seeds in the ground!

She gave those ideas some serious thought for about two minutes. How did people feel their way through the dark, shuck off the sleepiness, summon up the energy to do anything at this hour? She went back to bed. Once she finally roused herself five hours later, shook the sleep from her body with a series of exaggerated stretches, she felt good—wide awake. Malcolm would be in Medford or Ashland by now. Soon he'd cross the border into California. And Joanna would spend the day with soothing rituals: wash the sheets, remake Malcolm's bed, read trashy magazines and eat chocolate ice cream from the carton. Cry, perhaps, if the mood struck her.

That night she headed to her own bedroom to sleep, alone. Had it always been so cold in this part of the house? The overhead light cast unflattering shadows everywhere. And it was a mess. She'd been using it as a changing room for weeks—clothes lay in piles on the bed, on the floor. It would just be so much *work* to try to rest in this horrible place. It wouldn't cancel out the day's effort of cleansing practices if she were to sleep in Malcolm's room for a few more nights, would it? Sheets could be washed, beds remade. She loosened the freshly-laundered sheets from Malcolm's bed and fell asleep with her head on his pillow.

The next week Joanna received her first letter from Malcolm. She was surprised to see her chaste reflections on the nature of fog and rain, a spirited review of a new movie they had both wanted to see, and a rundown of some potential household projects met by a series of pen-and-ink nudes that Joanna immediately stashed in the top drawer of her dresser, under her socks. She had to admit he had a flair for illustration, a sharp attention to detail. She spent two days deliberating on the best way to respond: polite rejection? Indignation? She contemplated writing back without mentioning his letter at all—just scribbling out a few banal observations about the Christmas lights popping up all over the neighborhood, some funny anecdotes from her classes.

Two days later she went to the post office and mailed off a paperback romance novel she had found at a used bookstore, carefully illuminating the racy passages with a pink highlighter. She mailed another package at the same time, to her sister—a tiny snowsuit, made to look like sheep's wool, soft and gray, with an attached hood and little ears sewn on top. After she left the post office, she realized it was all wrong. Her sister's baby wasn't due until June. The baby would be too big to wear it by the time winter rolled around.

Joanna's last visit with Laura had started with Joanna showing up on Laura's doorstep the day after Thanksgiving and asking "why everyone feels the need to reproduce" and ended with her feeling like a complete jerk and a horrible sister. It turned out that Laura and Ted had spent Thanksgiving in the hospital, afraid they were going to lose the baby. She had already had two miscarriages in the past six months and she couldn't handle another one.

Joanna was shocked. "But why didn't you tell me you were pregnant? I didn't even realize you were trying!" This set off a huge fight. Laura yelled at her, saying she didn't think Joanna would care—she was always so dismissive of marriage and children. This infuriated Joanna. How could her sister say she didn't care? She didn't have a chance to care! More yelling, and then Joanna stormed out. By Monday she had cooled down and tried to smooth things over, but Laura wouldn't return any of her calls. Three weeks had gone by, and her sister still refused to speak to her.

Her mother had made reservations for them to eat Christmas Eve dinner at the casino steakhouse—a dark, wood-paneled restaurant tucked away from the patterned carpet and blinking lights of the gaming floor. Why Tess would want to celebrate at their old workplace where they had spent so many hours on their feet, breathing in second-hand smoke and pouring coffee, was beyond her. Maybe Tess enjoyed the idea of returning, revealing a new self, and getting a table in the most expensive restaurant in the joint.

The steakhouse was not the fluorescent-lit diner with its orange booths and forest wallpaper. No, the steakhouse was high class. Starched tablecloths, candles, the works. The waiters talked in hushed tones and wore tuxedos. This was, for Tess Robinson, somewhere special, somewhere to really treat her daughter.

Joanna had dressed up, as her mother had asked. Now they sat at a table for two. They had a bottle of wine, and her mother was in high spirits. Her eyes twinkled in the candlelight. "Order whatever you want! It's on me. And it's Christmas! Just like old times."

Joanna did not view these "old times," when she and Tess lived together, after Laura had gone off to college, as fondly as Tess apparently did. She ordered fettuccine Alfredo and her mom got a steak.

"Have you been seeing anyone?" her mother asked her.

Joanna rolled her eyes. Always the first question from her mother's lips. "No, Mom."

"No? Why not? I thought you were finding men from the Personals—"

"They weren't the *Personals*! It was online dating. There is a difference. And I stopped doing that … a while ago."

"Oh?" Tess raised her eyebrows, picking up on something, perhaps the vibrations in Joanna's voice. Tess had a bloodhound's sense of smell for a romantic story. She could sniff it out of her. "And what about Malcolm?" she pressed on.

Joanna tried her best to mask her alarm. "What about him?"

"Is *he* dating anyone?"

"Malcolm? Uh—no. I wouldn't say that."

"Aha!" Tess hit the table with both hands, causing all of its contents to tremble. The glasses made tiny ringing sounds that echoed through the room. "I knew it!"

"What?" Joanna couldn't keep up her neutral expression. Her mouth gave her away, forming into a smile.

"You two ... I knew something would happen. Especially since he moved in—"

"We're not dating, Mom. We're friends. It's just that—"

"You're also sleeping together? Yes. I know how that goes."

Joanna shook her head. "No, I don't think you do—"

"You remember Danny don't you?" Joanna remembered him. He had a dark, thick head of hair, glossy from some sort of gel or wax. He chewed gum, went around smelling like wintergreen. "Well, that's how it was with him," Tess said.

"I doubt that very much," Joanna responded.

"No, listen! We worked together."

"I know this story."

"Not the whole thing. We worked together—so this must have been right after the divorce. We just *talked*. Took breaks together sometimes, sat at the counter eating our lunches. This went on for a couple years. Eventually we did things together, too, after work. He never once made a move on me."

Tess had quite the knack for retelling history, for

inventing the supporting details of Joanna's childhood.

"Mom, trust me, this thing with Danny was nothing like my friendship with Malcolm—"

Tess cut her off. "So when it finally happened, it took me by complete surprise. Years of innocent chatter and then—I couldn't believe it. It was so intense, so amazing to be with someone you just knew, inside and out...."

"Ugh, Mom, I can't believe I'm hearing this! Do you not remember how it ended with him? He wouldn't even speak to you."

Tess lowered her eyes. "Well, he didn't have much of a choice about that."

"Right, Mom. Because he was *married.*" She should have felt sorry for her mother. Instead, she was angry. "How can you even compare that—that *affair*—to me and Malcolm?" She excused herself to go to the rest room and worked at calming herself down. She would not fight with her mother on Christmas Eve.

Joanna sat back down at the table, ready to smooth things over.

Her mom smiled secretively at her. "You know," she said. "I've been seeing someone, too."

"Oh, Mom."

"His name is Clive. He lives in Fallon."

"Fallon?" Joanna imagined someone tall, thin, in Wranglers and a black cowboy hat.

"He's great. Really a nice guy."

"I'll bet."

"Why can't you be happy for me?" Tess frowned and poured herself some more wine. She filled Joanna's glass, too. "This is really going somewhere. We've been spending almost every weekend together since September."

Joanna sighed. "Why do you need him anyway? I

thought you said you were done with men!"

"I never said that!"

Joanna knew her mom hadn't said that; *Joanna* had said it. She had wanted it to sink in. "What do you need a man for, anyway? Look at you—college educated now, with an office job. A nice townhouse you bought yourself. Can't you see how much happier you are now? How much *saner*?"

Her mother waved her hands, shooing away Joanna's concerns. "Oh, Jo-Jo, what's the point of sanity if you have no one to share it with?" Tess laughed and took a big sip of her wine, pleased with this retort. "Isn't that what it's all about? Losing yourself for a bit? Isn't that the best part— what makes falling in love so fun?"

Joanna stared at her mother.

At that moment, two tuxedoed waiters stopped by with a rolling dessert cart. Joanna tried to take a few deep breaths, concentrating on the elaborate production made over their orders. A waiter took a huge white plate, zigzagged berry coulis over it with a pastry bag. He placed a piece of cake on top of that, garnished it with whipped cream and a live flower, and presented it to Tess with a flourish. Then he went to work on Joanna's order—some sort of meringue-covered torte that required a miniature blowtorch to brown the top.

Tess dug into her flourless chocolate cake, waxing rhapsodic on the virtues of Clive: his beautiful green eyes, his charming way of calling her "darling." The more good things Tess had to say about him, the more upset Joanna got. She could barely sit there, listening. She twisted her cloth napkin in her lap, picked at the meringue on the top of her torte.

"Mom, I don't want to listen to this."

Tess pouted. "You want me to be alone. And miserable."

"I don't want you to be miserable! That is the whole point! These guys make you miserable. Don't you know how many nights—*years*—I spent not doing homework or hanging out with my friends? Because I was home, taking care of you!"

"I never asked you to do that," Tess said, so quietly Joanna could barely hear her.

"No one asked me. Who would ask me? No one else knew. No one saw how you unraveled whenever someone broke up with you."

"It's normal to cry when you lose someone, Joanna. Normal to get attached, and then to feel sad—"

"But it's not normal to stop buying food, Mom. Or call in sick for weeks at a time, or stop changing your clothes. Remember Brian?"

"That was a long time ago," Tess whispered.

"I was fifteen." One morning Joanna woke up to find her mother perched on the couch in the living room, wearing the same clothes she had had on the night before. A shiver ran through Joanna's entire body. She had the eerie feeling that Tess had been sitting in that very spot, in that very same position, with the very same lifeless look in her eyes, for the last eight hours.

She shook her mom's shoulders and snapped her fingers in her face. She didn't know what to do. She had to go to school—she had tests in calculus and American literature.

Her mother shook her head with a few jerky movements. Then she smiled weakly. I don't feel so good, Jo-Jo, she said. And then her eyes rolled back into her head, her back arched, and her whole body seized three times, then went limp. Her mother lay passed out on the couch, her chest heaving up and down. Joanna couldn't move. Her mind—strangely, inappropriately—fixated on the tests she would miss. Perhaps someone could explain, she thought. Someone could write her a note, allow her to retake the exams.

In the next moment, she uprooted herself from the floor and ran to the phone. She didn't know whom to call—not Brian, certainly. Her father? She tried reaching him at work, but no one was able to track him down. She dialed an ambulance next.

Laura flew in from Portland that very night, already sobbing as she stepped off the plane. How did this happen? she kept asking. A week later, Laura went back to Portland to finish up her semester. Joanna and Tess would be fine— hadn't they always been, up until now? And wasn't what had happened just a fluke, an allergic reaction to some commonly prescribed drugs? As much as she wanted— needed—her older sister's help with their mother, she couldn't help thinking of the future. One day it would be her turn to venture off to some distant city and start college. Something made her think that if Laura could do it, so could she. But if Laura came back, they'd all three be stuck there, in this miserable apartment, for the rest of their lives.

"Joanna." Tess reached across the table and held on to Joanna's hand. "Is this what you've been worrying about all these years?"

Joanna nodded.

"That was a fluke, you know. The doctors said I had a bad reaction to the anti-depressants they had me on."

"I know."

Tess gave Joanna a sad little smile. "I thought you didn't want me to be happy."

Joanna couldn't smile back. "I just didn't want you to fall apart."

They got home late and went straight to bed. Joanna sat on the daybed, surrounded by about fifty decorative pillows, upstairs in Tess's spare bedroom. During the day the room afforded a breathtaking view of the Sierras. But in the night it was so black outside she could see nothing but flickering lights scattered over the foothills.

Alone on Christmas Eve. Outside, the air blew dry and cold over hard brown dirt and sagebrush. Laura wasn't talking to her. Her dad was in Texas with Linda's family. Her mom was going crazy over a guy—again. And Malcolm was in California. Joanna searched her room for a piece of paper and a pen—she'd write him a letter, get it all out. She wouldn't even have to send it; it was essential to talk to someone.

Or she could call him. If she really wanted to, she could talk to him right now. It became urgent, suddenly. She needed to hear his voice.

She almost hung up after his phone rang and rang without going to voicemail.

"Joanna?"

"Merry Christmas."

"What's wrong?"

"Nothing," she said. "Nothing's wrong. I just wanted to talk to you—that's all."

"Good. Because I wasn't sure how serious you were about this phone ban. I was just going to call you, as a matter of fact."

Joanna smiled. "You were?"

"So nothing's wrong? You sound … sad."

She sighed. "It was nothing. Arguing with my mom, as usual."

"But it's Christmas!"

"Yes, I know it is, Tiny Tim."

"I mean, I would have thought you'd both be on your best behavior."

"We were." They were both silent on the line for a moment. "I want to see you," she said. This came out more desperate-sounding than she had intended. She realized then that she missed him, wanted to see him. And not just anyone—him in particular.

"That's actually what I was going to call you about," Malcolm was saying. "What are you doing over New Year's?"

"I'll still be here," Joanna said, working hard to make her voice sound steady, neutral. "Unfortunately. I don't know what I was thinking. Now my mom's saying she wants me to meet this new guy. He lives in Fallon, so I guess she wants him to come over for a few *days* while I'm here—"

"Okay, she won't miss you then. Come spend New Year's with me."

"In San Diego? With your mom and dad?"

"No. In Tahoe. My parents were trying to decide between Palm Springs and Tahoe. I talked them into Tahoe. Can you get a ride? I could come into Reno and pick you up."

"So I'd meet your parents, huh?"

"Yeah. They want to meet you."

"Hmm," Joanna said, stalling. She was already devising a way to spin this to her mother. They could use a little break from each other—and didn't Tess want some "alone time" with Clive? She swept away the thought that just a few minutes before, she'd been opposed to her mom even dating this guy. And that she and Malcolm were supposed to be *reflecting* ... But could she help it if telephone lines, cell phone towers, and satellites seemed to be conspiring together, hurling their words at each other over the distance?

18

her weightless body

Joanna drove her mother's car up into the mountains. Tess wouldn't need it—Clive was driving into Reno from Fallon so they could spend New Year's Eve together. She pouted about Joanna leaving but then brightened at the idea of both of them having "someone to kiss" at midnight on New Year's Eve.

Like everyone else who grew up in Northern Nevada, Joanna had spent half of her summers up at the Lake, getting sunburnt at over 6,000 feet, swimming in melted snow, sitting on golden sand under Ponderosa pines. But as she headed up into the Sierras, she began to doubt the wisdom of joining Malcolm and his parents. First of all, she didn't ski. And more importantly, she and Malcolm were supposed to be easing into a new, monkish phase of their friendship. The whole point of sleeping with him in the first place had been to get him out of her system.

But what if it they weren't out of each other's systems? In that case, they would be obligated to keep working at it, eventually burning each other out, leaving nothing but smoldering ashes. From these ashes, their new, improved friendship would rise up, ready to take flight.

But … this was a *vacation*. Things work differently on vacation, the rules become more relaxed. You might eat dinner every night at 6:00 p.m. at home, but go out at eight o'clock on a trip, for example. Perhaps it would make more sense to give up Malcolm as a New Year's resolution, along with starting the garden earlier and doing better about grading papers in a timely manner.

With the last shred of light still clinging to the sky, she pulled in to a snowy driveway. The house was built up the side of the mountain, with the entrance at the back. Her feet crunched over day-old snow, up a redwood plank leading to the entryway. She knocked and the door seemed to swing open almost immediately. Joanna had never seen a photograph of Malcolm's mother, but she recognized her at once: long-limbed and dark-haired. Her hair was twisted up and piled on top of her head, with a perfect streak of gray shooting out from her widow's peak.

"Joanna!" Maxine Martin smiled hugely and enveloped Joanna in a long embrace. Joanna could feel the ridges of her ribs through the luxurious softness of the cream-colored sweater Maxine was wearing. "We are so thrilled you could join us. Come in, come in. Where's your coat? Malcolm … has his hands full at the moment." She chuckled to herself then, as if on the verge of divulging a secret.

Joanna followed Maxine up a half-flight of stairs, leading into a huge, open room with vaulted ceilings and a postcard-perfect view of the lake framed by trees and a darkening sky.

"Malcolm! Stephen!" Maxine cried out. "Joanna's here!"

Joanna sat down at a stool on a granite-covered island

to observe Malcolm and his dad in the kitchen. Somehow, in the hour and a half since Malcolm and his parents had checked in, they had managed to litter the countertops with cardboard boxes, canvas shopping bags, pots and pans, egg cartons and shells. Malcolm was holding two eggs in each hand, his fingers curling around them like talons. "Check this out, Joanna," he said, holding the eggs up for her to see.

"Uh—nice," she said.

"We've been listening to NPR," his mom explained.

"We do that on road trips," his father elaborated. The three of them—Malcolm, Maxine, and Stephen—stood in a line on the opposite side of the island. They were so clearly a family, all so lanky with the same dark eyes. Variations of each other. And apparently Malcolm's love for layering had been handed down to him from his father, Stephen, who had on a button-down shirt under a forest green sweater under a corduroy jacket with patches at the elbows.

Malcolm waited until he had Joanna's full attention. She rested her eyes on him, her tall and lean friend, wearing a narrow red sweater she had never seen before, his hair slightly shorter than the last time they had been face to face. In a swift movement, Malcolm cracked all four eggs down on the side of a glass bowl, which Joanna now saw was filled more than halfway with yellow orbs floating in clear gel. The whites and yolks slipped free and joined the others in the bowl. In a final flourish, Malcolm shucked the shells to the side, then raised his hands up like a magician's. His parents hooted and applauded.

Joanna, impressed, clapped as well. "What is going on here?"

They explained, all talking over each other, that they had been listening to a fascinating radio program on their drive and learned (among other things) that breakfast cooks in

Las Vegas needed to crack four at once to stay on the top of their game, which had inspired the Martins to stop at the store on their way up. They had spent the last hour cracking their way through over four dozen eggs.

Maxine poured Joanna a glass of wine and pushed it across the counter. Joanna smiled her thanks. Malcolm raised his eyebrows and nodded at her, and she returned the gesture. During the discussion about the radio show, he had transitioned from egg-cracking to vegetable-chopping. He peeled the skin from an onion, attacked it with a gigantic knife, and slid the contents of the cutting board into a skillet his father was shaking and tossing over the blue flame of the stove. His mother cleared a space on the island, began to cut butter into flour, working without measuring or even looking at her own hands, chatting away.

They had all refused Joanna's offers to help make dinner, and she was relieved. She couldn't keep up with them. On her way over the mountain pass, Joanna had practiced a few short but polite answers to the questions she was sure his parents would want to ask her—all the boring small talk she detested so much—what do you do, oh do you like doing that, where did you go to school, what do your parents do, and so on. Instead she could just ease into the chatter, speaking up only when she had something useful to contribute, letting the flurry of activity settle around her.

And then—dinner was served: omelets, a green salad, and biscuits, straight from the oven. They would serve flan for dessert, for which Maxine apologized in advance. Already Joanna saw they'd be dipping into the clear glass bowl of eggs right into the new year.

Cleaning up after dinner brought on another production. This is how Malcolm's family operated. They clanged pots and pans, ran water, threw dishes in the dishwasher, yelled over each other, tossed sponges through the air, laughed and sang along to the radio as they worked. It was like a movie; she half expected birds to swoop in the windows with dishcloths in their beaks.

Once the dishwasher was humming and the flan was steaming in its *bain marie*, Maxine suggested that Malcolm fetch Joanna's bag and show her where to put her things. Malcolm went out to the car and returned with Joanna's bag. He gestured for her to follow him downstairs to the bedrooms.

She followed him down to the cool, dry depths of the lower floor. She had arrived at this house over three hours ago. In that time, she and Malcolm had not exchanged more than a few words. They hadn't hugged or even so much as brushed their fingers together as they reached for the salt shaker during dinner.

He switched on a light in a bedroom. "This room has a complete lake view in the daytime," he said. He set her bag down on the floor and walked to the front of the room, by a large picture window. Underneath the window was a double bed with a thin, navy blue bedspread. Shelves along the walls held books, games, and framed pictures of sailboats.

Malcolm's suitcase lay propped open on a chair next to the bed. She looked at the bag, his clothes arranged in neat stacks, then up at him. He was standing just a few feet from her. He held his hand out, and she took it. He pulled her toward him, slowly. "Hmm," he said, when their bodies finally made their way to each other. She put her arms around his neck and looked up at him.

He pulled her into him and then bent down to kiss her neck. They stumbled their way to the bed, kissing, and fell down onto the mattress. They both laughed. When his hands went up under her shirt, touching bare skin, she pushed him away.

"We can't do this with your parents right upstairs!" she whispered.

"Sure we can." Malcolm lifted her shirt, bent down to kiss her stomach.

She let this distract her for a moment but then shook her head. "Malcolm?" She ran her hands through his hair, trying to divert his attention from her navel. "Are you staying in this room?"

"Mm-hm."

"Where am I going to sleep?"

He lifted his head up then to look at her. "In here. With me."

"In here?" She tried to ignore the way his fingertips felt against her skin. "What did you tell your parents about us?" He pulled her shirt all the way over her head and threw it over his shoulder.

"I told them you were my girlfriend." He squinted at her, leaned in to kiss her.

"Malcolm!"

"What did you want me to tell them?" Malcolm put on an innocent expression. "I guess I could have told my mom that we're friends who fuck, but girlfriend just seemed easier."

"Or you could have said we're *friends*."

"Yeah, but then they'd expect you to stay in a separate room. Is it such a stretch to act like you're my girlfriend for a few days?"

She tried to give the impression she was thinking very hard about this prospect. It was difficult to appear angry when she wasn't wearing a shirt. "So what does acting like your girlfriend entail?"

"You know … holding my hand, laughing at my jokes, sleeping with me sometimes."

"I could probably handle that." She reached for his sweater and pulled it over his head. He wore a button-down shirt underneath. She started at the top button and worked her way down, revealing what she hoped was the final tier of his clothing: a T-shirt. "And what does the Boyfriend do?"

Malcolm let her unbutton the shirt, made no attempt to help her push it off his shoulders or take his arms out of the sleeves. He answered immediately: "Gazes at you fondly, tells you you're beautiful, makes you breakfast, bakes you cookies. Makes you furniture, fixes up your house. Fulfills you emotionally, intellectually, sexually. That kind of thing."

Joanna studied Malcolm's face. He was looking back at her, his expression unreadable. "Okay," she said. "I can't argue with that. If all I have to do is laugh at your jokes every once in a while. I guess you have an okay sense of humor."

"Good. I'm glad we've got that settled."

Absurdly, they shook hands. Shaking hands led to kissing, which led to other articles of clothing falling to the floor.

"We can't just do this with your parents making flan upstairs," she whispered. "They're expecting us to join them for dessert in a minute!"

"We can make them wait. They wouldn't mind. They know we haven't seen each other in a while."

"So they'd be fine with us getting it on down here while they sit and wait for us at the table."

"Yeah. They're cool. They'd probably enjoy it."

"Ugh!" Joanna pushed him off of her. "Okay. Let's go back upstairs."

Malcolm laughed and pulled her on top of him. "I was only joking. Come here."

"Let's just wait until later tonight!" she said when her mouth was unoccupied. She spoke in syncopated breaths. "After your parents go to sleep …"

"They go to sleep *very* late," he said. "So there's no use waiting. We can be very quick and quiet."

"Tonight!" she whispered, in her best seductive voice. "We won't have to be quiet—or quick."

Malcolm stopped caressing her. "Okay," he said. "Let's compromise. Quick and quiet right now—then a slow and soulful round at midnight or so." He unbuttoned her jeans, pushed them down over her hips. He reached back to pluck them off her legs and returned to her, running a hand down her stomach, then between her legs. She gasped as quietly as she could manage, then let herself sink back into the mattress.

"Five minutes," he said into her ear. "That's all I would need to guarantee your complete satisfaction."

"Five minutes, huh? This a skill you picked up from reading *Maxim* during our time apart?"

"Mm, no." He was on top of her now, pressing himself against her. "Just a few things I've learned over the last couple months. About you."

Sure enough, after just a few minutes, Malcolm was smirking down at her. He reached up and brushed back wayward strands of hair from her face. "Wow," he said. "You must have really missed me."

Joanna frowned and tried to squirm out from under him, but his weight was pinning her to the bed. "Why do you have to go and ruin it?" She turned her face away from him.

"No, no." He dotted her neck with light kisses. "I like it when you … demonstrate your enthusiasm."

She couldn't look at him.

"Look," he was saying. He twisted around to show her his back, pink from the pressure of her hands. His back was mottled with crescent-shaped indentations where her nails had dug into his skin—some drawing pinpricks of blood.

She reached up to feel the ridges, surprised. "Sorry," she said. He wasn't supposed to know that every time she was with him she needed more of him, had to stop herself from smashing her mouth onto his, digging her fingernails into his skin deeper and deeper until she broke him open. It was like her first months in Portland, when she could walk and walk all night and into the next day and still not know the streets, each crack in the sidewalk, every leaf and thorn and weed. She wanted to take off her shoes and feel the wet cement on the soles of her feet. Claw up a giant elm with her bare hands, scraping her face along the bark, higher and higher, sending raindrops glittering to the ground, until she collapsed on a branch thick with dark green moss and live there, tearing tender young ferns from the tree with her teeth and chewing them for nourishment.

"We should get dressed," she said to Malcolm. She offered him a tight smile and patted his thigh.

"Hey," he said. Joanna sat up and began rooting around for her clothes. The bed cover had gone askew, pillows and clothes lay scattered on the floor. She found her underwear and bra, slipped into them quickly. His jeans were crumpled up on the floor. She tossed them in his direction.

"You don't have to do that, you know," he said.

"Do what?" she occupied herself in straightening the room, pulling the covers tight over the bed.

Malcolm watched her the way a teacher observes a rowdy classroom—waiting for her to calm down on her own. She sat next to him. "Do what?" she asked again.

"You don't have to act like that."

They sat side by side on the edge of the bed, their bare arms touching. She hadn't noticed the hairs on his arm before, dark against his pale skin. Without thinking she began smoothing them down with her fingertips. "Listen," she said at last. "I just don't want things to get confusing. The whole point of this—"

She was interrupted by his mother calling them up for dessert.

When they went back upstairs, she felt exposed, as if she had grass stains on her back, leaves in her hair. "There you are," his mother said absentmindedly. Malcolm opened and closed all the drawers, looking for spoons. To make herself feel useful, Joanna took charge of the coffee.

As they sat at the table eating still-warm flan out of mismatched teacups, his parents began telling a story about Malcolm as a child. Joanna listened, nodded, and laughed at appropriate junctures in the conversation. She tried to catch Malcolm's eye, but he was entranced by his parents' tandem storytelling. They talked through dessert, spinning the tale of Young Malcolm, who had prepared breakfast in bed for them every morning on their anniversary. Early attempts had involved sludge-like instant coffee cooked in the microwave. Then as a twelve-year-old he'd successfully recreated a full English breakfast, complete with baked beans and a grilled tomato half.

Joanna couldn't remember seeing him quite like this before. He was happy, his eyes gleaming. He didn't return her gaze but seemed to sense her looking at him, and put his hand on her thigh. She leaned into him.

"Oh, young love!" his mom trilled out. Joanna's face flushed with heat. Maxine was laughing. Malcolm tightened his grip on her thigh. How long could she stand this—sitting here, pouring cup after cup of coffee, all this talking? When Stephen brought out a deck of cards she almost groaned out loud. She didn't know what had come over her. When Malcolm squeezed her thigh, she could swear she felt every bone in his hand, even the lines in his palm, through the fabric of her jeans. They couldn't go on like this. It was good she had come here—she obviously didn't have him out of her system. Getting him out of her system needed to be her top priority.

His father dealt some cards and she picked up her hand, began organizing by suit.

Finally, finally, his parents retired to bed. "Come on," she said, leading Malcolm downstairs by the hand. They went into his room and shut the door behind them.

"I don't think my parents are asleep yet."

She pushed him on the bed. "I don't care." She climbed on him and once again began the task of peeling away the layers of his clothing. "We had a deal, remember?"

He flipped her over and ran his fingers through her hair, cupping the back of her head with his hand before kissing her. "A promise is a promise," he said.

The next morning Joanna woke up with Malcolm's arms wrapped around her. It was early. She had grown so used to falling asleep to the sound of rain, waking up in thick gray mist. The sun streaming through the window had nudged her awake after just a few hours of sleep. The lake sparkled in the snow-covered mountains. Blue tea in a Dutch teacup.

She eased out of his embrace and propped herself on an elbow to observe him while he slept. He looked so worried, his eyes closed tightly, as if his subconscious had taken on the task of unraveling a complicated math problem.

Malcolm's eyes opened. He squinted up at her. "Hey," he said in a creaky voice.

"Hey." Joanna smiled, leaned down and kissed him on the forehead. "Good morning."

She reached for him under the blankets, leaned in to kiss his neck. He was warm from sleep and sun. So many days and miles from work, and he still smelled like sawdust.

"You're wearing me out," he said, closing his eyes and smiling.

"That's the point," she said.

When they went upstairs they found they had the place to themselves—his parents had gone skiing. Malcolm and Joanna went into town, walked up and down the sidewalks, breathing in the thin mountain air. By that time the sky had filled up with clouds. Adapting to her role as his "girl-friend," she took Malcolm's hand in hers; they swung their arms as they walked, like children. They stopped in a coffee shop in a wooden-shingled strip mall, ordered oversized coffee drinks and stale pastries. When they came out into the parking lot, hand in hand, it was snowing. She turned to him and kissed him on the lips, right in front of everybody.

She'd done it impulsively, because she had never kissed him in public before and never would get the chance again. She grabbed him by the pockets of his coat, pulled him closer. She kissed him again, harder this time, until she ran out of breath. She bit his lip so forcefully she tasted blood, hot and metallic.

He let go of her, startled. "What's gotten into you?" he said.

She looked at him, his hand held up to his mouth. For some reason this image made her laugh. "You, you, you!" she cried. "And I have to get you out!" She laughed crazily, ran across the parking lot, and spun around, still laughing. She looked back at him through the static of snow. He was just standing there, his hands in his pockets.

When they got back, his parents were sitting in front of the fireplace, sipping red wine from large glasses. Their hair was wet. They huddled under a thick quilt, working on a crossword puzzle. "You two should try out the hot tub before dinner," his mother said. "It's the perfect temperature. Did you pack a suit, Joanna?"

"Oh yes." She always packed a suit—one useful piece of advice handed down from her mother. She was more surprised that Malcolm even owned swim trunks. "We look like aliens," she said to him as they walked outside, towels wrapped around their waists. They sank into the hot water. It was almost dark. "Wow, this is the life," she said. She held out her hand to catch a lone snowflake making a lazy descent into the tub. She couldn't catch it; it landed in the water and melted on contact.

They sat for a moment in silence. More flakes started to fall, whirling over them, sticking in their hair. "You're so lucky, you know?" she said. "I can't believe you grew up like this."

"I can assure you I didn't spend my youth drinking wine and hot-tubbing with my parents."

"I know, I know." The funny thing is that she could hardly imagine Malcolm growing up anywhere else—she pictured the three of them here, in this house, Mom and Dad doing crossword puzzles by the fire, little Malcolm in the room with the sailboat pictures and the navy bedspread. She looked out, into the forest. It was too dark to see the lake now, just trees and snow. "I mean ... this is nice. I'm glad I came."

"Me too." He turned his face upward and closed his eyes.

"I don't know what I would have done if I'd had to stay with my mom this whole time. I probably would have killed her at some point."

"So that's why you came here? To avoid a homicide charge?"

"No. Not the only reason." She laughed. It came out strained, like a bark. "I had this crazy thought, when I was down in Reno, that I'd have to return one day. That in a few years I'd be living in that townhouse, spoon-feeding my mother canned soup. Laura is married, having a baby; she wouldn't be able to do it. So it would have to be me." She looked over at Malcolm. He was watching her, waiting for her to continue. "Anyway, I'm being ridiculous. But I had to get out of there." Joanna tilted her head back up to the sky. The snowflakes had already begun to thin out. One or two hard, white flakes drifted down. She lifted up her hand to catch one, but the breeze carried them away before they could land on her palm. "And I wanted to see you," she said. "I did."

"I wanted to see you, too." He was frowning. He reached over for her hand and pulled her weightless body to him.

On New Year's Eve, their last night together, Malcolm and his parents introduced her to "The Dictionary Game." This Martin family tradition involved a gigantic dictionary, scraps of paper, and an elaborate scoring system. Joanna caught on quickly, racking up points by scribbling down plausible-sounding definitions for archaic words. At ten minutes before midnight, Stephen poured them glasses of champagne. When the clock struck twelve they made a big deal over it, toasting and drinking and kissing.

But just five minutes into the new year, they sat hunched over the dictionary and scraps of paper again. By this point "penalties" had been added to the scoring system, and Joanna found herself knee-deep in a drinking game with Malcolm and his parents. Stephen emptied two bottles of champagne into their glasses. Then they switched to oversized shots of bourbon, measured out in juice glasses.

"You will sphacelate for this, Joanna!" Maxine cried, downing the last of her glass in one valiant chug. Joanna had won the game with the old medical term "sphacelate": to get gangrene, rot, and die. Malcolm and Stephen followed Maxine's lead, drinking in defeat.

"Thank you, thank you!" Joanna said, standing up and raising an empty glass into the air.

"Speech!" Stephen yelled.

Joanna laughed and dropped back in her seat. The room was spinning, which made whatever she was laughing at even funnier. She loved it here. She belonged here; she didn't want to go home. She should stay here pretending to be his girlfriend forever.

Years from now, Malcolm would have a wife, a kid. *They* would be the ones sitting around scribbling on scraps of paper on New Year's Eve with Maxine and Stephen. And what about her? She looked around the table, at her hosts' faces, their eyes happy and half-closed. There would be no place for Malcolm's dear old best friend at the table. No dark-haired, big-eyed kid calling her "Aunt Joanna" and begging for her Dictionary Game strategy.

A shiver ran through her. She had to stop thinking like this, like she had glimpsed into the future and couldn't find herself there. Like she was just a ghost.

Maxine and Stephen stumbled downstairs to bed. Malcolm put his arm around Joanna's shoulders. "Tired?"

She nodded and closed her eyes. They went down to the sailboat room. The air was cold and still. She shivered, quickly stripped off her clothes, and jumped under the sheets. "Come in here," she said.

Malcolm walked over to her and sat down on the bed on top of the covers. He looked down at her and patted her hair. "It's late," he said.

"Come on." She began yanking at the covers, trying to get them out from under him. Somehow she'd pull him under, wrap herself around him. "It's so cold in here without you," she said. This struck her as very funny. She tried to stop herself from giggling and then gave in.

Malcolm stood up, stepped away from the bed, and returned with one of his T-shirts and a pair of her underwear. "Here," he said. "Put these on."

"Aw." Joanna gave him an exaggerated frown. "Then will you come to bed?"

"You're drunk," he said, but he took off his jeans, pulled off his sweater, and climbed in next to her.

"So?" she said. She pressed herself against him, ran her hands up and down his torso.

"Joanna—"

"Come on," she said. "We need to do this. One last time."

He shooed her away, laughing, until he fell off the bed and landed on the floor, taking half of the blankets with him.

"We're both drunk," he said. "Wait here. I'll get us something to eat."

"No eggs!" she yelled after him. Joanna gathered the blankets around her again. She was tired; she tried to close her eyes but felt her insides lurch. Malcolm returned in a few minutes with a plate of buttered toast and two mugs of hot tea.

"Oh, Malcolm," she said, taking a piece of toast from the top of the pile. "You're such a good friend. Such a good, good friend."

The next morning she had to wake up early to drive back to Reno so Tess could take her to the airport. She had taken two ibuprofen to clear her head, to take away the sting from her eyes. Even that and two cups of coffee hadn't helped though. When she hugged his parents goodbye, she had to keep herself from crying.

Malcolm walked her out to her car and kissed her in the driveway. "It's cold out here," she said, but she didn't let go of him.

They sat in the car so they could have a few more moments together; she turned on the heat. They bent into each other, trying awkwardly to hug in the car, with their coats on. They laughed. He kissed her again, and she responded. Five minutes later, his hand up her shirt, she broke free, breathing heavily. "I should probably get going."

Malcolm frowned. "Too bad."

"You'll be back home in a week, right?"

"As far as I know. We're finishing up this job for sure. They had some more work for me, a property in the Bay Area. They seemed to like my work, but I turned them down."

"Malcolm," she said. She put her hand on his arm. "You can't afford to be turning down jobs like this."

He turned toward her. "Oh yeah? And why is that?"

Joanna's head pounded. His voice sounded muffled, far away. "It's just that—maybe it would be better for you to stay away for a little bit longer. It seems like we could use … a breather. A break." When Malcolm didn't respond, she kept talking. "The thing is, if you turned this job down for me—even if that was just a part of the reason—you might regret it. You'd resent me. That's just the kind of thing we need to avoid. Maybe what we need is a fresh start for the new year, you know?"

"A fresh start," he repeated in a flat voice.

"We can't keep going on like this." She willed herself to talk steadily, through the thick white cotton wadded up in her head. "We need—*I* need to get *over* you. This isn't good for us."

Malcolm sat back in his seat. He seemed to be concentrating on the text written on the sun visor, up at the top of the windshield. He shook his head with tiny movements while Joanna talked.

"I mean, all this time we've spent together—spent here—has been so, so great." Her eyes were red and stinging but remained dry. He was staring out of the front window, his jaw clenched. "But we agreed to end it before it went too far. Right, Malcolm?" she said. "Isn't that what we'd agreed on?"

19

what you do to forget

Outside, the sky tumbled with clouds in varying shades of gray. They moved quickly with a cold breeze, sometimes revealing a patch of blue or letting a ray of sun peek through. When the wind rose up, it sent petals flying across from the plum tree in the adjacent yard. A chain-link fence separated her and her neighbor. Through the metal diamonds she could see bright yellow daffodils, the garnet branches of the flowering plum, a deep green lawn.

All this would be very heartening if her own vegetable patch hadn't been ravaged over the winter. She had had to bring last fall's harvest in so early, and then she'd neglected it. Now in March the beds resembled abandoned graves— wet mounds of earth riddled with weeds and the withered remains of last year's crops.

She wore rubber gardening shoes that kept getting stuck in the mud. Her feet would step out of them, onto the damp ground. So now her feet were wet and cold, but she kept at it. She crouched in the soil and worked it with her hands, breaking up lumps of clay, making a pile of weeds. They had weak roots, pulled easily out of the ground. If she found a slug she'd pluck it between two fingers then hurl it into the lawn. She should kill them, but she didn't have the energy.

She was making little to no progress, and then the sky opened up, pelting hard, cold raindrops on her. It seemed to come at her sideways, whipping her hair across her face. "Agh!" she screamed. "Thwarted by Mother Nature again! The elements have won." Lately she'd been doing this—narrating her thoughts as if she were on camera. She took this not as a sign of mental instability, but of job preparation. She had decided on a new career path, which started with forming her own landscaping business and eventually segued into hosting her own televised gardening show: "Mud, Slugs, and Bugs." She'd already come up with several catchphrases, such as "It's a dirty job, and I'm here to do it."

On this program, she would transform her guests' weed-infested eyesores into veritable oases of calm and beauty. But unlike other shows, she would not shy away from the harsh realities of her craft. She was sick of the romanticizing of gardening in literature and popular culture. Tales of Victorian children—children!—smiling and pruning some forgotten garden back to its former glory enraged her. And just recently she'd read a book in which an Iowan opened her window in the dead of winter and scattered a handful of spinach seeds out onto the snow. The snow melted and tender salad greens popped out of the ground. What nonsense! Of all the suspending of disbelief she was required to do as a reader, this—*this*—was beyond credibility.

Her television program would highlight the feet-sticking, the slug-tossing. Through much anguished yelling and gnashing of teeth, she would tame the unwilling landscape into something better than nature could do on its own.

The wind and rain continued to pelt her. She could barely see. Her feet and hands couldn't move; they were frozen to the bone. She gave up and headed inside.

She entered the house through the back room—or what used to be Malcolm's room. It looked the same as it had before he'd left last December. He had sent her a text message telling her he could get his furniture moved out if she wanted to bring in another roommate. No, no, she had written back. She'd keep it here for him. He'd be back eventually. Right? She hadn't heard from him again.

She wished she could throw herself into her work. Isn't that what you do to forget? But her job made everything worse. What made her think she was qualified to teach writing? She'd taken on five classes this term; she was swamped with lesson planning and grading. Hours spent agonizing over those plans, those compositions, and for what? Were students rewarding her with polished apples, standing ovations, tears of gratitude? Quite the opposite. She'd just received last term's course evaluations. "Joanna doesn't have much talent as a teacher," someone wrote. The office had carefully typed out the comments so she couldn't sleuth out the author. It went on: "But that's okay because neither do I. No one's good at everything." To soften the blow, a smiley-face emoticon was included at the end of the comment.

But that wasn't even the worst one. "The teacher doesn't seem to know much about the subject so she can't help us with our writing. We NEED to learn grammer! [sic]

SHE DOES NOT TEACH US WHAT WE NEED TO KNOW ABOUT WRITING!" And the one that made her cry, almost, it was so unfair: "She just doesn't seem to care very much."

How could someone say such a thing? And what did it mean? Joanna had received the evaluations in the morning and then had to teach three classes in a row. After that, at a coffee shop next to the college, she rifled through the evaluations one by one, trying to make sense of them. Maybe they were right: she should quit teaching. If only she could hibernate through winter term, burrow into a blanket and survive on supermarket donuts. But going home didn't appeal to her so much these days.

Coming to no conclusion about the state of her career, she figured she should get something done. With a sigh, she heaved a folder onto her table and halfheartedly began reading student essays.

"Joanna?"

Three papers into grading and the interruption already came as a relief. "Wow, how long has it been?" Joanna asked.

Her friend Allison was squinting her blue eyes at Joanna. "I don't know," she said. "Maybe since last fall?"

"Here—" Joanna gathered up her papers and stuffed them back in the folder. "Sit down."

Allison took a seat and gave Joanna a hard look. "What's wrong?"

"Do I look that bad?"

"Not bad, exactly. You look worn out."

"Great."

"Just—sad."

Joanna didn't know what to say to that. Part of her wanted to break down sobbing, tell Allison everything that had happened with Malcolm. Instead she said she was feeling discouraged over the student evaluations. "What do they know?" Allison responded. She dove into a ten-minute rant about students and how they were incapable of recognizing the subtle genius of Joanna's methods. This made Joanna feel better, even if Allison was making it all up.

Running into her old friend got her through the last days of winter. They went out a few times. It helped to drink, to flirt with guys she'd never see again. She knew even while she was doing it how pointless it all was. But it made her feel like she was going through the motions of moving on.

She and Allison went out one Saturday and they ended up chatting with two college students; they couldn't have been older than twenty-one. Art school types, with unwashed hair and elaborate tattoos. And then somehow—it's not as if she planned it—she agreed to leave the bar with one of them, this kid who paid for his beer in quarters and crumpled-up dollar bills; she went back to his apartment without even telling Allison she was leaving. Let him take all of her clothes off, then lay back on the bed and allowed him to lap at her between the legs for forty-five minutes before she pushed him off of her, gathered her clothes, and ran down the stairs and out into the street. She hadn't even been paying attention on the ride over, had no idea where she was—she didn't recognize the streets.

She called Allison then. Allison was furious with her but came and picked her up once Joanna figured out where she was.

She counted the days down until spring break, whiling away hours looking up fares to possible vacation destinations—Rio de Janeiro, Paris, Tokyo! But she ended up driving down to Nevada—again. As a part of her effort to move forward with her life, she had vowed to patch things up with her sister. As teachers, they both had a week off, while Ted had to work. Laura said since she didn't go down for Christmas she wanted to see her parents before the baby arrived and Joanna had grudgingly agreed to accompany her. So she and Laura had been spending time together again. They'd resolved their differences not with a heartfelt talk but by simply pushing it under the rug. Not much had changed since they were kids.

They were on a scenic portion of the drive—out of the misty blue forests and into open skies, golden windblown fields, a view of Mt. Shasta to the east for miles and miles. They had driven the last half hour or so in silence, and then suddenly Laura spoke up. "So it sounds like Malcolm's pretty popular down in San Francisco."

Joanna's heart skipped a beat. What did this mean? That he was dating someone? That he was dating hundreds of women? "Mm," she answered.

"I mean, it's great that they admire his work so much. He should have no problem starting up his own business when he comes back to Portland."

Joanna kept her eyes on the road, trying to puzzle out Laura's comments without stooping to ask her directly. She couldn't figure out if Laura was speaking hypothetically or if Malcolm really did have plans to move back to Portland.

"So what ever happened with you two, anyway?" Laura asked.

"What do you mean?"

"I mean, it's obvious you haven't been speaking to Malcolm lately. He moved out last December. It's March now. What happened?"

"Nothing happened. He got those jobs down in California. Like you said, they love him down there. He couldn't pass that up."

"Right." Her sister rested her hand on her rounded belly, a gesture that irritated Joanna, though she knew almost all pregnant women did it. It just looked so affected. Joanna suspected they did it to draw attention to themselves, force people to jump up for them on the bus or let them cut in line at the restroom. "So you obviously had a falling-out," Laura pressed on. "Does this mean it's over between the two of you?"

"*What?*" She couldn't believe this. "How did you find out?"

"Come on, Joanna. Please. Everyone knew what was going on."

"What are you talking about?"

"It was obvious to anyone who saw you together. The way you made eyes at each other, the way you disappeared off to the bathroom at the exact same time, the way you—"

"Okay," Joanna interrupted. "And Mom never said anything?"

"Mom! You told Mom about this and didn't tell me?"

"She pried it out of me over winter break. I believe you weren't talking to me at the time."

"Well, it's all out in the open now. So let's hear it. We have a couple hundred more miles to go."

Laura sat back in the passenger seat and listened as they headed back into another forest, with pines outnumbering the firs. "But I don't get it, Joanna," she said when Joanna had finished speaking. "Why all this game-playing? Why not just—you know—be with each other?"

"I'm not playing games! And not everyone wants the whole marriage and kids with the white picket fence, you know!"

"I never said you had to marry him. I'm just talking about having a basic relationship with him. And don't tell me you're against that on principle because you've done it before, with other people. Why not him?"

"I told you. Malcolm and I are friends. That means something to me. I didn't want to ruin it—"

"Very ironic."

Joanna ignored the interruption. "Look around you. All these relationships—they end. Most people who find someone they get along with well enough to marry just wind up divorced."

She could sense her sister's eyes on her. "Well—so what?" Laura said.

Joanna was so shocked at this she didn't respond at first—kept both hands on either side of the steering wheel, driving on. She would have thought that Laura's current happiness with Ted would have blinded her to the possibility that it might one day fall apart. Or that even if it did fall apart, she'd rather suffer through affairs, separate bedrooms, and awkward family dinners than call it quits, satisfied that she'd toughed it out until death.

"So you're saying if this marriage and baby thing blows up in your face—you'd be fine with it."

"I'm not saying I want to get divorced, or plan to get divorced. I'm just saying it's not the end of the world. That years of potential happiness and partnership with someone—even if it ends five, ten, sixty-five years later—is worth it. I know you think that friends are forever but obviously that didn't work out."

"You don't know that."

"You can't be with someone forever when you go halfway like that," Laura continued. "You sort of have to take the plunge."

They drove through the forest without speaking. Finally they made their descent into the valley below—brown hills, squat sagebrush, huge sky with clouds billowing up over the horizon, making shapes. They stopped for gas in Susanville and then got back in the car for the homestretch. Eighty miles to Reno.

"You know," her sister said out into the silence. Joanna's mind had been wandering to her landscaping idea. The desert had made her think of it; how opposite this place was! Perhaps after some initial success in the Pacific Northwest, she could take her show on the road, gardening her way through the other hardiness zones. "This is how you tend to do things," she heard Laura say.

"What? What do you mean?" Joanna looked over at her sister for a moment, then focused back on the road ahead. Laura's blonde head was swiveled toward Joanna.

"I mean, this thing with Malcolm. It's part of a larger pattern."

"What are you talking about? I never had a friend like Malcolm before. I never slept with my friends before."

"I mean, you do things halfway. You always talked about going off to Vermont or someplace to college—but then you didn't even apply." Slowly, Joanna began to seethe. She clenched the steering wheel, staring at the yellow line in the middle of the road, breathing deliberately through her nose. "And then when you do get a chance to leave Reno, see the world, you come back early. You only had to stay in the Czech Republic a few more months—"

"I guess it doesn't matter that I was miserable the whole time—"

"You were right there in the middle of Europe! You act like it was the end of the earth, a Siberian prison! A lot of people would have been thrilled—"

"That's enough!" Joanna yelled out. It was lucky they were the only ones on the entire highway because she felt like smashing into something.

"All I'm saying is, it wouldn't hurt to follow through with something for once in your life," her sister said in a small voice.

Joanna could barely think straight. She took a few deep breaths and checked the speedometer: eighty miles per hour. She took her foot off the accelerator, watched the orange needle drop back down to the legal speed limit before answering. The words came out clipped but reasonably calm. "It's interesting that you don't think I follow through with anything, Laura. It seems to me that you are the one who left your fifteen-year-old sister with our crazy mother so you could run off and enjoy the whole 'college experience' without a care in the world." Laura tried to say something but Joanna kept on: "You know why I didn't apply for any private colleges or even out-of-state schools? Because I couldn't go out of state. Someone had to stay with Tess, and it sure wasn't going to be you."

"Joanna, no one asked you—"

"I know you didn't ask me. You had no idea. She kept it pretty much together right after the divorce, back when you were still around. But you had no idea because you *weren't there*. And you weren't there because I was. For *eight years*! So don't tell me I don't follow through with anything!" Joanna almost choked on the last few words. She brushed tears from her cheeks. She didn't look over at her sister, but she could hear from the sniffling sounds that Laura was crying, too.

When they arrived at their mother's townhouse less than an hour later, they had both calmed down, though they weren't speaking. They knocked on the door. No one answered. They stood on the cement step and waited. "That's weird," Joanna said. "I told her we'd be here for dinner."

Laura's mouth formed into an O. She slapped herself on the forehead. "You're going to kill me," she said.

"What?"

"I totally forgot. We're supposed to meet her at Dad's. Dad and Linda were having some sort of welcome-the-baby dinner for me tonight. They want us to stay with them tonight."

"And no one bothered to tell me this? *I'm* the one who's been driving you and your 'precious cargo' around for the last ten hours!"

"I offered to drive!" Laura reached over and grabbed the keys out of Joanna's hand. "That's not the point. I was supposed to tell you about the dinner—I forgot. Pregnancy brain."

Joanna rolled her eyes. So far on this trip, Laura had invoked "pregnancy brain" to explain why she'd put salt in her tea and left her jacket in the candy bar aisle at a service station. Joanna had been nice enough to turn around so she could fetch it, even though the detour had added an extra twenty minutes to their journey.

Laura got in the driver's seat and headed west through town toward their father's place, which was nestled in some brown foothills with views of the mountains and some cliff-like rock formations. The sun was sinking down into the Sierras, tingeing the clouds tangerine and purple. A band of bronze along the edge of the horizon burnt brighter and brighter as the sun descended, making it difficult to see the road before them. Both sisters turned down their sun visors at the same time.

They stopped at an intersection. "I can't see *anything*." Laura hunched over the steering wheel, trying to get a better view of the street.

"Why aren't you wearing your sunglasses?" Joanna didn't even try keeping the irritation out of her voice.

They lurched forward. Joanna looked over to her right a second before she saw it: a pickup truck hurtling toward them. The rest of it happened in a blur. A loud crash, like an explosion. The sounds of metal crunching, tires skidding over asphalt. Cars honking. Then it was silent.

Joanna batted the airbag that had burst open on impact. Already it was deflating, withering into a sad, limp sack. The air smelled like smoke and burnt plastic. "Laura?" Joanna turned to look at her sister.

Laura unfastened her seat belt and rested her head and hands against the steering wheel. She looked like she had slumped over the deflated airbag and fallen asleep. Or died. "Laura?" Joanna lowered her voice. "Are you okay?" She saw her sister's back rise and fall. She was breathing.

Laura turned her head to the side to look at Joanna. She coughed and fanned at the smoky air. "I'm okay. I think I'm okay. You?"

"It's going to be all right." She tried to make herself sound confident. Comforting. "Don't worry. Everything will be fine."

Joanna tried to open her eyes but then shut them again to stop the room from spinning. She opened them slowly, concentrating on a figure she made out in the corner of the room.

"You're awake," her mother said. Joanna focused on her face, now peering over her.

It took a few minutes for her mind to make sense of it, but then she was able to sit up in the hospital waiting room and look around without toppling over. Her mouth felt dry, her words came out hoarse. "Where's Laura?" she croaked.

Her mother poured some water from a plastic pitcher into a paper cup. "Laura's great," Tess said. "The baby is healthy, too. They just want to keep her here overnight to be sure."

Still groggy, she thought back to the accident. They'd called their mom, filled out the police report. Then Tess insisted they drive over to the hospital, too, just to be sure everything was all right. The force of the airbag had torn the cuff of Joanna's sleeve, and she was left with a large scratch on her wrist. Other than that, she was fine. Shaken up, but fine.

It took her a moment to register her mother's words. Laura was doing well. That was good. And the baby, too? "But it's too early for the baby!" Joanna blurted out.

"No, no. She didn't have the baby," her mother said in a soothing voice. "Everything is okay. You're all okay. Can't say the same for your car."

"What time is it?"

Her mom consulted a large clock on a wall next to a ceiling-mounted television set. "Almost midnight."

Joanna's head was beginning to clear. She took in the waiting room. A huge fake potted palm in one corner. An aquarium bubbling along the wall. Tess and Joanna were the only ones there.

"I've got to see Laura," Joanna said, "Can I go see her?"

"If she's still awake."

"Why aren't you with her?" Joanna sniffed. She felt strange, as if she was going to burst into tears like a child.

"Dad's with her. It's you we were worried about." Tess smiled and patted Joanna's leg. "You got a bit hysterical."

Tess walked her over to the front desk of Labor &

Delivery, where she had to sign in. She wrote her name on a nametag, stuck it on her shirt. Tess already had one. She saw her father's head through the door window and tapped on it softly. He let her in. After making a fuss over Joanna for a minute, he said he was due for a coffee break.

Laura was sitting up in the bed with a crossword puzzle out on the table next to her. She looked tired but miraculously unharmed. Her hair was even brushed smooth, as always. Joanna swallowed the lump in her throat.

"We're okay," Laura said to Joanna, smiling. At first Joanna thought she meant the two of them, sisters. But soon she saw Laura was patting her extended midsection: she meant her and the baby. Little wires connected Laura's rounded abdomen to a machine that was monitoring the baby's heartbeat with excited, jagged peaks and valleys. Laura looked over at the machine. "I have to stay here overnight, just to make sure I don't go into labor or something."

Joanna started crying then. "I didn't mean it!" she blubbered. After she blurted it out, she wasn't sure what, exactly, she didn't mean. The quip about Laura's "precious cargo"? The whole thing about marriage and kids and the picket fence? That Malcolm had ever been just a friend? None of the above? All of the above?

A tear trickled down Laura's cheek. "I'm sorry for wrecking your car."

"I shouldn't have let you drive. Not in your condition."

They looked at each other, and then both sisters started to laugh.

Laura wiped the tears from her eyes. Her laughter stopped, suddenly.

"What is it?" Joanna took a terrified look at the baby monitor, but it was blipping along as usual.

"Oh my God," Laura said. "You will never guess who's here."

"What are you talking about?"

Laura paused dramatically, then whispered. "I can't believe I didn't tell you first thing!"

Joanna was about to reach over and strangle her sister—pregnant or no. *"What?"*

"Malcolm!" Laura explained that when their mother had called Ted to tell him about the accident, he'd freaked out. He'd tried to book a flight into Reno but it was too late. Rather than wait until the next morning, he jumped in his car and started driving. He called Malcolm and made him promise to drop everything and go to Reno; he was closer, he'd get there first.

"Well," Joanna responded after a moment, "That was nice of him to drive all the way over here to check on you."

Laura gave Joanna a look. "I'm sure that's not the only reason he had to hightail it over here in under three hours. Just to check on his friend's wife? Come on."

Joanna concentrated on her hands. They looked dry, uncared for. Her knuckles were raw and red. "So where is he?"

Laura gestured toward the door. "Around here somewhere, I'd imagine. Maybe you should find him."

20

how far from reno, how close to home

Joanna found Malcolm peering through the window of the nursery at a few babies, all wearing little hats and bundled up tightly like burritos. "Kind of cute, I guess," she said.

Before speaking, she had watched him for a few moments. There he stood in the dim hallway, his hands stuffed in the pockets of his jacket. His hood was pulled up over his head, though it wasn't cold at all in the hospital, especially not in the maternity ward. This, combined with his solemn expression, lent him the appearance of someone who didn't belong there. If he wasn't an excited new father or a doctor, what was he? A hooded infant enthusiast, a hospital loiterer, a baby snatcher? When he turned to her, his visitor nametag came into view. He'd printed his name in neat block letters. She smiled. So that was who he was.

He turned to her, surprised to hear her voice. When he saw her standing there beside him, every feature in his face fell, and for a moment Joanna thought her sister must have been mistaken about the reason he came—that he was simply being a good friend to Ted, checking up on his pregnant wife. Malcolm took a hand from his pocket and grazed Joanna's cheek with his fingers. He lifted her hand and examined her torn cuff, the scrape on her wrist.

How terrible she must look—her hair a matted mess, bags under her eyes. His arms opened and she fell into them. He pressed his body into hers gently, as if she were breakable. Closing her eyes and hiding her face in his neck, she held on to him until he let go.

His voice came out sounding hoarse. "Listen, your dad said I should take you back to his place."

"Okay," she said.

Her dad's house felt cold, the air still. They entered the kitchen through the garage, using the key hidden behind a fencepost outside. When she flipped on the light, the dining table came into focus. It was set for a party, with pastel pink and blue streamers strung through the chandelier. "We should put this food away," Joanna said, picking up a platter of mini quiches, now glossy and congealed.

Malcolm took the plate from her and set it back down on the table. "It's late. You should get some sleep."

Too tired to argue, she shuffled down the hall to the room Linda had set up for her and Laura, with matching twin beds covered in scratchy store-bought quilts. Malcolm followed her and set her suitcase on the nearest bed. Then he slipped away. Her last shred of energy went into changing her clothes, brushing her teeth. When she caught a glimpse of herself in the mirror, a sharp laugh burst out of her, foam bubbled from her lips. She looked rabid, deranged.

Heavy-lidded, dinged and scratched. Like an abandoned car at the side of the road, stripped of parts and left to rust. She spit into the sink, then rinsed. Her stepmother always kept piles of fluffy washcloths, folded precisely, on the étagère above the toilet. She pressed a dry washcloth to her face. It smelled comforting, like detergent and dust. After washing her face and brushing her hair, she assessed herself in the mirror again. Better.

She took the bed at the far end of the room, under the window. Her head sunk into the pillow, softer than she was used to. Malcolm appeared at the doorway a few minutes later, his body backlit by the light in the hall. "All settled in?"

She tried to turn up the corners of her mouth, though it was too dark for him to notice. "Yes," she answered. It sounded formal.

"Good." His silhouette hovered outside the frame of the door; then the door inched closed, slowly. He was being careful with her, she realized. No sudden movements or noises.

"Malcolm?" The light from the doorway widened, a sliver. "You're not leaving me here, are you?" She had a sudden childish fear of staying in here by herself, in this big house, coyotes howling in the hills above.

She heard him exhale softly. "No. Sh-h. Go to sleep." The door closed with a muted click. "Thanks," she murmured to the sound of his footsteps down the hall. A part of her had hoped he'd feel sorry enough for her, in this tender state, to sleep next to her. But aside from the initial hug, he had kept a careful distance from her.

The next morning she woke up, unaware of how long she'd slept. Her head was pounding. There was no clock in the room. The glare of the sun didn't help—the days blazed bright from dawn until sunset here. The twin bed on the other side of the room hadn't been slept in—the patterned covers still smooth, pillows piled against the headboard just so. Inexplicably, her heart picked up, although it was broad daylight, and there was no need to fear being alone in an empty house.

She crept down the hall, peeking into the other bedrooms, all of which appeared undisturbed. Her sister, she knew, had spent the night in the hospital. Her father and Linda must have stayed there too, slouched in waiting room chairs.

"Dad?" her voice echoed out into the living room. The dining table had been cleared, the food and dishes put away. "Malcolm?"

At the kitchen sink, she filled a mug with water and set it in the microwave to cook. No tea kettles and teapots in this household. At least the tea would disguise the mineral taste of Reno's water. She peered out the window at the backyard, half hoping to find everyone there, gathered out in the bright cold. The patio furniture still wore its protective covers from the snow and chill of winter.

The door into the kitchen creaked open. Joanna jumped.

"Sorry," Malcolm said, entering the kitchen.

"Where were you? Where did you sleep?"

Malcolm ignored her questions. "Everyone is over at your mom's place now. Ted came in early this morning—he'll probably crash all day. Laura's there, too. She's fine; they let her check out this morning."

Joanna let her head nod, taking it all in. "Wow," she said. "Great."

"So if you get dressed, I'll take you over there."

"Okay."

"I'll probably take off right after that, though. I've got to get going."

She studied his face. He was regarding her politely, as if she were a stranger stopped on the side of the road in need of assistance and he was doing the right thing by giving her a lift across town to the nearest service station.

"Where are you going?" She hadn't expected him to be leaving her so quickly, before they'd even had a chance to talk, to sort anything out. She couldn't stand it; she took in a quick breath to stave off tears. If she had just a few moments with him, or a day, at least, she could fix this.

"Back to Portland."

"Portland?" She tried to make her voice come out neutral. Maybe he meant he needed to go there to fetch his things, scoop her out and leave her empty, the way she'd been before he'd moved in. She'd have to start over again. Live in a barren house or buy furniture. Both prospects sounded equally dire.

He nodded. "I finished up that last job a few weeks ago. I don't know—I'm probably going to start my own company. Furniture commissions, built-ins, things like that."

"Wow." She smiled into her teacup. She hadn't taken a sip, but she set the mug down on the counter. "Okay, give me fifteen minutes." Her headache had disappeared; she felt fine. Better than ever.

In the room, she threw her clothes into her suitcase without folding them. Then she plucked everything out again, furiously, realizing she needed something to wear besides pajamas. She debated whether to shower or not. Yes, she definitely should shower. She cranked the plastic dial as far as it would go. The water was too hot. Blistering. The scratch on her wrist, now bordered by a dark purple bruise, stung. She didn't care. She liked it; she wanted to be scalded clean.

Hair still wet but brushed, cheeks flushed from the heat

of the shower, she ventured down the hall, suitcase in hand. She found Malcolm outside in the driveway, rearranging the contents in the back of his car. She set her suitcase down at Malcolm's feet. "Ready," she said. "Let's go."

"You look better." He frowned at her suitcase. "I think your dad and Linda wanted you to stay the night here. Especially now that Ted and Laura—"

"I don't want to stay here," Joanna said. Malcolm shrugged with a suit-yourself gesture. "I'm going with you."

"What do you mean?"

"I want to go home. Back to Portland."

"But you just got here. And you were in an accident—"

"I know. But I'm fine. Just a little achy is all. And I was here over Christmas. I came to keep Laura company, and now her husband is here so I'm no longer needed."

"That's not true."

"Come on. Don't make me ride back up with the two of them. I couldn't take it." Malcolm's head shook slowly, back and forth. "Come on," she said again. "Hey, it's spring break! We don't even have to go home right away! We could go camping!"

"Camping?"

"Yes!"

"But we don't have any equipment. And it's March."

Joanna ran into the garage through the side door and banged her hand against a switch. The garage door grunted and screeched its way up, revealing stacks of cardboard boxes, outdoor furniture, tools, sporting equipment, and—yes—camping gear.

"We can borrow everything we could possibly need from my dad!" Joanna ran over to a shelf, took down two sleeping bags, tossed them into Malcolm's car, and darted back inside. What would they need? A propane stove? A tent? Backpacks with aluminum frames? Water purifiers?

"Joanna—" Malcolm stood to the side while she filled every remaining space in his hatchback.

After a few trips into the garage and back, she ran into the kitchen for provisions, emerging with a gallon bucket of mixed nuts and two jumbo bags of dried fruit. They could live off this for a few days, she figured. "I think we're ready."

Finally he relented. "Okay," he said, "I'll take you with me if you call your parents and let them know." She clapped her hands. "But we're not camping."

Joanna settled herself in the passenger seat and fastened her seat belt. They had ten hours, at least, to patch their friendship back together, piece by piece. Even longer if she could talk him into camping.

She slept a good part of the drive; she was exhausted, still shaky from the accident. They didn't talk much, but she felt like it was a companionable silence, not an awkward one. Progress, she thought. They didn't stop for lunch—just ate salted nuts straight from the plastic jug as they retraced the journey Joanna had taken the day before. Already it seemed like a lifetime ago.

They exchanged very few words. When they passed through a town, he asked if she needed to pull over. And when she put her hand to her head, he asked if she was feeling okay. No, no, she would say. She didn't need a thing.

Her shout interrupted the cozy calm. "Stop! Turn around!"

Malcolm slammed his foot on the brake. "What?"

"We have to go back there."

She made him turn around and stop at a restaurant on the side of the highway, nestled under pine trees. It was nothing more than a log cabin set up like a diner inside, with a few tables and a long counter. She'd been there with her dad once, when they were driving back from Portland after dropping Laura off at college. It was exactly as she remembered it, with a rotating glass case stocked with every flavor of pie imaginable. Joanna and Malcolm ordered four different kinds, washed down the blackberry and chocolate and banana and Dutch apple with cups of coffee. If only we could live on pie and coffee and salted nuts, Joanna mused. And Malcolm had smiled at her.

When they got back in the car the mood felt lighter, easier. "Since when are you so into camping?" he asked as they ventured back onto the highway.

She hesitated before answering, wanting to get it right. She had a few hazy memories of the whole family camping together, all snuggled up in sleeping bags in a big green tent. Hot chocolate on cold mornings, swimming in mountain streams. After the divorce they'd gone on trips with just their dad, then their dad and whatever woman he was seeing at the time, and then, eventually, Linda. Camping had lost its charms by then. It might have had something to do with adolescence—the indignity of finding a place to squat in the woods, scraping hard ground with a rock to make a suitable toilet. Smelling like a campfire, covered in a layer of dust, she'd spent those trips reading novels on a dirty canvas chair.

But if she admitted her history with camping, he'd never agree to it. And here is what she needed—she needed him to agree to it. It all hinged on his agreeing to it. She didn't know why, exactly. The plan had arrived to her, fully formed, in her father's driveway. Take him camping. That was it, the whole plan, but she knew it would work.

"I do like camping," she said cautiously. "I just haven't gone in a long time. Since I was a kid."

"Well, if you knew anything about camping you'd know

not to do it this time of year. We'll go in the summer. You don't want to die out there."

"Sounds like you're a real camping expert."

"Somewhat." He was smiling, but his eyes stayed on the road ahead.

"You went to art school. How much of an outdoorsman could you be? You wouldn't last a day in the wild."

He laughed and looked over at her. This was good. Engaging in ridiculous conversations. "And I suppose you would."

"Sure," she said. "If I had to. I've read *Alive*. I can identify ten kinds of edible mushrooms."

"Sounds like a plan. So you'll live on dead bodies and fungus."

"At least I *have* a plan. You wouldn't last a day out there."

"I could last two weeks."

Joanna regarded Malcolm. "Go on," she said.

"It was this survival camp my parents sent me to one summer."

"Survival camp? You went to something called 'survival camp'? And you *survived*?"

"Two weeks. *In the wild*, as you say."

"And how did I not know this about you?"

He shrugged. She spent the next twenty minutes grilling him. What did he eat? Where did he sleep? What did he do all day, by himself, a teenage boy wandering around the San Bernardino mountains, fending off grizzlies with a chiseled stick? "I just never saw you as the survival type. Two weeks, by yourself!"

"Okay. So maybe I didn't make it for the entire two weeks."

"Aha!"

"Maybe it was more like four days."

"Well, still. You were a kid."

"And maybe I wasn't entirely alone. They had guides tracking us, keeping an eye on us."

"This is making more sense now." Her eyelids began to feel heavy. She pressed her thumb in the middle of her forehead, trying to make her headache go away.

"Take another ibuprofen," he said. "Try to sleep if you want. It will help."

Her eyes closed. Malcolm had said "we"—we'll go camping in the summer. They'd never spent a summer together. He was gone for two years, and last summer they were barely speaking. If they were friends again in time for summer, he could build things in the garage while she gardened out back. At the end of a perfect July day, they could sit out on the porch swing (Malcolm could build them one), drink raspberry lemonade from raspberries she would plant along the fence. Garnished with some wild mint she would gather from the easements. Back and forth, they would swing, waiting for night to fall....

Her eyes opened when she felt the car pull to a stop. They were in a forest, with gigantic narrow pines towering above them. If she studied her surroundings hard enough, she could figure out where they were. It was better not knowing—how far from Reno, how close to home. The sun had already sunk below the horizon, but the sky was glowing, still infused with light. She sat up.

"Bathroom break," Malcolm said, getting out of the car.

Joanna shook herself awake and stepped out onto the pavement. She shivered and took in a huge breath, that intoxicating smell of evergreens. She could gulp the air down, it was so clean. It forced every slumbering part of her awake. Her stomach was empty, and her muscles ached, but she was alive, the edges of everything crystal clear.

Malcolm found her waiting for him in the covered area between the men's and women's restrooms. "Hey," she said, "are we going to camp here?"

"Here? Joanna, it's a rest stop, not a camp ground." He walked back toward the car, and she reluctantly followed.

"So?"

"So we're not camping here." They stopped at the car.

"Please. It's perfect!"

"We'll get buried by snow in the night. They won't find us until July."

"Come on. It's not that cold. Burrow under a pile of leaves like you did at survival camp. Rub two sticks together and make a fire. Or just use a sleeping bag." She hit the back of the car. "Open up."

He shook his head, but then unlocked the back of the car. "We can stay here for a few minutes. Then we have to get back on the road."

"Okay," Joanna said, happy to have won a fraction of the argument. She found a sleeping bag, unfurled it, and presented it to Malcolm. "Bundle up."

They walked down a narrow path behind the restrooms, into the forest. Malcolm wore the unzipped sleeping bag like a shawl around his shoulders.

Silently, they approached a picnic table in a small clearing. They sat side by side on the tabletop, their feet on the bench. Joanna gazed up into the darkening sky, glowing like blue glass, somehow dark and bright at the same time. It was so beautiful she couldn't speak. She looked over at Malcolm and his face was turned up, too. She nestled closer to him.

He looked down at her, then reached his arm around her, enfolding her in the sleeping bag. This was all she really wanted, to feel his body warm against hers and look out at the sky. They sat there like that for quite some time without saying anything. She couldn't tell if ten minutes or an hour went by. As the light faded the stars popped out, one by one. Maybe this was it, the resolution she had been looking for. They had muddled through different stages of their relationship to arrive at this, a silent communion.

He seemed to sense her looking at him and turned to her. It was now so dark, she could see him only because he was right there, inches away. His expression unsettled her. She closed her eyes, then leaned in and brushed her lips against his. They barely made contact, but her stomach dropped. She froze, waiting for his reaction. She thought she heard him exhale. He pressed his forehead to hers, and they sat like that for a minute before he seemed to make a decision. He pulled her in, roughly, and kissed her.

Joanna kissed him back. She grabbed onto the front of his shirt to bring him in and the sleeping bag slipped off his shoulders, collapsing onto the table in a heap. So *this* was exactly what needed to happen. This was her whole plan, even if she hadn't realized it back in Reno. She simply needed to show him how much they needed each other. Then they could go back to Portland and live happily ever after. He could start his business, she'd do something. Go back to work, start that gardening show—something. She'd figure that out later. Whatever it was, they'd be together. They'd have their friendship or their romance or whatever he wanted her to call it.

So she kissed him back, hard, and soon she was reaching down to unbutton his jeans. His hands were under her shirt; she felt the pressure of them on her back.

She was fumbling with his zipper when he stopped her. She had known he would push her away a second before he did. It happened quickly. One second they were all tangled up in each other, the next there was a foot of space between them.

"Why are you doing this?"

She was surprised to hear anger in his voice. For a minute all she could hear was their breathing, fast and jagged.

She couldn't look at him. Instead she focused on the picnic table. She ran her hands over the splintered wood, carved with the initials of all the travelers who had stopped before them. Her dad used to sleep on rest stop picnic tables when he traveled; he said they always provided a perfectly flat surface.

"Seriously," Malcolm said. "I want to hear you say it."

"Say what?"

"Tell me what you want."

She knew what he wanted to hear. She opened her mouth to tell him. It would be easy. It *should* be easy.

Malcolm rushed in before she could say anything, his voice low and modulated. "And don't tell me we're just friends. I swear if I hear you say one more time—Let me tell you something, Joanna: we were *never* 'friends.'"

"Of course we were friends," she snapped. Suddenly she was angry, too. "We still *are* friends. Or we could be. *You're* the one—"

Malcolm cut her off. "We made out within hours of meeting each other. You couldn't keep your hands off me—"

"We were better than friends!" Joanna yelled. Her voice had nowhere to go. It rang out and disappeared into the woods. "Why can't you get that? Why doesn't anyone get that? So what did you want—you wanted to play house? You wanted to be boyfriend-girlfriend?"

Malcolm exploded. He jumped off the table, stomped around in the dirt. "Is that really such a bizarre idea? We lived together. Slept together. Why is that such a fucking stretch?!"

She took a deep breath in attempt to regulate her voice.

"You want to know *why*?" Her hands began to tremble. She balled them into fists. "You left me. You slept with me, then you left me. The very next day."

Malcolm took a step toward her, then stopped. "I should have known you'd hold that over my head. God, what do I have to do to make it up to you?"

"Apologizing might be a good place to start."

"Listen, I'm *sorry*, Joanna. I've always been sorry. That should be pretty clear by now."

"And you never even explained it."

"I tried—"

"Just tell me why you did it. Why you left." She held her breath, waiting for him to answer.

Malcolm ran his hands through his hair. "What do you want me to say? I wanted to be with you. I did. I freaked out. It killed me that it happened like *that*. I mean, you were crying about Nate. Drunk."

"I knew what I was getting into."

"You were wasted. Inconsolable."

"But I wanted you," Joanna said. Almost under her breath she added, "You have to know that."

"Well, you have to admit, my timing sucked. I could barely face you the next morning. So I left."

"Well, luckily you found Nina to make it all better."

"God Joanna, I know I screwed everything up, but how long are you going to make me pay for it? We're obviously in love with each other, but you want to go around being 'just friends.'"

Her heart stopped for a moment. She tried to speak, but he wouldn't let her.

"What do you want from me? I made your *breakfast* every morning, fixed up your entire house, built you that bench hut you wanted so much. What next? How long do you expect me to keep this up, for our precious *friendship*?"

Her throat constricted. It was difficult for her to gauge her own reaction to everything he had said, but she chose to focus on just the last part. That, she could manage. "Malcolm, we've been over this. I didn't—*don't*—want to lose you again, is that so difficult for you to understand? I didn't want to ruin it."

He came up to her. In the darkness, she could barely make out the features of his face, just inches away from hers. She felt heat come off of him when he spoke. "It's ruined," he said. "You ruined it."

She reached up to him and succeeded in grasping the edge of his sweater. The fabric slipped out of her fingers.

Malcolm swiped the sleeping bag from the table. Its nylon fibers brushed over her as it snapped through the air. And then he was gone. She heard some rustling, his feet crunching over pine needles, and then it was quiet.

It was so dark out Joanna couldn't see anything. The sky gaped above her, black and endless, glittering with stars. No moon. He had left her to survive on her own—or die trying. She put her hands out, feeling for the table underneath her. The trees swayed overhead, hundreds of feet above her, creaking in the wind. It threw her off-balance. If she left the table, she'd fall into nothingness. She was so unused to this darkness.

She took in a few deliberate, deep breaths, filling her lungs with the crisp forest air. Then, before she lost her courage, she stepped off the bench. Her hands stayed on the table; it would anchor her. Her eyes could not focus— only look up to see the sky. Where the stars ended, the tops of the trees began, cutouts that melted into the ground where she stood.

"Malcolm?" she called out. She craned her neck, listening

for an answer. She couldn't hear anything. A cold breeze picked up and the trees shuddered and groaned.

She was shaking now. "Malcolm!" she shouted as loud as she could. Then she took her hands from the table. It was like stepping into space. Above she could see the stars, but all around was nothing. She had no idea how to move forward, but she didn't reach back for the table. She didn't need the table anymore. She would survive out here on her own if she had to, fling herself into the great unknown. If she never found him she would be devastated, of course, but she'd get by. She'd be like that kid in *My Side of the Mountain*, live in a hollowed out tree, wear underwear made from rabbit hides.

But she would rather not. She could make it out here if she had to—she'd read enough survival stories by now—but she would rather not. She lurched forward, waving her hands in front of her. "Malcolm?" She wasn't yelling now. She said his name softly. "Malcolm!"

She took another step, less shaky this time, and then she crashed right into him. He was standing not four feet from the table, waiting for her. Her whole body unraveled, trembled with relief. "I thought you'd left me out here to die."

She heard him sigh, and then she felt his hand on her face. "You wouldn't die."

"Right. I'd subsist on trail mix."

Malcolm didn't laugh. She couldn't see his face, but she knew he wasn't even smiling. She felt him press his lips to her forehead. Then his hand dropped away from her cheek.

"Malcolm." She paused. "You asked me what I want."

"Joanna—"

She needed to say it. Quickly, before she lost her nerve. "I want you. That's what I want. I want to *un*-ruin it—us. I think we can. I think it's possible."

He didn't answer, but she could hear him breathing.

Slowly, she pulled him in by the edges of the sleeping bag, still draped around his shoulders. She'd bring him back. He would fold his arms around her, wrap the two of them up in a fabric cocoon. They'd fall to the ground, sleep like that on a bed of pine needles, live off each other's warmth, hibernate under the snow. They could survive out there. She knew they could.

acknowledgments

To all my early readers of *Broken Homes & Gardens*, many of whom read draft after draft—Coral Anderson, Abby Schmidt, Gina Kelley, Anne McKee Reed, Felisa Salvago-Keyes, Lynne Nolan, Angie Culbert, Andy Henroid, and Christi R. Suzanne—thank you!

Many thanks to all the members of Writers Anonymous, past and present, for their advice and encouragement over the last five years. I am so lucky to be a part of this supportive and somewhat drunken writing crew.

To my agent, Jennifer Chen Tran, without you, this book wouldn't be published. Thank you so much, for everything.

And of course, I want to thank the team at Blank Slate Press, for believing in this book and making it happen.

about the author

Rebecca Kelley grew up in Carson City, Nevada, wandered for a few years, and eventually landed in Portland, where she teaches writing at Oregon College of Art and Craft. She is the co-author of *The Eco-nomical Baby Guide*. *Broken Homes & Gardens* is her first novel.